BOUND BY BLOOD

Anthology

Cora Reilly

Copyright ©2020 Cora Reilly

All Rights Reserved. This book or any portion thereof may not be reproduced or used in any manner whatsoever without the express written permission of the author except for the use of brief quotations in a book review.

This is a work of fiction. All names, characters, businesses, events and places are either the product of the author's imagination or used fictitiously.

Cover design by Hang Le

AUTHOR'S NOTE

This is a collection of short stories featuring different couples plus a novella about Matteo and Gianna.

I don't like to give trigger warnings because they spoil the storyline, but this book deals with a topic that might be upsetting to some readers. I can't say more, so proceed with caution.

BOUND BY
BLOOD

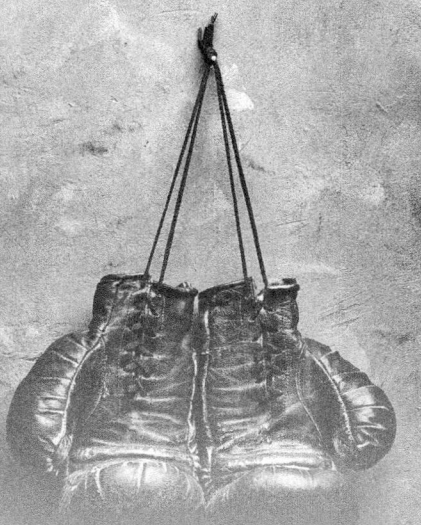

SHORT STORY # 1
Aria & Luca Gym Scene
(from the Books for Boobies Charity Anthology, 2015)

Aria

Luca and I entered the shabby brick building that harbored the gym of the Famiglia, the mob family that ruled New York and most of the East Coast. Behind the rusty steel door, one of Luca's soldiers sat guard, a middle-aged man who was busy cleaning his guns; outsiders weren't really welcome, not that I thought anyone ever came here by accident. This wasn't the most inviting part of New York after all.

The guard straightened in his chair when he spotted his Capo. Over time, I'd grown used to the looks of respect and fear that Luca evoked in others. Even if he weren't the head of one of the most notorious mob families in the country, his tall frame and imposing muscles intimidated most people. Not to mention the fierce brutality in his gray eyes. They only ever softened when he looked at me.

Luca's hand on my waist was light as he led me past his soldier and into the main part of the gym, a huge hall that had been transformed into a place where Luca's men could work out and practice their fighting skills. There was a boxing ring, all kinds of exercise machines, dummies for fight and knife training, and a corner with mats where a few men were sparring. They greeted us friendly, but apart from that, they hardly glanced our way. It wasn't the sensation it used to be that Luca took me here to teach me how to fight. Most of the men probably still found it strange or even inappropriate, but they knew better than to share their opinion.

Men in our world preferred their women docile and helpless; easier to control. Nobody wanted a woman who could defend herself, least of all against her own husband. Not that any fight training in the world could ever make me stand a chance against Luca. My sister Gianna always said he was a beast, and she was right. I loved his strength, his fierceness, and yes, even his deadliness. Watching him fight always made wetness pool between my legs. I peered up at my husband, his broad shoulders, strong jaw, black hair. He met my gaze, gray eyes holding the same fire I could already feel simmering in my belly. His mouth pulled into that familiar almost smile, then he gently nudged me into the changing room. It was men only, seeing that I was the only woman who came here, but nobody was crazy enough to walk in when the Capo's wife was getting dressed. Luca was a possessive bastard as his brother Matteo so nicely put it.

The low ceiling of the changing room always made me feel slightly claustrophobic and the smell of sweat usually worsened that sensation, but today I was distracted by the burning need between my legs that had only grown worse since I'd felt Luca's morning rod pressed into my lower back this morning. Luca closed the door behind us, walked past me, and dropped our sports bag on the wooden bench before he turned to me and pulled his shirt over his head, revealing inch over inch of perfectly sculpted stomach and chest. I wanted to trail my tongue over every ridge. From the look on Luca's face, I could tell he knew exactly what I was thinking. I strolled over to the bench, snatched my workout clothes out of the bag, and pretended to ignore my arrogant husband. Of course it was close to impossible. There were people you simply could *not* ignore. Luca was one of them. He removed his pants and underwear. His cock was already half-erect, and he didn't bother hiding it, or getting dressed. He was trying to provoke me. He knew how turned on I was by him. Sometimes I could hardly stop myself from jumping him in public.

I slipped out of my jeans and shirt, then unhooked my bra and lowered it slowly, knowing Luca was watching *me* now. His gaze practically burned a trail down my skin, lingering on my nipples, which hardened under his scrutiny. I turned my back to him and then I inched my panties down ever so slowly, bending forward and jutting my butt out so Luca got a good look at what he was doing to me. My panties had only reached my knees when I felt Luca behind me. One of his hands curled around my shoulder, gently pushing me down until my hands shot out to brace myself against the bench. I knew this position was giving him an even better view. Luca brushed two fingers over my opening before spreading my wetness over my folds and clit. I shuddered and stifled a moan. I didn't want his men to know what we were doing, though a part of me was turned on by the idea of getting caught in the act. Luca dipped his fingertip into me, then added a second. I tried to move my butt to make him push into me all the way, but his hand on my shoulder held me fast. I threw an annoyed look over my shoulder, hoping he'd get the hint.

He returned my gaze steadily, eyes hungry but relentless. He wanted to drive me to the brink, make me beg for more. I pressed my lips together, determined to win this game. My hand shot out and grasped Luca's erection before he could stop me. He twitched in my palm. Slowly I ran my thumb over his tip, coating it with precum. Luca let out a low growl and eased his fingers all the way into me. I almost cried out. Instead I let my head fall forward and released a long breath through my nose. Luca curled his fingers in me and pressed his knuckle against my clit. He moved slowly. Despite my best intentions, I ground myself against him, at least as much as his hold on my shoulder allowed.

I tightened my grip on his cock and started pumping up and

down. Luca's fingers sped up. I could feel myself getting closer; my arms started shaking and my breathing was coming fast. Then without warning, Luca pulled his fingers out of me and released me. My legs almost buckled. I jerked up, whirled around, and glowered at Luca.

"We are here to teach you how to defend yourself. Maybe the frustration you're feeling now will give you the necessary motivation to fight."

I crossed the distance between us and fell to my knees. Luca's hands shot out to grip my head and stop me, but my tongue darted out and licked the precum off his tip before he could do any such thing. After that, he only raked his fingers through my hair and moaned quietly. I only took his tip into my mouth while my hand worked his shaft; that's how he liked it best. Occasionally I'd pull back to lick the underside of his cock from bottom to top. Luca began thrusting lightly, a good indicator that his release was getting close. With an audible 'plop' I let his cock slip from my lips and stood. "And this should distract you enough for me to land a few good hits," I said with a wicked grin.

"Aria," Luca growled. "Don't leave me hanging like that."

"From what I see, you're not hanging at all."

Luca tried to grab me, but I jumped back and snatched my gym clothes before I darted away to the other end of the changing room. Luca didn't chase me but his expression was that of a jaguar watching its prey. He looked so damn sexy that it took all of my self-control not to throw myself at him. Instead I calmly put on my workout shorts and tank top. Luca watched me the entire time.

I raised an eyebrow and nodded toward his erection. "I thought we were going to work out."

Luca shook his head with a chuckle. "What's become of the shy girl I married?"

"You corrupted her," I said with a smile.

Luca put on black sweatpants and a tight white shirt. I approached him, suddenly insecure. Did he think I'd become too forward?

"Did you prefer her?" I asked, trying to sound teasing but failing spectacularly.

"I love you exactly as you are," Luca said. He grabbed my arm and pulled me against him before he kissed me firmly.

Luca frowned when he pulled back. "That sounded fucking cheesy."

I grinned. "You're turning into a softy."

"We'll see about that. Let's go before I cancel our training and have my way with you right here on the bench."

That didn't sound too bad, but Luca took my hand and led me out of the changing room, probably to show me how good his self-control was.

We headed straight toward the sparring mats as we always did. When we faced each other, my eyes darted to Luca's crotch even without intending to, but his bulge was gone, which shouldn't have disappointed me as much as it did. The Capo could hardly prance around with his erection in front of his soldiers. Luca's eyes flashed, but he didn't give me the grin he reserved for when we were alone. His face remained the hard mask he almost always wore when he was around his soldiers. I wasn't sure why Made Men thought showing any kind of emotion that wasn't anger or hate was some kind of weakness. Luca motioned for me to attack him. As usual, I tried to land a hit, which was impossible with his fight experience and reflexes. My third try landed me flat on my back with Luca crouching over me. His hand brushed my mound through my shorts, only the barest touch, but it sent bolts of lightning through my body.

It hadn't been an accident. Luca's eyes said it all. I let him pull me to my feet and made sure to brush past him in a way that my hip touched his groin area.

After that, it was pretty clear that our fight training had turned into a game of who could drive the other wilder with secret touches. The other men in the gym seemed oblivious to our activities, or they knew better than to pay too much attention to us. My body was practically bursting with need when Luca finally ended our session. I wanted to drag him into the changing room with me, even if that meant I'd lose our little game. But one of the men came over to us, a teenage boy at his side.

Luca sent me a look of regret. "He's a new initiate. I'll have to talk to his father and him for a moment."

I smiled. "I'll go ahead and shower."

It was the last thing I wanted but it would have been rude for Luca to disappear without a word. I gave both man and boy a smile as I walked away. Once I was inside the changing room and had closed the door behind me, I let out a sigh. My panties were sticking to my skin and not just from sweat. After I'd listened for sounds that I wasn't alone, I undressed, grabbed a towel and then headed for the shower stalls. I turned the water to cold and hopped under the stream, gasping for breath. The cold didn't help with my desire. I wasn't sure if a cold shower worked like that for anyone, or if that was only urban legend. I turned up the heat and tried to relax. I lathered myself in shower gel but as my fingers brushed my folds, I couldn't resist. Who knew how long Luca would be gone? I needed some relief now. The second I touched my clit, I slumped against the wall and exhaled, my eyes falling shut. I was already close; all the teasing touches had driven me to the brink. I rubbed myself faster and my legs began shaking. God, I was so close.

A strong hand curled around my wrist and pulled my hand away moments before I could reach my peak. I groaned in frustration and my eyes shot open, only to find Luca in front of me, naked and with a raging hard-on, his eyes flashing with hunger. I almost came because of that look. He raised my hand to his lips and sucked my fingers into his mouth, but his gray eyes burned into mine with the same need I felt.

"That's my job," he growled.

I shivered in delight. He grabbed my thighs and lifted me up. I wrapped my arms around his neck and my legs around his waist. Luca positioned my opening above his erection but he didn't lower me. Instead his lips claimed mine, and he kneaded my butt cheeks. I ground my pussy against his abs, hoping it would get him moving. His tip brushed my folds and I sucked in a breath. Luca growled into my mouth but he still didn't move. Of course he had no trouble holding me upright.

I raked my fingernails down his back, pulled back from his mouth and whispered into his ear, "I need you now."

"You do, hm?" Luca murmured as his lips traced my throat. I ground myself against him once more and felt his abs constrict under me. This was torture for him too.

I kissed the spot under his ear. "Don't you want to be inside of me? I'm so wet."

Luca's fingers on my thighs tensed. He caught my lips for another kiss, and then finally started lowering my body. His tip eased into me, then slowly the rest of his shaft followed until he filled me to the hilt. I threw my head back with a moan and Luca let out a low groan. We stayed like that for a moment, relishing in the feeling of being united like that, almost reluctant to move.

"Fuck, you feel so good, Aria," Luca rasped. I shivered at the sound of his voice and goose bumps covered my body despite the warm water.

Luca gripped my butt and supported my back against the shower stall before he started to slide out of me. He halted with his tip against my opening again. I parted my lips for a protest but before I could utter a word, he slammed back into me. I dug my fingers into his shoulders as I cried out in pleasure. I didn't even care if someone heard us. This felt too amazing.

Luca claimed my mouth, silencing my next moan as he thrust into me hard and fast. My back rubbed against the tiles and Luca's grip on my butt was almost painful, but that only heightened my pleasure. I wrapped my arms around Luca's neck to pull myself even closer. Our bodies were pressed against each other so tightly I could feel Luca's heart pounding in his chest. We locked gazes, and I knew the look in Luca's eyes had only ever been for me. Our breaths were coming faster and as Luca slammed into me again, I fell apart. I tensed and moaned into his mouth, and seconds later Luca's own release followed. Afterward, we still clung to each other as the water slowly turned cold. I slid my legs down, even though I wasn't sure if they could hold me yet. I leaned against the stall just in case.

Luca released my butt and leaned over me, stopping the water from splashing my face. He kissed me again, lightly this time, and our eyes met. In the beginning, I'd found his gray eyes cold and terrifying, and I knew it was what others still saw in them, but not for me, not anymore.

"What are you thinking?" Luca murmured. He turned the shower off but didn't move away from me.

"That I love you."

Luca raised an eyebrow. "That's what you were thinking?"

"Not in those exact words, but it always comes down to it," I whispered before I grasped Luca's neck and pulled him down to me for another lingering kiss.

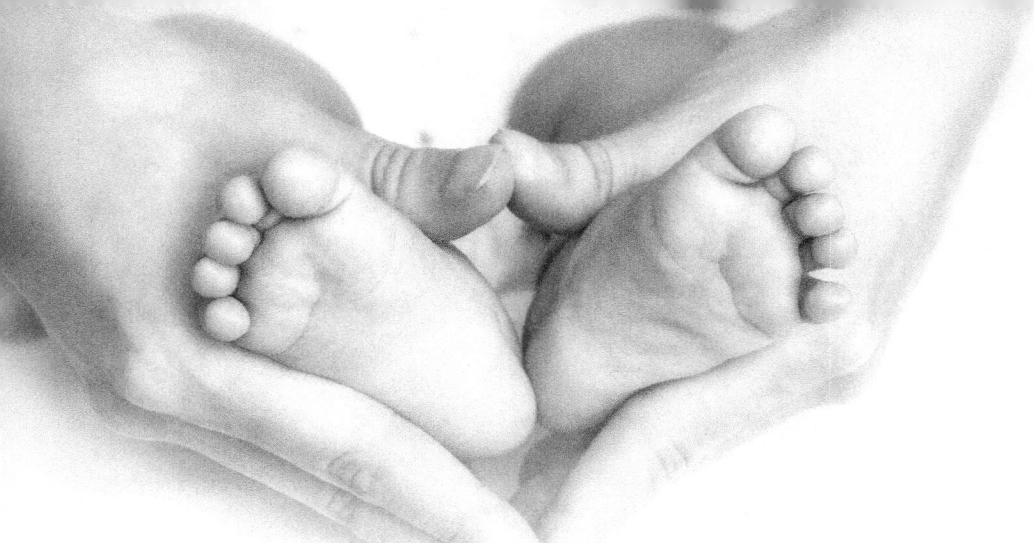

AMO'S BIRTH BONUS STORY

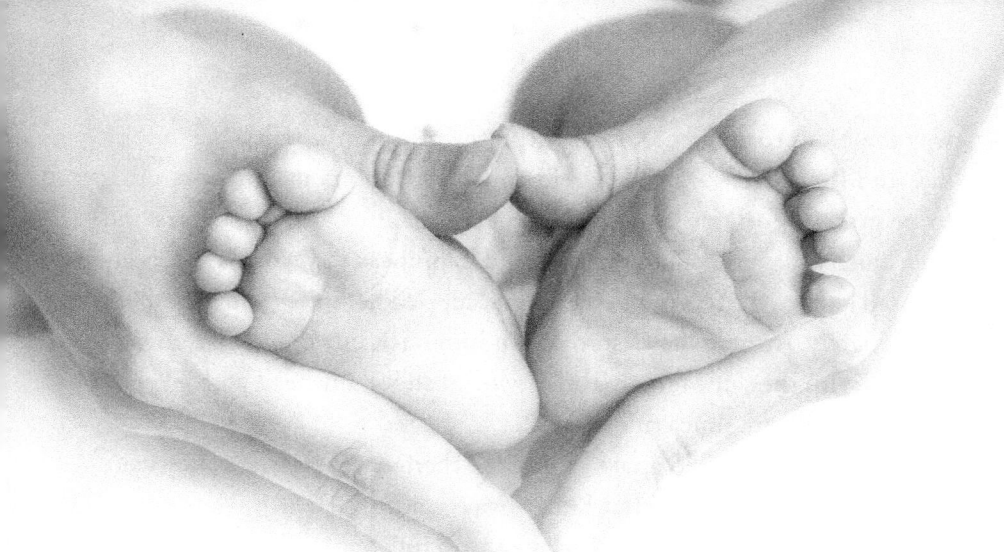

PART ONE

Aria

Romero, Lily, Gianna, Matteo, Luca, and I had gathered on the roof terrace to celebrate New Year's Eve as a family. It was becoming a beautiful tradition.

"I love New York at night," Lily said as she leaned back against Romero who had his arms wrapped around her waist, looking at her as if she was the center of his world. Those two were such a harmonic couple, I'd never seen them argue.

"It's grown on me. I thought I'd hate it but I really don't," Gianna said, propping her elbows up on the railing. Matteo bent down and whispered something in her ear that made her slap his arm but she was obviously fighting a smile.

"New York is home," I said quietly. Luca squeezed my hip and our eyes met. Because of him, this city had become a place of happiness and the home of our small family.

"Ten, nine," Matteo began the countdown to midnight, quickly handing us glasses with champagne.

"Four, three, two, one," we finished together, grinning.

We clinked glasses and toasted the New Year. I took a sip, loving the way the New York sky bloomed with fireworks. Luca pulled me in for a kiss and I relaxed against him, relishing in this moment. I had so much to be grateful for, not just Luca and Marcella, but also my sisters and their husbands. We'd all found love and happiness in a world that rarely granted either. Matteo grabbed Gianna, cupped her head, and kissed her passionately. At first she tried to push him back but then she returned the kiss with the same fervor. Those two… I shook my head with a laugh.

"Get a room," Luca muttered.

They finally pulled apart, neither of them embarrassed. They were a match made in hell, is what Luca always said.

Gianna shrugged and pulled me into a hug before she moved on to Lily. Celebrating with them was the most wonderful gift I could imagine, even as my chest squeezed tightly when I thought of Fabiano. I hoped he'd find happiness too.

We watched the fireworks in silence, Luca's arms creating a warm cocoon around me.

"I can't believe the kid doesn't wake with all the fireworks," Matteo said, shaking his head.

"Marcella sleeps like a rock," I said.

"Speaking of the devil." Gianna nodded toward the living room. Marcella stood behind the window with her little palms pressed against the glass, staring up at the sky with big eyes.

Luca chuckled and went over to the terrace door, sliding it open before he scooped up our daughter. With her being two-and-a-half years old, she had no trouble climbing out of her bed and down the stairs. She wrapped her tiny arms around Luca's neck and peered up at the fireworks in wonder. My heart squeezed with happiness seeing her and Luca. When I'd found out about my pregnancy, I'd harbored so many worries but luckily none of them had proven true. Luca was the best father for Marcella I could hope for, and he'd be a wonderful father to more kids, even a boy.

Lily immediately headed over to Luca and Marcella, tugging at my daughter's tiny toes and smiling. The way Romero watched her, I knew kids would definitely be part of their future.

Marcella giggled as she pointed up at the sky then she looked at me with a wide grin. "Mom, look!"

I nodded and peered back up to the sky and the colorful explosions.

Gianna leaned beside me against the railing. "Planning on getting knocked up again?"

Taking another sip from my champagne, I gave a small shrug. In the last few weeks, I'd thought about a second child more and more, and now that Marcella wasn't as dependent on me anymore, I felt like I could have another baby.

"Your expression says yes," Gianna whispered. "I never thought Luca was a family man, but now I think the two of you will end up with five kids and still do fine."

I laughed. "Definitely not five. I'm really not too excited about being pregnant that often, and even less about giving birth."

Gianna considered that with a wrinkled nose. "Yeah. Squeezing a baby out of you that often… I can't imagine doing it once."

I regarded her, then Matteo who'd joined Luca and the others, doting on Marcella. "You don't have to if you both don't want kids."

"We don't. And if Matteo and I feel like spoiling a kid, we've got Marcella and soon more. You and Lily are going to pop out more babies soon enough."

"Don't spoil her too much. Luca's already having a hard enough time trying not to spoil her rotten. She's got him wrapped around her tiny finger."

Luca handed Marcella to Romero who lifted her up over his head to her obvious delight before Matteo took over. Marcella was beaming like the little princess that she was.

After everyone had left and Marcella was asleep in her bed, Luca and I decided to take a long shower together. He went ahead into the bathroom while I headed for the nightstand where I kept my contraceptives. I fumbled with the pill package then glanced at the open bathroom door before I put it back down and followed Luca. He was already naked and turning the shower on.

I joined him in the shower, pressing up against his muscled body and peering up at him as the warm water streamed down on us and he ran his hand down my spine. His brows drew together when he scanned my face.

"What's wrong?"

He knew me too well. It was a curse and blessing. I wasn't sure if Luca was up for another baby yet. The Famiglia kept him busy—war with the Outfit, the Bratva and the MCs was taking its toll, but when would there ever be peace?

"I don't want to take the pill anymore."

Luca paused. "Okay."

"I'd like to have a second baby," I added quickly, feeling the need to justify myself. "Marcella will be three this year. I think it would be good for her to have siblings. She'll have someone to play with and she'll learn to share our attention, which will be good for her as well."

Luca stroked my cheek, then brushed a kiss across my lips. "If you want a baby, you'll get one. How about we start working on it right away?"

Surprise filled me. I'd expected more resistance from him for some reason. "I thought I'd have to talk you into it."

"I love Marcella and I love building a family with you, a family like it's meant to be. I want Marcella to have siblings like we do."

I smiled, relieved and excited. Life without my siblings would have been bleak, and even though Luca and I loved Marcella with all our hearts, we couldn't replace a sister or brother. Standing on my tiptoes, I kissed Luca, tugging at his neck, wanting him closer. His tongue in my mouth, his strong hands on my back and ass, they banished any trace of tiredness. I drew back and knelt down in front of Luca so his erection bobbed in front of me. I curled a hand around it then took him slowly into my mouth and began sucking, casting my gaze up to watch Luca as I did. He leaned back against the wall, lips parted, muscled chest heaving. I loved giving him head like that because I could admire the entire length of his incredible body that way. Working him deeper into my mouth, I cupped his balls with one hand while my other pumped the base of his cock.

Luca stroked my hair away from my face. "Fuck, as much as I love this, it won't help our baby mission if you suck me dry."

I pulled back. "You're always up for a second round."

Luca's eyes darkened with hunger. "With you looking at me like that, I'll probably manage a third and fourth round as well."

I laughed then closed my mouth around his tip once more, but Luca gripped me under my arms and hoisted me to my feet.

"Enough. I want to be inside of you."

Luca slipped his hand down my belly, between my legs before he dipped two fingers into me, finding me already wet. With a growl, he lifted me off the ground, so I wrapped my legs around his waist before he pushed me up against the wall and entered me. I dug my nails into his shoulders, my head lolling back from the sensation. This position always allowed him to go so much deeper.

Luca held me up with his arms as he began slamming into me, long, hard strokes that sent shockwaves through my body. I pressed my lips together, trying to keep my moans in, not wanting to wake Marcella, but after another deep thrust I cried out, my toes curling. Luca silenced me with his mouth, his tongue plunging in, stroking mine, stirring up the fire in my belly.

I dug my heels into his backside, my inner walls clenching so tightly I was sure I'd snap until finally everything burst forth. Luca possessed me with his eyes as I moaned into his mouth and rocked myself desperately against his cock, even as he slammed faster into me. With a harsh groan, he ripped away and spilled into me. He kept pumping, his breathing ragged as he kissed my throat then pulled my nipple into his mouth to suckle on it. I arched into him, loving the feel of his tongue circling my nipple. His fingers cupped my ass and he lifted me higher so only his tip remained inside of me and he had easy access to my breasts. I leaned my head back against the shower stall as I watched him lick and suck my nipples.

"Up for another round?" he murmured with a hungry twist of his mouth. I could only nod.

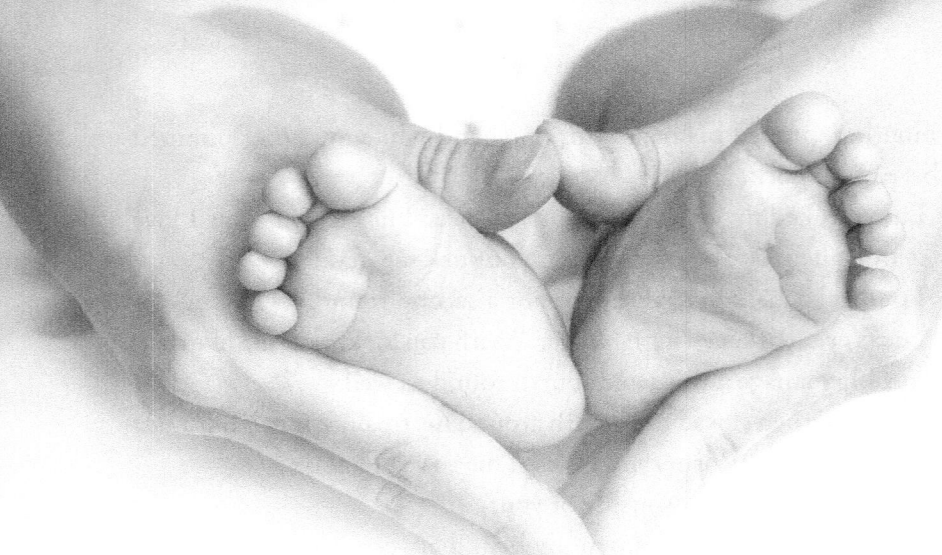

PART TWO

Aria

It was late March when I started to feel small changes in my body, like tension in my breasts and just the subtle sensation that something was off. I suspected at once that I was pregnant but I didn't mention anything to Luca that morning because I wanted to be certain before telling him. The moment he left, I texted Gianna, asking her to come up and bring a pregnancy test from her stash. She usually had a pregnancy scare at least every other month so she always kept a few tests on hand.

Since Demetrio would leave soon to become Underboss of Washington, Luca and Matteo had decided to change the way we were guarded. Gianna and I didn't want new guards around us constantly so for a few weeks now, Demetrio and the other guards had moved into a room on the ground floor of the complex from where they could follow several cameras that showed them images from the elevator, underground garages, lobby as well as the immediate surroundings of the building. It guaranteed our protection while allowing Gianna and myself more freedom. I woke Marcella and went through our morning routine of brushing our hair and teeth, before I dressed her in a cute red wool dress and white tights and headed downstairs.

"Gianna will come over for breakfast this morning."

"Yay," Marcella screeched, clapping her hands. Having Gianna over meant fun activities and fewer rules but recently my sister had been busy becoming a yoga instructor, which I still found funny. She'd never struck me as someone who had the patience for something like yoga, but the activity seemed to ground her and gave her something to keep busy in addition to her online studies to become a nutritionist.

The elevator arrived on our floor shortly after, and Gianna got out, waving two tests in the air. Dressed in tight black leggings, an oversized black pullover with a huge glittery *Kiss* tongue and black boots, she looked like a rock band groupie. I doubted she owned a single piece of clothing that wasn't black. Gianna had really found her own style, and most women in the Famiglia didn't approve of it. Not that they had liked Gianna before.

"I can't believe he got you knocked up this quickly. That guy only needs to look at you and you're already pregnant."

Marcella frowned up at me. "What's that mean?"

"I don't know if I'm pregnant," I told Gianna, then to my daughter. "Nothing, sweetheart. Let's have breakfast." I put Marcella into her high chair before I grabbed everything for her banana oatmeal.

Gianna gave me a one-armed hug then shoved the tests at me. "Go pee on them. I'll make breakfast for little miss princess." She tickled Marcella's tummy, who giggled delightedly.

"Here, give her a few of these to keep her busy until then," I said as I handed Gianna a handful of raspberries.

"You should add Brazil or macadamia nuts to her breakfast for the healthy fats," Gianna said thoughtfully.

"Check the cupboards. I don't know if we have any." Laughing, I slipped into the guest bathroom. It was wonderful to see Gianna being passionate about something. Life as a woman in our world could get monotonous very quickly if you didn't find something to occupy yourself with.

Once I was done peeing on the tests, Gianna joined me inside to wait for the results, leaning against the doorframe with crossed arms.

Marcella was busy eating her raspberries but I could tell that she was growing impatient from the way she bounced her little legs.

"Usually I find it nerve-wracking to wait for the test, but now that it's for you, I'm actually excited," she said.

"Are you that scared of getting pregnant?"

She shrugged. "I wouldn't say scared but I don't want kids so I don't want to be put in that position."

"If you and Matteo are absolutely sure you don't want kids, why don't you opt for a more final solution?"

Gianna scoffed. "You know how men are… especially Made Men. Matteo doesn't want to be castrated, how he put it."

"Hmm," I said, my eyes darting to the pregnancy test on the sink once more. The time was up by now, wasn't it?

Gianna wasn't as patient as me. She stepped forward, grabbed the test and grinned. "Congrats, your vajayjay is getting shredded again."

"Really?"

Gianna snorted. "Never thought anyone could be this excited about the prospect of *that*." She held out the test to me and indeed, I was pregnant. Smiling, I hugged my sister.

She held me tightly. "I'm happy for you."

Excitement bubbled up in me. I hadn't expected things to happen so fast and I couldn't wait to tell Luca. It would definitely boost his ego, not that he was in need of that.

"Come on. Let's have breakfast together," I said, suddenly starving now that my nervousness had evaporated.

Gianna and I settled at the table beside Marcella, whose lips and cheeks were tinged pink from eating the raspberries. I wiped her face with a napkin then brushed a few strands of her black hair from her face. Gianna set a bowl with oatmeal down in front of my daughter, then two bigger bowls in front of us. They were sprinkled with nuts, so she had actually found them in our cupboards. I'd have to thank Marianna tomorrow for always making sure our shelves were stocked with an array of food.

Marcella hummed when she shoved her spoon with oatmeal into

her mouth and I smiled, trying to imagine how I'd be sitting here with two children soon.

"Marci is already ridiculously beautiful. Luca needs to build a tower where he can lock her in once she hits puberty," Gianna commented.

I snorted then took a spoon of the oatmeal. It tasted better than mine. Maybe I should ask Gianna to come over and cook us breakfast every day. "Do you take cooking lessons with your college classes?"

"God, no. I prefer telling people what they're supposed to cook and not cook it myself, but oatmeal isn't really rocket science."

"If you say so…"

Gianna rolled her eyes then we both burst out laughing. "I wish Lily lived closer so she could just come over like you do."

"I know," Gianna said. "But Romero needs to protect his mother and sisters… yadda yadda."

"Well, he's the only man in the family, and his youngest sister and mother still need protection. You know how it is."

"We all need protection, always."

"Tell me about your classes. Are you still happy with them?" I asked, deciding to distract Gianna from the topic that always riled her up, and at once, her expression transformed.

"I love it. It's super interesting to learn about the different effects macro and micronutrients have on our well-being."

"Have you thought about what you're going to do with your degree once you're done?" I lifted Marcella out of her high chair because she was getting bored and set her down on the floor so she could get something to play.

Gianna crossed her arms, leaning back in her chair. "Do you think it's a waste of time like Luca does?" She huffed. "I get it. I can't do the Famiglia's books like you do…"

"I didn't say that." Luca definitely had, though, but he and Gianna were like cat and mouse anyway, so it was a given.

"I've actually thought it through. I can be useful for our cause with my degree. Our men are protective maniacs; every man in our circle is, so it's difficult for women to go out by themselves. Not every Made Man has as many soldiers at his disposal as Luca and Matteo do, but they all have wives who want to look pretty so they can make their husbands happy."

I cocked an eyebrow at Gianna's derisive tone, even if she had a point.

"So I was thinking of opening a ladies' gym only for Famiglia women where I can give yoga classes and diet consultations. Money isn't really an issue so I'd pack it with amazing equipment, look for staff among our women, and Matteo could make sure that we always have a few guards who keep us and the gym safe."

"That sounds great."

"I know," Gianna said with a grin. "I hide a clever brain behind my pretty façade."

"You're as vain as Matteo."

Gianna poked out her tongue at me.

"That's bad!" Marcella shouted, pointing an accusing finger at her aunt, who turned to her and poked out her tongue again.

Marcella giggled then her own tongue darted out with a cheeky grin.

I sighed, stifling a smile. Maybe it was for the best that Gianna and Matteo didn't have kids…

When Luca returned from work that evening in time for dinner, I was practically bouncing on my feet and the second he spotted me, his brows drew together.

"What's the matter?"

He headed over to where I was stirring pasta into a bowl of tomato sauce, and kissed me. Marcella was busy watching an episode of her favorite show. She was allowed to watch it while I prepared dinner and barely looked away from the screen, completely mesmerized. Setting down the spoon, I grinned up at Luca.

"I'm pregnant," I whispered, remembering the last time I had found out about my pregnancy with Marcella. Luca and I had been fighting during the first few months of the pregnancy so I didn't tell him until much later and it had been horrible.

Luca blinked then a slow smile took over his face and he lifted me off the ground to crush me against his chest. His lips found mine, soft and warm, and when he pulled back, he looked as happy as I felt. It was a look only very few people ever saw on Luca's face; Marcella, Matteo, and I were probably the only ones who knew Luca's honest smile; not the smirk, not the cold smile, not the arrogant smile or the one that was full of threat. No, this one reflected true happiness. I swallowed hard, overcome with emotions.

Luca touched my still flat belly and shook his head in apparent amazement. "How far along are you?"

I laughed. "Only about five weeks. It's still very early. We should wait until we tell the others. I don't want people to find out before we are certain that the baby is fine."

Luca shook his head. "We won't tell them until you're farther along but not because we'll lose our child. Nothing will ever happen to you or our baby, Aria. I won't allow it."

He sounded absolutely certain, as if even Mother Nature, even my body, would listen to his command, but we both knew that wasn't the case. Still Luca's certainty made me feel better and I smiled.

Luca seemed even more nervous about the doctor's appointment than me when I settled on the examination table. I was in my eighteenth week and the chances were good that we'd find out the gender of our baby today. If it was a girl, Luca and I would definitely try for a third child because he needed an heir, and I was actually not against the idea. A big family was something I wanted more and more since we'd had Marcella. I loved being surrounded by family: Gianna, Marcella, Lily... I wanted a house full of laughter.

The doctor smiled at me when she entered the room but spotting Luca her lips pinched. She didn't like the way he threatened the staff so they accommodated us outside of the usual office hours and kept their silence about us. He gave her a curt nod, but didn't move from his spot beside me, nor did he sit down.

I squeezed his hand and his eyes softened ever so slightly when they settled on me. The doctor began the ultrasound and I watched the screen with bated breath, but I couldn't see if it was a boy or girl.

"Is everything all right?" Luca asked with a hint of impatience after a minute of silence from the doctor.

She peered up at him with a tense smile. "Everything is as it should be. You're expecting a boy, congratulations."

For a moment, I didn't move. Marcella would be a wonderful big sister to a baby boy. Maybe she wouldn't be as jealous if she remained the princess in the family, and I loved the idea of having a small Luca in my life, a tiny version of the man I loved more than anything else in the world.

Luca stroked his thumb along the back of my hand, the only sign of affection he'd allow himself in public. Luca and I would make sure that our boy had a better childhood than Luca and Matteo. Luca's face was stone but in his eyes, I could see the hint of wariness. I could imagine the worries going through his head. Even with Marcella he'd worried he'd be like his father, would be too harsh or cruel, but nothing could be further from the truth. Maybe he wouldn't be as lenient with a boy as he was with a daughter, but that was it.

Now wasn't the time to discuss the test results, not while the doctor did the ultrasound and we weren't alone.

The moment we were back in our car, I took Luca's hand. "You will be a wonderful dad to our boy. I just know it. You'll love him like you love me and Marcella. I know you will be patient and loving and you won't hurt him."

Luca raised my hand to his lips and kissed my knuckles but he didn't say anything.

Luca

Aria sounded absolutely certain and I wished I could feel the same way but I knew raising a boy in our world required me to make him strong, to make him tough, to make him ruthless. Our boy would become Capo one day, he would rule over the Famiglia and the entire East Coast. For him to be ready for that task, he needed to be a killer, he needed to be cruel and brutal, resistant to pain and fear. My father had loved torturing Matteo and me like he loved torturing our mother and later Nina. He'd relished in our pain, in our fear; hardening us had happened automatically. Matteo and I became used to pain from an early age, had seen horrible things in our own home, had seen our father commit horrendous crimes when we were barely old enough to walk.

How would I handle a boy?

Aria was still smiling at me with a face full of kindness and love. It let my own heart swell with the same emotions. Though, Aria and Marcella were the only people I was kind to, the only people I wanted to treat that way. But a boy, a small version of me… that was another story.

If he was anything like me, like the men in my family, he'd be difficult to handle, would love the kill and inflicting pain. Showing him kindness would be difficult. I'd have to encourage his dark side, his brutality, would have to make sure he became even more bloodthirsty. How could I harden a boy for our world, for the task of becoming Capo, if not with violence?

I didn't know and I wasn't sure if there was even a way, if I would even try going the gentle route. Maybe I wouldn't feel the same hesitation, the same revulsion when thinking about hurting him, as I did with Aria and Marcella. When I looked at them, at their innocent faces, I couldn't imagine hitting them, or worse. The idea of inflicting pain on my daughter or my wife made me sick to my stomach while inflicting pain on other people had always only brought me joy.

"What are you thinking?" Aria asked softly.

I drew my eyes away from the traffic, realizing I hadn't reacted to her earlier comment, too lost in my whirring thoughts. "Just about how it's going to be with a boy."

"It's going to be all right." She squeezed my thigh and I put my hand on hers. "Have you thought about a name for him? With Marcella, you wanted your grandmother's name, so I wondered if you want to do the same with a boy."

"Name him after my father or grandfather? After men who tortured their children and wives?" I released a dark laugh. Those names would never be part of our family again. They'd died with their despicable owners.

"Well, I don't want to name our son after my father or grandfather either."

"We'll find a name for him that doesn't carry the baggage of the past," I said.

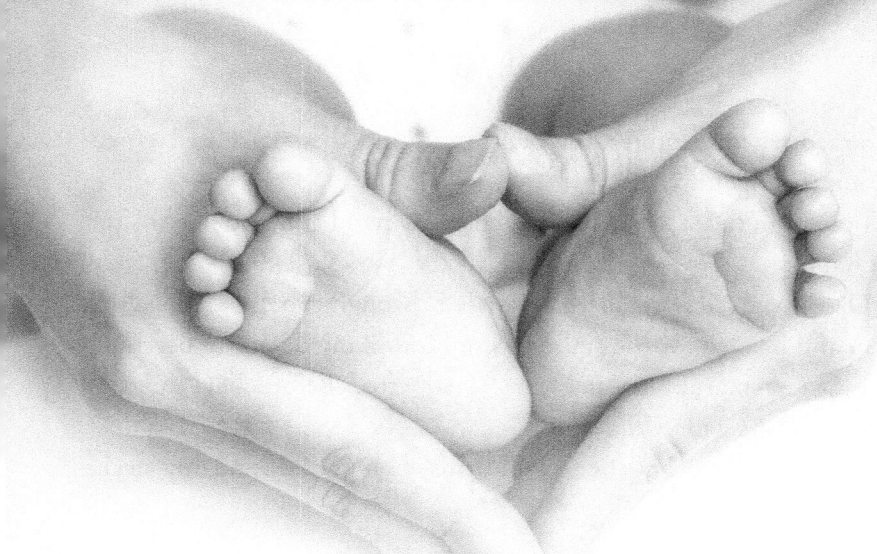

PART THREE

Luca

It was way past midnight when Matteo and I entered the elevator in our building. We'd tracked down a gun depot of Tartarus MC in Jersey and burned it to the ground. Despite my hit to their chapter three years ago they were still being a pain in our asses.

Their cooperation with the Russians was shaky but they still had us as their common enemy.

Matteo yawned as he leaned against the mirrored wall. "Any luck on your house hunt?"

I shook my head. "Not yet. Most houses with a yard are too far out of the city."

"Aria will pop out your kid soon so you better find something."

"Still two months to go," I muttered, but he was right. We'd been looking for a new home for us for three months now. The penthouse was too small for us and two kids, and they needed a yard where they could play, even if Aria and her sisters spent the weekends and the summers in the Hamptons.

The elevator stopped on Matteo's floor and he left with a wave. I felt drained when I entered the penthouse, and the stench of burned wood hung in my nose.

A noise on the stairs made me tense, my hand going to my holster out of habit.

"Dad?" Marcella's small voice carried through the dark. I lowered my arm and headed for the stairs where I found my daughter perching on the last step, rubbing her eyes. I squatted before her and she opened her arms wide. "Hold me."

I picked her up and her small arms wrapped around my neck. "Why are you down here?"

"Can't sleep."

"Why didn't you join your mom in bed?"

"I did, but you weren't there... I wanted to wait for you."

My heart swelled and I kissed her forehead. "I'm here now."

She nodded in the crook of my neck. "Where were you?"

"At work, princess."

"You smell like smoke."

Fuck. Good thing I didn't come home covered in blood today. That was something Marcella didn't need to see. Eventually she would understand what I did but not yet. I didn't want to taint her innocence so soon. "We had a bonfire."

"Can we have one too?" she said in her soft, high voice.

Fuck.

I chuckled. "Next time we're in the mansion."

"Okaayy," she murmured, her body already going soft. I carried her upstairs into the nursery and put her into her bed then covered her with her pink bedding. Her entire room was a girl's dream of rose and white with unicorn drawings on the walls. Five years ago, I'd have never thought that any room in my penthouse would ever look like that. After a kiss on her forehead, I walked into the master bedroom.

The moon illuminated Aria's sleeping form. As usual, she was turned toward my side. I quickly undressed and put on new boxers before I crept into bed. Aria had stuffed the blankets under her belly while her breastfeeding pillow was wedged between her legs. I supposed I'd sleep without covers again. Smiling, I pressed a soft kiss to her protruding belly then halted when I felt a small kick. My boy.

I lightly rested my forehead against Aria's baby bump, marveling at the small wonder growing inside of her.

"Luca?" Aria whispered sleepily.

I lifted my head, kissed her mouth and stretched out beside her. Reaching around her, I carefully pulled her as close as her belly allowed. She pressed her forehead against my chest then kissed the skin lightly. "Bad day?" she asked, her voice drowsy and her breathing slow and even.

I drew in her comforting flowery scent, ran my fingers through her silky hair then down the soft skin of her arm.

"Not anymore," I said quietly. "Now sleep."

She did, and eventually I fell asleep as well.

I woke covered in sweat. Blinking against the early morning light, it took me a moment to figure out the heat source.

I was stretched out on my back and Marcella was sprawled out across my chest, her hair sticking to my throat and chin. It was incredible how much heat her little body gave off. The second heat source was Aria, pressed against my side, her head on my shoulder and one arm thrown over Marcella and me.

Before Aria, I couldn't even fall asleep with another person in the room. Now I didn't even wake when my daughter snuck into our bedroom and used me as her mattress.

It must have been a deeply buried instinct that allowed me to differentiate because the few times I'd had to sleep somewhere else, I'd woken the second someone had as much as moved in the next room. It was as if my body knew I could trust Aria and Marcella and didn't have to wake when they were around.

While I loved having my two girls as close as possible, I was going to have a heat stroke soon if they didn't give me some space. Shifting,

I tried to move Marcella off my chest without waking her. Tough luck.

Marcella opened her blue eyes, blinked at me then yawned.

"Shouldn't you be in your bed?" For a while she'd crept into our bed almost every night but I wanted some privacy for Aria and myself, so we'd put a stop to it… mostly.

She gave me a sheepish smile and batted those long lashes. "I had a nightmare."

"Did you really?" I asked sternly, or as sternly as I was capable of when Marcella was concerned. I was getting better the older she got because I knew she'd have to learn the rules of our world and couldn't act like a spoiled princess.

She bit her lip, grinning cheekily. "No."

"What did I tell you about lies?"

"They are bad," she said, pushing into a sitting position on top of me. A few strands of her black hair stood off to the side.

I touched her chin. "No lying."

She gave a nod then she slid off me and dashed away.

I chuckled.

"She's got you wrapped around her little finger," Aria said with a laugh then kissed my collarbone and chest.

"Like her mother."

Aria raised her eyebrows and I kissed her mouth before I touched her belly. "How is he?"

Her expression softened further. "Amo's kicking up a storm. He's more active than Marcella was. He'll be a little daredevil."

I nodded as I stroked Aria's belly, wondering how difficult he'd be. If he were like Matteo, we'd have our hands full. I still worried about the way I'd handle him. With Marcella I felt such a strong sense of protectiveness, I'd never be able to punish her harshly, but a boy? A boy who pushed my buttons and needed to be strong for the Famiglia.

"Stop worrying," Aria said gently.

I sighed. "You know me too well. I'm not sure I like it."

Aria propped herself up on my chest. "You love it."

She was fucking right. I loved that Aria knew me better than anyone else, but I still tried to keep certain things from her—like the extent of my concerns about having a boy.

"I like Amo better every day," I said to distract her.

Aria beamed. When she'd first suggested the name, I had hesitated because it wasn't a very common name in our circles but then I'd figured that it was for the best. I wanted Amo to be special, wanted him to be better than Matteo and I, than everyone else. A better Capo and man than any Vitiello before him.

Aria

The pressure in my lower belly had gotten increasingly worse through the night. My due date was in three days. Staring up to the dark ceiling, I wondered if I should wake Luca but I worried that this was only a false alarm. He'd had a hard day and needed sleep. A strong contraction made me flinch and I cradled my baby bump, pressing my lips together.

Luca stirred beside me. "What's wrong, love?"

"It's probably nothing. I didn't want to wake you. But I'm having contractions."

Luca turned on the lights at once then rolled around to me with worried eyes. He touched my belly lightly as if he thought it would explode if he put too much pressure on it. "Should we drive to the hospital?"

If this wasn't the real deal, we would spend hours in the hospital for nothing and Luca would lose a whole night of sleep. "I don't think—"

Another, *a stronger* contraction cut me off and I panted, my fingers digging into the bedsheets.

Luca shook his head. "We're going now."

I could only nod. Luca helped me get out of bed and called Matteo while I got dressed in a summer dress, merely because it was comfy and could be taken off without hassle.

"Mom?" Marcella called from her room. "Dad?"

"I'll get Marcella," Luca said and disappeared before returning with our little girl on his arm, who was half-hidden behind her favorite teddy bear.

"You'll be cold in this," Luca commented when he saw what I was wearing.

I shook my head. "Trust me, being cold will be the last thing on my mind soon."

Luca grabbed the hospital bag with one hand as he held Marcella with the other. Her dark hair was all over the place and she was rubbing her blue eyes sleepily.

Slowly I made my way down the staircase, taking one step after the other while Luca kept throwing worried glances over his shoulder at me.

Another contraction made me grab the banister for balance. Luca quickly rushed down the remaining steps and set Marcella and the bag down. "Wait here. I need to help your mom."

Marcella nodded with big eyes, looking lost as she stood in her pink pajamas where Luca had left her. She didn't understand what was going on and I wasn't sure how to explain it to her. She knew she'd get a brother soon but for her he'd magically appear like a present. I wished it could be like that.

Luca wrapped an arm around me and slowly helped me down the remaining stairs. The elevator started moving up and a moment later Matteo stepped into our apartment in sweatpants. His eyes darted from Luca and me to Marcella who was clutching her teddy bear against her chest.

He strolled over to her. "There's my favorite girl," he said, grinning, but Marcella didn't smile, only peered at him with big watery eyes. My heart ached but I wasn't sure how to make this easier for her. Maybe if I hadn't been in this much pain already, we could have made something up, but now I drew a blank.

Matteo squatted in front of her with a smile. "How about you spend the night with your favorite aunt and uncle? Gianna's making chocolate chip cookies as we speak."

I supposed tonight was a good time to break the 'no chocolate after brushing teeth rule'.

"Are they good?" Marcella asked, tilting her head in that cute way she had.

Matteo chuckled. "Well, the dough is store bought, some fancy organic stuff, so chances are they're going to be edible if we head down now and make sure your aunt doesn't burn them."

"Okay," Marcella said in a gravelly voice. Then peered back at Luca and me.

"Go ahead, princess. I'll make sure your mom is all right."

Matteo opened his arms and Marcella immediately moved toward him, snuggling close. Matteo's face softened as he scooped her up and pressed her to his chest. "Make sure my brother doesn't get into trouble without me."

I smiled. "Don't worry. I'll keep an eye on him."

Matteo grinned then turned serious as he looked at Luca. "I'll keep her safe."

We stepped into the elevator together and descended to Matteo's and Gianna's floor. My sister hurried over in what looked like Matteo's boxers and a cut-off tank top when the doors slid open and kissed my cheek. "Keep me updated."

I nodded because I could feel another contraction fast approaching. Gianna turned to Luca. "Keep her safe."

Not waiting for his reply, she tousled Marcella's hair and kissed her cheek. "How about we paint our toenails? Maybe you and I can even convince Matteo to let us paint his as well."

She gave Matteo a cheeky grin.

"Yes, please, Matteo. Pleeaase," Marcella said, batting those long dark lashes at her uncle.

Matteo sent Luca a tortured look. "Hurry up for my sake."

"I'll think of nothing else during labor," I muttered as I clutched Luca's arm in a death grip.

Luca jammed the button that would take us down and the doors closed to Gianna's and Marcella's smiling faces and Matteo's resigned one. The moment we were hidden from view, I released a sharp gasp and bent forward, propping myself up on my thighs as I tried to breathe through the contraction.

Luca rubbed my back. When we arrived at the underground level, he gently steered me toward the car because I could hardly think straight from pain. "You're doing great, Love."

I couldn't even put into words how grateful I was for the man at my side. Without his support, this would be twice as hard. With him at my side, I just knew everything was going to be all right.

Luca

Seeing Aria in pain was the fucking worst thing I could imagine, even if I knew it would be worth it in the end and that the pain would be forgotten once Aria held our son in her arms. Still I wished I could bear the pain in her stead.

We arrived at the hospital within fifteen minutes and were taken into the delivery room at once. Soon two doctors joined us and started checking the baby's vital signs. One of them shook his head then turned to us. "We need to do a C-section. The heart rate and the oxygen level has gone down and your wife isn't dilated enough."

"Do what you have to do to guarantee my wife's and our son's safety," I said quietly, giving them a warning look they couldn't possibly misread. None of them would survive tonight if something happened to my family.

Aria's eyes were wide as she breathed through another contraction. "I want a natural birth."

"I know, Love, but this is for the best for you and the baby."

It didn't take long until everything was prepared for the operation. One of the doctors turned to me before they began. "Usually we warn the fathers that they shouldn't look over the barrier unless they can stomach a lot of blood, but I don't think that's necessary with you."

I didn't like his tone one bit and gave him a cold smile. "I can handle blood, don't worry."

After that, I focused all my attention on Aria, cradling her head and whispering words of adoration in her ear. I could see the worry and fear in her eyes, probably not for herself but our unborn child. "Everything will be all right."

I wasn't sure how much time passed until the doctor finally lifted our son, all wrinkly and blue. For a moment, I thought he wasn't breathing but then he let out a loud wail and the doctor turned to do checkups. He was much bigger than Marcella had been, definitely my son.

Aria released a harsh breath and I kissed her forehead, then her ear, whispering, "I love you more than life itself, principessa. You gave me the greatest gift of all, your love and our children."

Tears filled Aria's eyes and she put her hand over mine.

The doctor carried our son over to us and put him down on Aria's chest. She stroked his back then looked up at me in wonder, and everything else seemed to fade to black, becoming irrelevant. "He looks like you."

He did.

His hair was pitch black and his eyes gray, and he weighed at least nine pounds from the look of it.

I nodded. Like me, but innocent and tiny. I reached out and stroked his cheek. My finger appeared huge against it.

Aria looked exhausted and pale. "Would you like to hold him?"

"Yes," I murmured, my voice strangely hoarse. I gently picked our baby boy up from Aria's chest and held him in my arms. I'd forgotten how tiny and vulnerable babies were, how much they depended on our care. I wasn't sure why I'd thought my feelings for my son would be different than for Marcella. In the few minutes that he was on earth, I already loved him with a fervor I only reserved for Aria and my daughter. He still needed my protection like they did, and I would keep him safe as much as I could.

"Amo," I murmured as I put my finger into his small palm.

Aria watched us with tears in her eyes while I kept checking the doctors who stitched her up to make sure they were focused on the task at hand. When we were finally admitted to our private room, I bent over Aria and kissed her forehead then her lips. "You are incredible, principessa."

She gave me a tired smile. "Will you stay the night?"

"Of course. I won't leave your side."

Cradling Amo in my arms, I watched over Aria as she fell asleep. I wouldn't close my eyes until we were back home. They would be safe; nothing else mattered.

Because of the C-section Aria wasn't allowed to leave the next day, but Gianna and Matteo took care of Marcella, probably stuffing her face with chocolate and letting her watch TV until her little brain was completely frazzled. We decided not to have any visitors to give Aria time to heal and agreed to meet in our penthouse.

I carried Amo on my arm and Aria's bag in my other hand as we stepped into the elevator.

"I hate that I can't carry him because of the C-section," she said, looking longingly at our son.

"It's only a couple of weeks. Your sisters will be around to help you, and Matteo will take care of business as much as he can so I can stay home."

Gianna, Liliana, Romero, and Matteo were already in our penthouse when we stepped inside. Someone, I assumed Liliana, had decorated everything with balloons and baked a cake with blue frosting.

Aria's eyes widened in surprise. She moved carefully into our home, trying to hide that she was still in pain, but I caught the occasional wince.

Gianna and Liliana, who carried Marcella in her arms, hurried over to Aria and hugged her while Matteo and Romero joined me. Romero touched my shoulder, regarding Amo with a smile. "He looks like you."

Before I could say anything, Matteo spoke up.

"He looks like a fat little Buddha with black hair." He lifted one of Amo's stubby arms.

Aria sent Matteo an incredulous look and I would have hit him over the head if I hadn't been carrying Amo.

Matteo flashed the girls a grin. "Come on, it's the truth. It's not like he's an ugly baby but he's a little Michelin man with all those fat rolls."

"If he gets as tall as Luca, he'll grow quickly, then he needs the additional weight," Romero said diplomatically.

"Let's hope so. On the other hand, maybe we can torture our enemies by letting your little sumo wrestler sit on them."

"How about you shut up?" I muttered.

Gianna stalked over to us and pinched Matteo, who flinched, then rubbed the spot. "Look at him and tell me he doesn't look like a baby Buddha."

Gianna rolled her eyes then gave me an exasperated look. "Congrats. I hope you don't drop your kid on the head like someone must have done with Matteo when he was a baby."

"I'll do my best," I said then peered down at Amo who was deep asleep, oblivious to Matteo's comments.

Liliana came over with Marcella in her arms. "Look, that's your little brother."

I gave Marcella a smile, lifting Amo so she could get a better look. She watched her brother with her head tilted to the side as if he was a new toy she was trying to figure out. "Why isn't he doing anything?"

"Because he's a baby. They sleep, poop, and eat," Gianna said.

Aria sighed, but I could tell she was fighting a grin.

"That's boring," Marcella said, looking disappointed. Then she glanced over at Aria and stretched out her arms. "Mommy, arm."

Aria's expression fell.

"Mommy isn't allowed to carry anything at the moment," I said. Marcella's lower lip began to tremble. Fuck. I couldn't stand it when she cried.

Gianna sighed and came over to me. "Come on, give me your little poo machine. I'll carry your future sumo wrestler while you snuggle with Marci."

I handed Amo to her and her widened eyes flitted over to my wife. "How did he ever fit inside of you?"

Aria laughed. "I don't know."

"Good thing you didn't have to squeeze him out of your vajayjay."

"Hey," I said in warning as I took Marcella from Liliana who went over to Gianna to hold Amo's tiny hand.

"What's a vajayjay?" Marcella asked immediately. I sent Gianna a death glare.

"Nothing you have to worry about."

Gianna and Aria burst out laughing, and Marcella peered up at me with a small frown.

Matteo winked. "Missing your bachelor days, huh?"

"Never," I said as I kissed Marcella's frown, causing her to giggle then looked at Amo who'd woken and was staring up at Gianna with huge eyes. Aria was smiling as if this was perfection… and for me, it was.

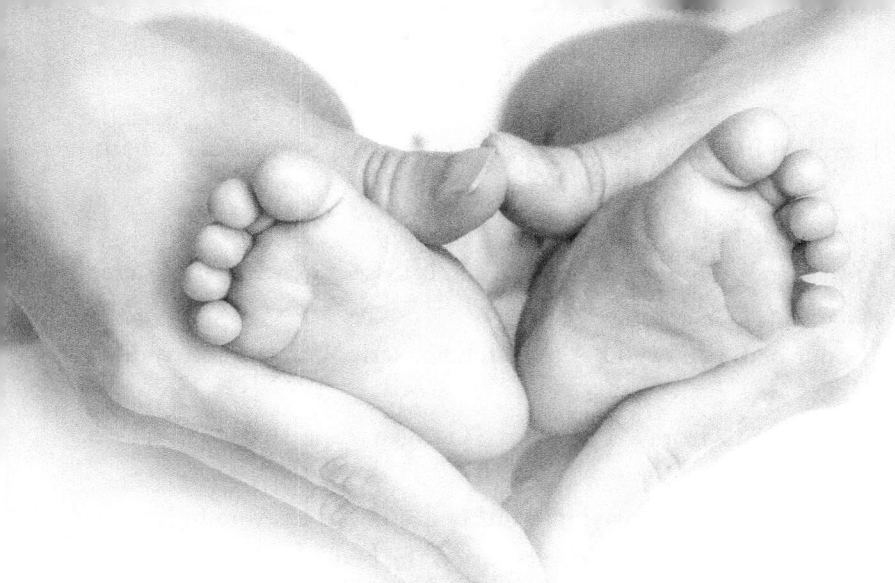

PART FOUR

Luca

ARIA'S HEALING PROCESS TOOK LONGER THAN LAST TIME but with her sisters' help things soon fell into place. Still I could tell that Aria was trying to not be a burden and do things on her own.

This was the first day I wasn't home before six because the Tartarus MC had thrown a Molotov cocktail into one of our whorehouses. They weren't as organized as they used to be. My hit to their local chapter had almost banished them completely from this area—almost.

Amo was eight weeks old and a fussy baby, so I tried to help Aria during the nights as often as I could.

The second I entered the apartment after midnight I could hear his wails. I took the steps two at a time and rushed into the nursery where I found Aria in the armchair, covered in sweat, eyes red from crying and a red-faced Amo screaming and squirming while Aria tried to feed him.

"Aria?"

"I can't get him to calm down. No matter what I do. He's been crying for hours."

I stroked her head. "Shhh. Let me take care of him. Take a bath, Love."

"I'm failing him."

"You're not failing anyone, Aria." I kissed her hair. "Where's Marcella?"

"In our bed. I allowed her to watch her series because she couldn't sleep."

I pried Amo from Aria's arms. "Go, get some sleep. Or take a bath. Now."

She nodded then moved into our bedroom. I put Amo in his carrier before I followed her. Marcella sat on the bed, watching her series on the tablet, but looked up from the screen when I entered. "How about you, Amo, and I drive around the city for a bit?"

Marcella jumped off the bed. "Yes!"

Before I left with our kids, Aria gave me a grateful smile as she sank down on the bed.

As I'd hoped, both Amo and Marcella fell asleep in the car after thirty minutes of driving in circles around the area. After bringing Marcella into her bed, I stretched out on the sofa in the nursery in case Amo woke up again.

"Luca?"

My eyes shot open. Aria's face hovered over me, her brows drawn together in concern. "Don't tell me you slept like this all night?"

I glanced at my watch. A few minutes after nine in the morning. "Amo kept me busy most of the night." I shook my head at the look of guilt on Aria's face. "You needed sleep more than I did. You've been taking over most nights and now it was my turn." I sat up, peering toward the crib but Amo wasn't in it.

"I grabbed him three hours ago and took him downstairs with me. Gianna and Matteo will watch him and Marcella for a few hours so we can have breakfast together and have some time for us," Aria said with a hopeful smile. Standing up, I pulled her against me and kissed her.

"How about we have breakfast in bed? Why don't you go ahead and order a few things while I take a shower?"

Aria nodded and dashed off after another kiss. Watching her in her sexy shorts and camisole, blood rushed into my dick. We hadn't been intimate since Aria had given birth, and it was slowly starting to kill me, but I didn't want to put additional pressure on Aria. I stalked into the shower and jerked off, even if it hardly satisfied my hunger for my gorgeous wife anymore.

When I emerged from the bathroom, Aria sat cross-legged on the bed, two steaming mugs of coffee on a wooden tray in front of her. "Food will be here in about ten minutes."

My eyes were drawn to the way her shorts gathered between her ass cheeks, accentuating her pussy. I took the cup and gulped down some coffee. Aria regarded me with a knowing look but didn't comment.

Thirty minutes later, we were done with our waffles and pancakes and I was sprawled out on my back with Aria lying on top of me. We'd been kissing for a couple of minutes and Aria's warmth and her scent rekindled the desire I'd tried to kill earlier. I wanted nothing more than to sleep with her, but I held back.

Instead my hands rubbed Aria's back, her sides, and her ass, trying to ignore the small rocking motions of her pelvis.

With a soft sigh, Aria pulled back, her lips red and swollen. "I want to try to have sex."

"Are you sure?" I rasped, even as my hand kneaded her ass cheek and my cock sprang to attention.

Aria answered with a firm kiss, her tongue slipping in. I rolled us over so I hovered over her, desperate to worship her and get her body ready. Soon I'd worked my way down her beautiful breasts to her pussy. After a kiss to her shorts, I dragged them down her legs, laying her bare to me.

I stroked Aria, parting her so I could rub her clit and stifled a groan at the sight of her need for me. Aria moaned softly as I stroked her.

I pushed my middle finger into her but paused when Aria exhaled shakily. "Okay?"

She nodded and I began to move slowly while I drew small circles on her slick clit. I loved watching my finger fuck Aria's pussy, loved seeing how it glistened with her juices. It didn't take long for Aria to become undone, rocking her hips, pushing my finger even deeper into her. She came with a cry, nails scratching over the sheets and I almost came in my fucking boxers. I quickly pulled out my finger then bowed my head down and ran my tongue along her slit, licking up her arousal.

"Luca," she gasped.

"Did you miss me eating you out?" I rasped before dipping between those delicious pussy lips.

"God, yes," she moaned. I smirked against her pussy and fluttered my tongue over her opening. Aria rewarded me with more of her sweet juices.

"You taste so good, principessa. I could lick your pussy all day."

Aria whimpered, rocking her hips, pressing her pussy closer against my mouth. "Do you want me to suck that little button?"

"Yes, please."

I closed my lips around her clit and started suckling the way Aria loved it. Soon she was writhing and moaning, and I couldn't take my eyes off her, even as my own need became almost impossible to ignore. She arched up as her release hit her, looking wild and gorgeous. I pushed up and shoved down my briefs, then kicked them off impatiently, dying to be inside of Aria.

Spreading her open with my thighs, I groaned when my tip pressed up to her heat. Three months since I'd last been inside of her. Fuck. I couldn't wait. Before I started to push in, I lowered myself so our bodies were flush together and kissed Aria.

She curled her fingers over my neck and lifted her ass. I shifted my hips, sliding into her slowly, my gaze intent on her face to see any hint of discomfort but there was only lust and need. I moaned when I was buried all the way inside of her and Aria squeezed her eyes shut with a shudder. "Is this okay?"

Aria gripped my shoulders, opening her eyes with a look of desire. "Please fuck me, Luca. I need you."

Our mouths clashed and I pitched my hips forward. Aria wrapped her legs around my hips, bringing us even closer as I started to thrust into her, deeper and harder, until we were both panting and sweating. Neither of us lasted long, coming at the same time, overwhelmed by the sensations. Afterward, I held her in my arms, trying to catch my breath, but my cock had a mind of its own and so did Aria's fingers as they trailed down my abs…

Aria and I picked up our children two hours and another round of sex later. It was strange how much more relaxed Aria appeared, and I, too, felt less stressed. We'd have to make sure to arrange time for ourselves even with two small kids.

When we entered the apartment to pick up our children, Gianna looked as if she'd done a nosedive into a paint box. Her bright red lipstick extended to the skin around her mouth, giving her a grotesque smile, and her eyes were surrounded by so much color it was difficult to make out her actual pupils and irises. "Marcella decided to do my makeup for me today," she said.

Aria laughed.

"She looks pretty, right?" Marcella said, beaming.

Aria stroked Marcella's head with a nod before she took Amo from Matteo.

"Yes, Luca. I look pretty, don't I?" Gianna piped up, batting her lashes the same way Marcella always did. She looked like a murderous clown doll.

Matteo chuckled and I gave him an exasperated look.

"I remember a time when your name was whispered in fear…" he said.

"I'm satisfied with the list of people who fear me."

Marcella came up to me and wrapped her arms around my leg. "Dad, why do people fear you?"

Gianna snorted. Marcella's eyes darted toward her aunt and she dashed toward her. "Tell me, why?"

I tensed, worried what Gianna would say. She motioned toward me. "Look at him, Marci. He's a giant. Everyone's scared of giants, right?"

Marcella regarded me for a moment before she nodded gravely as if truer words had never been spoken. A smile pulled at her mouth and she rushed back toward me. "But I'm not scared of you, Dad!"

I lifted her. "Good."

Aria shook her head with a grin then pressed a kiss to Amo's head. "Thanks for taking care of them."

"I hope you two lovebirds had time for some lovin'." Matteo wiggled his eyebrows.

"Bye, Matteo," I said as I stepped into the elevator. Aria joined me with a wave toward her sister and my brother.

Later that day, we settled on the sofa with our kids. Aria read a picture book to Marcella who sat on her lap while I leaned against the backrest with Amo in the crook of my arm. I rubbed his belly gently and was rewarded with a toothless smile and a few leg kicks against my outstretched palm. "You are a strong boy."

Amusement flashed across Aria's face before Marcella asked another question about the butterfly featured in her book. They both focused on the image with a small frown and pursed lips, looking so much alike in that moment, my fucking heart throbbed harder. I kissed Amo's forehead then murmured, "When you're older, you need to help me protect your sister and mom. They're too beautiful for this world. We'll have to kill all the boys who think they are worthy of your sister."

"What did you say?" Aria asked curiously.

"That I need to invest in more weapons to keep you all safe."

"I think you and Matteo own enough weapons, not to mention soldiers, to invade a small country. No need for more weapons."

Marcella tilted her head, her black hair curtaining half of her face and contrasting strongly with her blue eyes and pale skin. Then she smiled.

I raised Amo above my head. "Definitely more weapons, right, Amo?"

He gave me another toothless grin.

FORBIDDEN DELIGHTS

A stepbrother forbidden mafia romance

(Love in Lockdown Charity Anthology, 2020)

Stella is a forbidden fruit Mauro isn't allowed to taste.

Not only because she isn't promised to him but also because she's his stepsister.

She used to be his annoying shadow, the little girl he needed to protect and babysit. Now she's all grown-up and he can't stop noticing. Being locked into a panic room with her might be the ultimate test of his self-control…

Mauro has always been her protector and ally until she starts to see him as more. Afraid of his reaction, she hides her attraction. But can she keep doing so when they're trapped in a small room all alone?

CHAPTER ONE

Mauro

THE MAFIA WORLD WAS BUILT ON RULES.

Rules never to be broken. They'd outlasted generations, resisting the ever-occurring changes of modern society. They were like the Colosseum. The foundations of our traditions remained steadfast even as we adapted to our surroundings.

One of those rules was not to desire a girl that wasn't promised to you, especially if said girl was your stepsister.

As Underboss of Cleveland, my father needed to remarry after his first wife, my mother, died. I was eleven when she passed away, still a boy and yet well-acquainted with death. Growing up in the mafia, especially if your father was one of the Famiglia's Underbosses and ruled over hundreds of men, you were introduced to the dark underbelly of the business early, to harden you for future tasks.

Father waited exactly the expected year before he married Felicitas and disappeared into their cocoon of wedded bliss, leaving me to deal with something I hadn't bargained for: a kid-stepsister. The first time I met Stella, she was seven with braces and ridiculous pigtails, and so goddamn shy, she didn't talk to me for a week after she moved in. That changed quickly though and as her mother began popping out three babies in short succession, forgetting about her oldest daughter's existence, Stella became my shadow and I, her—at first not so willing—protector and companion.

Stella had always been a kid in my eyes, a girl I needed to protect because we were family, albeit not by blood and not even by choice because nobody asked us before our parents sealed their bond. Being five years my junior, I hadn't noticed the gradual changes in her body because I didn't pay any fucking attention to her body. Small shifts right before my eyes just didn't register. Until Father sent me away to help our family in Sicily in their fight against the other mob famiglias. I was gone for a little over a year and when I saw Stella for the first time after all that time, I did a double take. She rushed toward me with a huge smile and flung herself into my arms. I hugged her back after a moment, suddenly feeling her curves, her breasts pressing against my chest. When I pulled back, I actually checked her out. Something I'd never done. She was Stella, my stepsister, not a girl I checked out. And yet my eyes lingered on all the right places, and fuck, they were spectacular. Stella shared her mother's breathtaking beauty, but luckily not her self-centered vanity or air-headedness.

Had I just never noticed her curves or had Stella developed them all in only a year?

It seemed impossible. I must have been oblivious, and it was a state I needed to reach quickly again. Stella was completely off-limits. Fuck, we shared a last name. We were family.

After that day, I made an extra effort to not look at her body, focusing only on her face. Yet, even that didn't help matters. Because Stella's blue eyes and teasing smile haunted my nights, and sometimes even popped up when I fucked another woman. It was maddening.

Stella had become a fucking star, shining so brightly that she'd burned herself into my mind. No matter what I did, the image of her smile, of her curves, flashed up, even when I closed my eyes. It was like closing your eyes after you'd looked directly at the sun for too long:

speckles of light kept dancing against the dark of your eyelids, reminding you of the enticing brightness you'd closed off.

I cleaned my hands of the blood. The cleaners took care of the body and the cut off parts. Torturing Bratva assholes for information was one of the perks of my job, which currently was jack-of-all-trades because at twenty-three, my father wanted to show me the ins and outs of every area of the business in our city before I'd take over from him in a few years.

My phone rang and I dried my hands before I took the call.

"Mauro, I need you to come over right away to watch Stella."

I paused. "I thought you were leaving for Vermont today?" At every family dinner, I'd been forced to attend in the last few weeks, Felicitas hadn't shut up about their upcoming ski trip to one of those uptight luxury resorts.

"We are," Father said impatiently. "But Stella's not coming with us."

"What about the midgets?" That's what I called my three little half-siblings.

"Of course, they are coming with us. Felicitas would go crazy if she had to be separated from her children for a week."

"Stella is her kid too, she knows that, right?"

"I don't have time to talk about this. Come over. You need to stay here the days we are gone and protect Stella." He hung up, not waiting for my reply. Naturally, he expected obedience. His soldiers always followed his command after all, and as his son, I was little more than that in his eyes.

I grabbed my car keys, left the torture room and hurried toward my car, a new Aston Martin model that Father had given me on my last birthday. What he lacked in praise and affection, he made up with money and pricy gifts tenfold. I wasn't a little kid anymore who craved his love or approval, so I was fine with our arrangement. I froze with my pointer finger against the start engine button when I realized what Father's newest task of babysitting meant for me. I'd have to spend an entire week under a roof with Stella, my off-limits stepsister who visited my dreams almost every night.

Fuck. I was so screwed. Something I couldn't do with Stella—never.

Stella

Mother didn't deign me with a single glance as she ushered my three half-siblings into the lobby where their luggage waited for the bodyguards to pick them up. She'd never been this motherly to me, not even when I had been younger. Maybe it was because she'd been only nineteen when she had me, or maybe she just didn't like me very much because half of me was Dad. She'd never looked in love with him while she seemed infatuated like a teenager with Alfredo.

"Where is he?" Mother asked, annoyed, as she peered at her Rolex, matching the Rolex around Alfredo's wrist.

Alfredo knew that tone, and he took out his phone to call Mauro.

Excitement bubbled in me when I thought of spending a week alone with Mauro. When he'd moved out, and worse, spent a year abroad, I'd been devastated. He'd always been the only one who sided with me in this house. As a Made Man he was busy, so I only saw him once a week when he visited for family dinner. Before his time in Sicily he'd occasionally picked me up so we could do something together, but that never happened anymore.

A ring sounded and Mauro appeared in the open doorway, rolling his eyes at his father. "I'm here. I came as quickly as I could. Unfortunately, I'm not the only car on the street."

"We're going to be late for our flight," Mother said. I hovered on the last step of the staircase and gave Mauro a quick smile, trying to ignore the way my belly fluttered. For three years, I'd been in love with him, a completely insane, impossible crush I couldn't shake. It was a good thing that Mauro didn't see me as more than his little stepsister, someone he now had to babysit as if I were eight and not almost eighteen.

Mauro cocked an eyebrow at me over my mother's head and I

had to bite back laughter. She'd probably have grounded me eternally if she'd discovered I wasn't half as sad as she wanted me to be because I wasn't allowed to go on their ski adventure with them.

"Will you be gone the planned week?" Mauro asked.

"Of course," Alfredo said as if it was a stupid question.

Mauro's eyes tightened, his brows building a V and a muscle in his left cheek twitched in a way that showed his displeasure over the situation. Was it so bad to spend a few days with me?

"Stella's birthday is in four days. Isn't it tradition to celebrate with the family?"

Oh. He was pissed on my behalf. The stupid butterflies in my stomach rioted.

Mother made a small noncommittal noise. "She should have thought about it before acting out."

My little sister had hit me with her Barbie doll because I didn't do what she wanted, which was why I'd taken the thing away. Mother had spoiled her and my other half-siblings rotten and obviously preferred to keep it that way.

I was glad to stay home. If I'd come along, they would have used me as a nanny and their metaphorical punching bag whenever something didn't go as planned. A few chill days with Netflix, fast food, and Mauro sounded like pure bliss in comparison.

Mauro shook his head again. Sometimes I got the feeling my mother's lack of interest in me annoyed him more than it did me. It had bothered me for a long time, and it still occasionally did, but I'd come to terms with it. Mother wouldn't miraculously become more caring or affectionate, and if I didn't want her neglect to break me, I needed to accept it and move on.

Mother, Alfonso, and the three spoiled little brats finally left the house. Mauro threw the door shut with more force than necessary, shaking his head. Then his gaze settled on me.

"You look as if you got a jail sentence. Is it really so bad to stay with me?"

Mauro ran a hand through his dark hair, those milk-chocolate brown eyes locking on mine. "No. But I hate to be called away from business because of last-minute theatricals."

"You had plans?" I asked, wondering if he was currently seeing a girl.

He couldn't really date. Women from our world were only allowed to be with their husband, and Outsiders could never be more than an affair. Still, it bothered me that Mauro was with other girls when it decidedly shouldn't. He wasn't mine, never would be. The butterflies stopped their maddening fluttering as if someone had ripped their wings off, and that's how it felt whenever I considered how doomed my feelings for Mauro were.

I couldn't stop myself from checking him out. He was tall, more than a head taller than me, and muscled but not bulky. He was lithe, deadly, and just ridiculously handsome. His shirt hugged his six-pack, his pecs, and his strong biceps. Because the shirt was white, the outline of his Famiglia tattoo that every Made Man got for his initiation shone through.

Born in Blood. Sworn in Blood.
I enter alive and leave dead.

Why couldn't I stop looking at him as if I could ever be with him? It was wrong. Our parents would never allow it. Mainly because of the major scandal it would cause. I wasn't sure how long I checked him out, but Mauro seemed lost in his own thoughts. He was watching me in a way as if I was his nightmare come true, and I didn't understand it. We'd been so close before he went off to Sicily and we were still close while he was there, but things had become tense, almost awkward at times. I wasn't brave enough to ask him why. Maybe it was something that happened with all people in my life. They eventually lost interest in me.

CHAPTER TWO

Mauro

I stared out into the night. Fuck, I wasn't scared of anything, but now I was acting like a goddamn pussy. Too scared of sleep. Too scared of my mind's torturous fantasies that only got more creative with every passing day in close proximity to Stella. We'd spent three whole days together so far. I was torn between wanting our time alone together to be over as quickly as possible—to prevent a misfortune from happening—and wanting to prolong it.

Stella was my drug of choice. She was oblivious to my dirty thoughts, to all the ways I'd already fucked her in my fantasies. Today she was still seventeen, tomorrow she'd finally be of age. *Finally?* Another barrier crumbling, another hit for my dwindling self-control.

Fuck. Father had given me one job: keep an eye on Stella, protect her physical well-being and her honor. The latter probably more than the former. After all, a girl in our circles was judged by her fucking pureness. That was the reason for the disgusting bloody sheets tradition. He still wanted to marry her off to the highest bidder one day. If I acted on my fantasies, that could ruin his plans.

My eyes registered a moving shadow on the premises. At first, I was sure my mind was playing a trick on me. We had an advanced alarm system for the yard and house, which went off as soon as anything bigger than a cat tried to get over the fence. It was necessary because our territory bordered on enemy land, and the Outfit had been attacking frequently since the truce had been broken.

Another shadow, then another. What the fuck?

Glass shattered somewhere in the house. No alarm. Nothing.

I whirled around, grabbed my Berettas from the nightstand, and stormed down the hallway toward Stella's room, shoving one gun into the waistband of my sweatpants. I barreled inside and staggered toward her bed, grasping her arm. I jerked her upward, and she awakened with a gasp, her eyes wide with fear. Her lips opened to cry out, but my hand clamped down on her mouth. Finally, her eyes settled on my face and her brows pulled together in confusion.

"Attackers are in the house. Come on, I need to get you to the panic room."

"The alarm?" she asked. I pulled her out of bed when she didn't move.

"Stella, follow me!" After another moment of hesitation, she finally acted on my orders. Pulling my second gun out, I handed it to Stella. She shook her head. "I don't know how to shoot."

"Point at an attacker and pull the fucking trigger, that's it."

She took the gun, and I led us into the hallway. "Stay behind me at all times and don't shoot me in the back by accident. And for fuck's sake, do what I say, no questions asked."

She nodded mutely, obviously stunned by my dominant demeanor.

We hurried toward the staircase. Hushed male voices were coming from the living room.

"Quick," I rasped. I grabbed her wrist because she looked frozen. I hurried down the staircase, dragging Stella after me.

The entrance to the panic room was in Father's office on the ground floor, the last door on the right, branching off from the lobby. An attacker appeared in the doorway to the living room when we reached the last step. I pulled the trigger and sent a bullet through his left eye. He tumbled to the ground with a resounding thud. I dragged Stella past the body, hearing steps of several more intruders in the living room. I ran faster even though Stella panted desperately behind me. With a hard shove, I pushed the door open, ran inside and entered a code into the keypad beside one of the bookshelves. The floor parted beside the desk, revealing a narrow staircase and an underground panic room.

"Go in!" I shoved Stella in the direction of the opening. She clambered down a few steps.

"Don't leave me alone." Her eyes were wide and fearful.

"Down!" I snarled.

She disappeared, and I quickly climbed down as well. Only my head peeked out from the hole in the floor when another attacker glimpsed into the room. Like the first attacker, I didn't recognize his face. I shot, but he jerked back and the bullet collided with the wall behind him, sending plaster flying everywhere. I pressed the close button, and the floor slid shut within seconds, then I punched a code into the pad that would guarantee no one got down here who didn't know the correct numbers. A flicker of a face peered down at me a moment before the door clicked shut. Was it the Bratva or the Outfit? Both were giving us trouble.

Gritting my teeth, I turned and tensed.

Stella stood in the middle of the hundred-twenty square foot room, her arms wrapped around her middle, looking completely out of it. Her breathing came out in sharp bursts, panic flickering in her eyes. Her gaze darted around the room restlessly.

"It's okay. This room is safe." I tried to calm her, but my words barely registered.

She seemed to be going into shock, her chest rising and falling rapidly. I tore my eyes from her breasts, shoved my gun into the waistband of my sweatpants and moved toward her, carefully prying the gun from her clenched fingers. Pushing it into the back of my waistband, I touched Stella's cheek. She tilted her head up, her gaze meeting mine.

She was more than a head shorter than me, and my protectiveness reared its head. I stroked a few strands of her caramel brown hair from her sweaty forehead.

"You are safe, Stella."

"You are here," she whispered as if that affirmed my words.

"I'll protect you."

She looked around again. The room was meant for a short stay. Six bunk beds lined the walls to our left and right. The back of the room had a small kitchenette and a narrow closed-off bathroom. Though it was the size of a broom closet, no more. You could pretty much shower while you sat on the toilet.

Right beside the steep ladder was a sofa and a small TV. That was all.

"We're trapped under the floor," she whispered, looking up at the low ceiling and swallowing hard. Only a light bulb dangled above our heads.

"Just think of this as a normal apartment."

"It doesn't have any windows."

"A shitty apartment then."

She giggled nervously. My fingers found her throat and her fluttering pulse beneath her satin-soft skin.

"We won't have to stay down here long. Soon reinforcements will arrive." But the alarm hadn't gone off. I went over to the small console beside the ladder and pressed the alarm button which was connected to our main security system. A red light flashed. No connection. Fuck. I glanced up the ladder, hearing footsteps above us. They couldn't get down here unless they blasted the entire house into smithereens. But if reinforcements weren't alerted, Stella and I were stuck down here until our parents returned, and that was in three days. A long time to be stuck in an underground room, especially with your tantalizing half-dressed stepsister. My eyes registered Stella's flimsy nightgown for the first time. This was a nightmare, and not mainly because of the attackers who potentially wanted to torture and kill us.

"I didn't hear an alarm," Stella said, searching my eyes.

Damn. I sighed. For some reason, I never liked lying to her. "It didn't go off. They disabled it."

Her eyes darted up to the trapdoor. "But they aren't going to come in?"

"No, not without a code."

She nodded, biting her lip, still looking so fucking lost and scared.

I returned to her side and stroked her cheek with the pad of my thumb. Fuck, why couldn't I stop touching her? "I swear you're safe."

Again that small trusting smile, which was giving me ideas and at the same time reminding me that I had a responsibility for Stella. She trusted me, had miraculously done so for a long time.

I glanced at the clock on the wall. It was past midnight.

"Happy Birthday," I said.

Stella blinked, her brows crinkling. "If the start of my birthday is any indication for the rest of my year, I'd like to skip it."

I smiled, shaking my head, my fingers still on her skin. My gaze darted to her lips, the way they curved up in a half-smile despite the anxiety in her eyes. I dropped my hand as if I'd been burned and stepped back, clearing my throat. "I'm going to check everything. It's been a while since I've been down here."

"Does that mean you don't have a birthday present for me?"

An image of my head buried between her legs popped into my mind. Not the birthday present she had in mind. I needed to drag my mind out of the gutter. "Not down here," I got out.

CHAPTER THREE

Stella

My heart beat wildly in my chest as I kept listening to sounds from above. Muffled footsteps sounded on occasion, but the door held fast. Slowly, I made my way over to the sofa and sank down, trying to calm myself. Mauro meticulously checked every drawer of the kitchen and the narrow wardrobe.

The muscles in his shoulders and back flexed as he leaned forward. Scars littered his back from knife and gun wounds he'd suffered over the years as a Made Man. Slowly my gaze dropped to his firm ass and a flush heated my cheeks. I quickly dragged my gaze away when Mauro turned, his brows furrowed in concentration. His chest was chiseled, tanned and a small splattering of dark hair trailed from his navel down into his low-cut sweatpants. It was the first time I saw him without a shirt in a long time. He'd always worn a shirt around me. My stomach warmed.

Mauro's eyes cut to me and I blushed, feeling caught, as if my inappropriate thoughts were written all over my face. I was glad he didn't know how I felt toward him. He'd think I was being silly. "We're well equipped with canned food and a change of clothes. A few days down here won't be a problem."

I nodded, then flinched when something crashed over our heads.

Mauro narrowed his eyes.

"What was that?"

"I think they threw over one of the shelves. They might be looking for a safe. Maybe this attack isn't about us, but about information they hope to acquire."

Again, I nodded. I'd never much cared for mob business. I'd never gotten a taste of what it entailed—until now. Mauro had been risking his life for years, since he was younger than I am now. Maybe that was why the age difference of five years between us sometimes felt so much bigger.

"Try to get some sleep. I can dim the light," Mauro said.

I quickly shook my head. There was no way I'd fall asleep now. Adrenaline pumped through my body.

"Why don't you watch some TV while I try to figure out a way to send out an emergency signal?"

I dropped in front of the TV like a five-year-old, but what else could I have done? My legs were shaking and my brain capacity close to zero. I took the remote and began to mindlessly flip through the channels. But I kept the volume low so I'd hear what went on above our heads, and my gaze kept returning to the trapdoor, the only thing between us and our potential murderers.

That and Mauro. He was a good shot. He'd protect us.

Mauro

I was interested in modern technology, but trying to send out an emergency signal past whatever block our attackers had installed was well beyond my knowledge.

Stella's eyes kept alternately following me and checking out the ceiling. She was still shaking and goose bumps pimpled her skin. Her nipples peeked through her nightgown in the most distracting way possible.

"Aren't you cold? You can change into other clothes," I suggested eventually.

Stella followed my suggestion and surprised me when she put on one of my sweaters. For some reason, the sight of her in my too-big clothes was even more of a turn-on than her flimsy nightgown had been. Damn it all.

I spent the night and most of the day going over the manual for the keypad and turning on the heat. More to distract myself than for any practical purposes. I sat on one of the bunk beds while Stella had curled up on the sofa, only her shins and feet peeking out from my sweater.

She dozed off twice but jerked up shortly after, her breathing shaky until her eyes settled on me. "Can't you read beside me?"

I got up and walked over to her, then sank down next to her feet. Stella propped them up on my thighs, and without thinking, I put my palm on her calf. Her skin was soft, warm and now that I felt it, I couldn't stop thinking how much better it would feel if I trailed my hand up to her sensitive inner thigh or even higher.

I shoved the thought out of my head and focused on the tiny font of the manual. Stella sat up and caught me off guard by turning around and settling her head in my lap. For a moment, I stared down at her caramel hair, half torn between shoving her away because I really didn't need additional images of her face close to my dick haunting my nights, and tugging my waistband down and sliding my cock into her mouth.

I shifted when I felt the treacherous blood flow down into my groin area.

"Anything interesting?"

"No," I gritted out. Stella met my eyes, frowning. My sudden tension didn't make sense to her. "Did you hear something? Are we in danger?"

I was in danger of losing my sliver of self-control, and she of losing her honor.

Something in her expression shifted, as if she knew what I was thinking.

I'd on occasion thought she'd looked at me with more than step-sisterly affection, but had blamed it on my own forbidden desires. Now I wasn't so sure anymore.

After an early dinner of a can of cream of mushroom soup and some crackers, Stella slipped into the tiny bath-cupboard. The door was thin and I could hear every muttered curse as she tried to change in the narrow space. I tried not to imagine how she undressed, how she'd look naked.

"Ouch!" Stella muttered.

I chuckled despite the situation.

Silence followed behind the door.

"Can you hear me?"

"Of course, I can hear you."

More silence. "You have to cover your ears."

"Stella, I'm not going to cover my fucking ears. I know how it sounds when someone pees, so get on with it and don't you dare turn the water on to cover up the sounds."

"I'm not going to pee if you can hear everything!" She turned the water on. I stretched out on one of the bunks, wondering what the attackers were doing upstairs. Undoubtedly trying to get down here. Why hadn't Father thought of installing monitors down here that were linked to cameras on the premises?

The door opened and Stella stepped out. My heart skipped a beat. What the holy fuck was she wearing? I sat up slowly, wondering if my mind was playing tricks on me. Stella was in some kind of flimsy red negligee made of thin silky material. It only reached her upper thighs and clung to her breasts. Fuck.

Stella shifted on her feet, her face turning red under my scrutiny. "Only my mother would choose this as her nightwear for a lockdown situation. The clothes in my drawer are a few years old and don't fit me anymore."

I barely registered her words. Most of my blood had left my brain. Of course, I'd noticed Stella's curves before, but having them shoved into my face like this, it would definitely stir up a whole new onslaught of dirty fantasies I had absolutely no business entertaining.

I pushed to my feet and headed over to the drawer with my clothes, ripping it open with a bit too much force. I pulled out a T-shirt and boxer shorts and flung them at Stella. She barely caught them, her eyes wide in surprise.

"Here. Put that on. It'll be more comfortable than that thing."

As if Stella's comfort had anything to do with my need to cover her with one of my T-shirts.

Hurt flickered in her expression, catching my half-functioning brain by surprise. I didn't get the chance to analyze the look because she whirled around and returned to the bathroom.

Stella

I clutched the clothes to my chest, stunned by the wave of disappointment I felt. At first, when I'd realized I'd have to wear my mother's ridiculous negligee I had been embarrassed, but after putting it on, I'd secretly been excited about Mauro's reaction.

I hadn't expected him to look almost appalled. Trying not to take this to heart was difficult, even when I should have been relieved. Mauro's reaction was normal. Mine wasn't. He acted like a stepbrother should.

I peeled out of the negligee and got into Mauro's clothes. The shorts hung very low on my hips and the T-shirt reached mid-thigh. Taking a deep breath, I emerged again, determined to get a grip and stop seeing anything more than family in Mauro.

I couldn't read the look Mauro gave me. It was only a few minutes past seven, but I felt tired. I'd barely slept last night, and I wasn't sure if I'd get any sleep tonight. It had been silent above our heads for a while now.

"Do you think they are gone?" I asked as I headed over to Mauro's bunk where he sat hunched over a semi-automatic from the rifle cabinet behind the ladder, putting it back together after dismantling it.

He glanced up, his eyes dragging over my body in a way that sent a little shiver down my spine. Did his gaze linger on my bare legs?

Do not go there…

"I doubt it. They could be taking apart room after room in search of something useful. Like the code to this room."

My eyes widened.

Mauro shook his head. "It's not written down anywhere. Only Father and I know it, as well as a few trustworthy men."

I sank down beside Mauro and his body became taut. I mourned the fact that he'd put on a shirt. Our eyes met, and I held my breath, not even sure why. Something in Mauro's brown eyes sent a spear of longing through my body.

"Aren't you tired?" he asked. His voice held a strange note.

"I am," I admitted. My eyes burned from lack of sleep and the dry air down here.

"Why don't you take the bed over there?" He nodded toward the bunk across from his.

"Do you want to get rid of me?" My joke backfired because Mauro didn't laugh.

He focused on the gun, and his lack of a reply was all the answer I needed. "I need to check the remaining guns to make sure we have enough firepower."

I stood. I didn't want to push myself on Mauro when he obviously wanted to be alone. Hiding my disappointment, I slipped under the blanket in the narrow bunk. The coarse material was cold and smelled faintly of disuse. I rolled over, away from Mauro, needing privacy.

The click of him working on the guns rang in the panic room. It wasn't what kept me awake, not even the light—which he dimmed a bit later. My thoughts whirred in my head. Thoughts about Mauro, about my feelings for him, about the men in the house, about their horrible motives. And worry that Mauro's and my relationship would be even worse off after this. It felt as if something was shifting between us—again.

I stared at the gray concrete, listening to Mauro until he, too, seemed to have lain down. He turned the lights off except for a faint glow, probably the lamp he'd prepared for use in the afternoon.

I wasn't sure how long I'd been lying motionless in the bunk before I couldn't take it anymore. "I can't sleep. I keep thinking about them upstairs, waiting for a chance to get to us. And it's freezing down here." The blanket wasn't very thick.

Mauro sighed. "I can't turn the heat up. I don't know how long the generators can keep up all the essential facilities and we need to stay for three days unless someone checks on the mansion sooner."

I shivered again and turned around, peering over to Mauro in the bed across from mine. He was facing my way as well. The dim gas lantern on the floor between us threw shadows on his face that made it impossible to read his expression from where I lay. "Can I come under your blanket? I'm shaking so bad."

Even as I said the words, alarm bells rang in my head. Considering my feelings for Mauro, sharing a narrow bed with him seemed like a dangerous option.

Don't be stupid.

Mauro only saw me as his little stepsister. I wasn't a woman to him. He probably didn't even realize I had breasts and a vagina.

Mauro tensed. Not only did he have to babysit me and was now stuck in a panic room with me, now I wanted to intrude on his personal space.

My cheeks burned at the resulting silence. I was glad for the dark that hid my mortification from his vigilant eyes. Why couldn't I stop acting like a stupid kid around him?

When I'd given up hope that he'd reply, his low voice sounded. "Sure."

I scrambled out of my bunk, shivering when my bare feet touched the cold stone floor, and hurried the few steps over to Mauro. He lifted the covers, and I crept under them. The bunk was small, and our bodies brushed despite my butt dangling over the edge. Mauro shifted back until he bumped against the wall, allowing me to lie down more comfortably.

Suddenly I was caught in the reality of the situation. Mauro looked down at me with a tight expression. He was lying ramrod straight, his arm resting awkwardly on his side. Our faces were close enough to kiss, and I wanted nothing more, but I wasn't insane. I wouldn't make a fool out of myself again.

I cleared my throat, which was the equivalent of an explosion in the silence of the room. "I'm going to turn around." Mauro didn't say anything. I quickly rolled over and my ass bumped against his crotch.

His low exhale made me swallow. God, this bunk was too narrow for two people who weren't intimate. "You can wrap your arm around me."

What was wrong with me?

But I wanted him to wrap his arm around me.

He shifted again and hesitantly touched his palm to my hip. It was warm and big, and more distracting than I thought a touch like that could be.

Mauro was almost… shy? Though maybe shy was the wrong word. He was careful. Maybe he was worried to scare me? He knew I'd never been in bed with someone. Heat washed over me.

He finally wrapped his arm around me, his heat singeing my back and stopping my trembling. I released a soft sigh, snuggling closely against him. His palm against my belly felt perfect.

"You're so warm and strong."

Had I just really said that?

Mauro let out a strangled sound that might have been a laugh.

Of course, I couldn't shut up because when I was nervous, and for some reason, Mauro suddenly made me very nervous, my mouth always ran free. "I'm glad we're family so nobody can construe any crazy rumors when we share a bed. It's not like something could happen between us. I mean, we're practically sister and brother." But damn it, my feelings weren't sisterly in the slightest.

"But we're not," Mauro said in a low rumble that made me melt.

"No, we're not," I agreed quietly.

Mauro's scent engulfed me, his warmth was everywhere. And the feel of his body shielding mine, it was better than anything I'd ever felt. Despite my worry about what was going on in the house, I drifted off, knowing Mauro would keep me safe.

CHAPTER FOUR

Mauro

Stella fell asleep, her body softening against mine. Sleep was out of the question for me. My body thrummed with adrenaline and worse, desire. Feeling Stella's body so close to mine, her firm, little butt pressed against my crotch, my dick was getting ready to rumble.

I tried to bring at least a few inches between my hardening cock and Stella's ass, but the wall behind me made that impossible.

With a sigh, I tried to get some rest. Stella was oblivious to my body's reaction to her closeness. She released a small sigh and moved closer to me once more, bumping into my cock. Knowing it was a losing battle, I wrapped my arm more tightly around her middle and settled comfortably against her.

I must have fallen asleep because sometime later I startled awake. Stella stirred at my sudden move. She had turned around while we were both asleep and now faced my way. She blinked up at me, disoriented, her face so close to mine our lips were almost touching. I'd never woken beside a woman. It was too intimate and too risky for someone as distrustful as me.

"What's wrong?" Stella mumbled, yawning before flashing me an embarrassed smile. She shifted and dug my morning erection into her lower belly, causing me to groan. Her eyes widened and her cheeks turned red. Even in the dim light of the gas lantern, her embarrassment was unmistakable.

I had no way of pulling back with the wall against my back. Gritting my teeth, I pushed up on my elbow. "Can you sit up? I need to check on the door. A noise woke me."

It was a fucking lie. I wasn't sure what had woken me from my dream—a dream with Stella in a leading role. Stella scrambled back and sat up, slanting me a quizzical look. I slipped out of the bunk and stood, glad to be rid of her tantalizing warmth. Her gaze darted to my sweatpants then jerked back up and she got even redder, which seemed hardly possible. I stifled a laugh. She pointedly avoided looking at me after that and I went over to the door, peering up. It was still safely locked. I didn't hear a sound above our heads.

"You're not thinking about opening it, right?"

Stella stood and came over to me, her arms wrapped around her chest.

"No," I said. The silence above could be a trap. The attackers could be lying in wake. Even though I was a good shot, it would be near impossible to win against several opponents.

Stella yawned again.

"Why don't you try to sleep again? It's still early."

"Won't you join me?"

I shook my head. "I'm not tired." In truth, I just needed some distance between us.

Nodding, she returned to the bed and closed her eyes.

I watched her for a few seconds. We'd have to spend at least two more nights down here. Two nights in which I needed to get a grip on myself.

Stella

When I asked Mauro the next evening if we could share a bunk again because I couldn't fall asleep alone in my cold bed, he hesitated. Maybe he was embarrassed because of what had happened this morning? It surprised me. Mauro didn't strike me as someone who was easily embarrassed. And a morning erection was pretty common from what I knew.

Still, a silly part of me hoped he'd been hard because of me and not a dream of another woman.

Eventually he nodded and lifted the blankets. With a smile, I slipped under them and settled with my back against his chest. I wasn't tired. Locked in the panic room, we hadn't done much all day, except to eat and talk about Mauro's past missions or funny childhood memories. Mauro wasn't asleep either. Sometimes I wondered how he'd react if I told him about my feelings. If he'd laugh at me, it would maybe end my crush, but I was too scared of it.

Mauro's hand on my hip shifted, and I realized his thumb was lightly tracing my skin over my shirt. The touch sent a tingling straight to my core. I bet he didn't even realize what he was doing, probably lost in thought.

I wanted him even closer. I shifted until our bodies were completely flush, and then something hard pressed into my butt.

I'd never been with a man, not even been allowed to be alone with anyone who wasn't family or an elderly bodyguard, but I wasn't oblivious or completely unworldly.

Did I… did I actually turn him on?

The thought was exhilarating and delusional at once. Mauro wasn't into me. But the firm pressure against my lower back told a different story.

I should have ignored it, but I simply could not. Overwhelmed with curiosity, I rolled over until his bulge bumped into my lower belly. Mauro gritted his teeth and I let out a surprised gasp at the harsh look on his face. "Mauro?"

My voice shook with… nerves? Triumph? Excitement? Too much was happening in my body all at once to figure it out. His mouth was set in a tight line, his brows furrowed as he glared down at me. He looked angry, not aroused, but somehow that made him look even hotter.

Mauro

Stella sounded terrified, and what else would she be? She was stuck down here in this windowless prison with me and I was sporting the fucking king of all erections. Feeling Stella's firm butt rubbing all over my dick had fired up all of my fantasies. First this morning and now.

Now she peered up at my face curiously, as if she was trying to figure me out. Fuck. I swallowed hard and shifted, trying to bring at least a bit of space between our bodies. "That wasn't supposed to happen."

"Why did it happen?"

If she hadn't figured it out by herself, I wouldn't tell her. As long as she remained in her oblivious bubble, the better for us.

"Try to sleep. I'll keep you safe." I probably wouldn't catch any sleep tonight anyway, not with Stella's body so close to mine and my dick eager to claim her.

She pursed her lips. "Mauro, why—"

"Sleep," I growled.

Stella settled against the pillow but kept her eyes open. I needed her to stop thinking about my fucking erection and why I'd gotten it.

"If the attackers get down here, they're going to rape me, and torture and kill you."

Tension shot through my body at her sudden topic change. The thought of anyone hurting Stella like that turned my stomach to stone. I wouldn't allow anyone to touch her. I wrapped an arm around her. "No. They can't get down here."

But they had managed to shut off our entire security system. What if they hacked the panic room system as well? It was a closed system, but what did I know? Fuck.

"Do you think it's the Russians?"

"It could be the Outfit." It was telling that I wished it was them. They never touched women. Stella would be safe even if they got down here. Their boss, Cavallaro, had a strict policy regarding harming innocent women. Me, they'd dismember and kill, of course.

"It's sad that yesterday wasn't even my worst birthday."

My hold on her tightened, knowing what she was referring to. Her dad had died a day before her sixth birthday. "You'll get your present once we're out here."

"What did you get for me?"

"That's a secret."

She cast her eyes up and something in them went straight to my dick. Maybe it was the dim light, but desire and need reflected on her beautiful face. "If we never get out of here alive, I won't get a birthday present from you."

"We're not going to die," I said firmly.

"But we could."

She inched closer, her breasts brushing my chest. What was she doing?

She lifted her face, her lips coming closer to mine. I needed to stop her, but I didn't move a single muscle. "There's one thing I've wanted to do for a long time…"

She took a deep breath and pressed a kiss to my mouth. Her eyes widened. Her lips were satin-soft and she smelled absolutely delicious. I lost it. My arm tightened around her and I pulled her against me, then really kissed her. My tongue plunged into her mouth, discovering her, tasting her, losing myself in the sensation. I slipped my hand under her T-shirt and stroked her back. She shivered, her eyes fluttering shut, her body completely motionless in my embrace. Her tongue met mine and she moaned into my mouth, an eager sound straight out of my dreams. My brain short-circuited. I rolled on top of her, settling between her thighs, feeling the heat of her center through our clothes. My dick twitched and I kissed her even harder, cupping her head.

I jerked back when I realized what I was doing.

She'd given me a shy, innocent kiss, and I'd taken it up another level. Fuck, I'd dragged her from the ground floor to the fucking top level of the Empire State Building with me.

Stella was innocent. I was supposed to protect her, not manhandle her when she was at my mercy.

Maybe it was cabin fever. I shoved myself off her and stood, trying to rearrange my dick so it was less obvious. As if that still mattered. I'd dry-humped her like a fucking dog. Turning my back on her, I took a few deep breaths. "I'm sorry," I got out.

"Don't go," she whispered.

"There's nowhere I could go."

"I mean, come back."

I slanted her a look. She was propped up on her forearm, her hair all over the place and her lips swollen from our kiss. Fuck, she looked absolutely irresistible. Better than in my fantasy.

"Stella—"

"I don't want to stop kissing you."

I blinked, not sure if this, too, was part of my overeager mind.

I stepped up to the bed and leaned over her, my arm braced beside her head. Narrowing my eyes, I said, "You know the rules. You know what it means to break them."

"I don't care."

Neither did I. But I should. I damn well should.

She curled her hand around my neck, trying to pull me back down. I resisted. My eyes trailed down her body, lingering on my boxers, which looked fucking perfect on her. "If you knew what I've done to you in my fantasies…"

She took a deep breath, then licked her lips in the most tantalizing way possible. "What did you do?"

Nerves and excitement rang in her voice.

"I could show you," I said. What the hell was I thinking? I wasn't. That was the problem.

She gave a tiny nod. I still didn't trust my eyes. I leaned down, claiming her lips again, and like last time, she kissed me back. I slid my palm up her thigh, needing to feel proof of her desire for me. Stella didn't wear underwear beneath my shorts and my fingertips brushed her pussy lips.

She was completely soaked. My fingers glided smoothly over her folds and I groaned, completely lost in the sensation. I'd imagined this moment so often.

"Are you wet for me?" I growled.

Stella blinked at me, lips parted. Small pants fell from her mouth as I traced her pussy lightly, spreading her wetness.

"Tell me, is this..." I slid my pointer finger along her slit, gathering her juices and holding it up for her to see. "...because you want me?"

"Yes," she admitted breathlessly. "I've wanted you for so long." A dark blush stained her cheeks, but she held my gaze.

I groaned because she'd torn down my last defense. If she'd been hesitant, I would have kept my distance, but like this, with the prospect of dying in this hellhole? I had no power to resist.

I knelt down in front of the bunk and dragged her toward the edge, my fingers stroking up her soft thighs. I hooked my hands in her boxer shorts and slid them down, catching a whiff of her musky-sweet aroma. My cock twitched with need. Fuck.

"I'm going to give you a good lick before I show you how to blow me," I rasped. I wanted more than that. I wanted to bury myself in her heat, wanted to mark her as mine, but I couldn't.

I didn't wait for her reply. I parted her wide and dragged my tongue from her opening up to her clit. Stella bucked up with a hoarse moan. Her hand flew to the top of my head, her fingers raking through my hair. I smiled against her pussy, ignoring my warning voice. In this moment, I didn't want to consider the consequences of our actions. The outside world and its rules seemed light-years away.

She said my name over and over again as I licked her. Stella was my forbidden treat. Sweet as sin. A forbidden delight I wasn't allowed to have and she tasted all the better because of it. Her throaty moans, her fingers tangling in my hair, her dripping arousal drove me near insane with desire. For the first time since losing my virginity at fourteen, I felt like I might come in my pants.

"Oh Mauro," she said, her hips bucking, pressing her pussy closer to my open mouth. I dipped my tongue into her, wishing my cock could do the same.

"Do you like my tongue in your pussy?" I rasped.

"Yes."

Her voice dripped with desire, with the need to come. I circled her opening then dove back in. Slipping my hands beneath her ass cheeks, I lifted her for better access, burying my face in her lap.

Every moan, every twitch of her body as I devoured her pussy made my dick swell more. Soon, Stella writhed beneath me, her cries bouncing off the walls as she arched up. I groaned against her as she came, feeling fucking triumphant about giving her first orgasm to her.

I didn't want anyone else to see her like this—ever.

Stella

I tried to catch my breath, staring up at the underside of the top bunk. Whenever I'd tried to imagine how it would feel to have Mauro go down on me, it hadn't been nearly as intense. I tilted my head. Mauro was still wedged between my thighs, his tongue trailing over my sensitive flesh lazily. It was almost too much, and yet still too good to stop him. Mauro looked up, meeting my gaze. With a dark smile, he parted me and took a deliberate lick. I flushed, torn between embarrassment and arousal.

"Are you ready to return the favor?" he asked in a growl.

Biting my lip, I nodded. Mauro pressed a kiss to my sensitive flesh, then to my hipbone before he stood. The bulge in his sweatpants was huge. Standing right in front of the bunk, he removed his shirt and dragged down his sweatpants. His erection bounced when it caught on the waistband. My eyes grew wide at his size.

I stared, lying frozen on my back.

Mauro tensed. "Stella? You don't have to do—"

"I want to," I choked out and slowly sat up. Now his erection was only a few inches from my face. He cupped my head with one hand while he braced himself against the top bunk with the other. His six-pack flexed and pure hunger reflected in his eyes.

Under his lustful gaze, I curled my fingers around his base, surprised at how wide he was.

"Take me into your mouth," he rasped.

I parted my lips and cupped his tip. Taking my time to discover every inch of him with my lips and tongue, I relished in the small impatient thrusts of his hips, in his sharp breaths. Soon he began to pump into my mouth lightly. "Fuck, I want to fuck your mouth."

He looked on the verge of losing control, dark and irresistible. I wanted him to lose himself with me. "Then do it," I whispered, wanting to show him that I wasn't the little kid he needed to protect anymore.

His eyes flashed with need. I cupped his ass, feeling a rush of heat between my legs. He gripped the board of the top bunk and began to thrust his hips, slow at first, then faster and harder.

I clung to his ass as he took my mouth. His eyes burned into mine, his expression twisted with pleasure, his muscles flexing with every slam. I had trouble taking in even half of him, but he didn't seem to mind, judging from his grunts and moans.

Soon his movements became jerkier. He moved back without warning. "On your knees!" he barked.

Rattled, I scrambled onto my knees. I didn't get the chance to wonder what was going to happen because I felt something wet and sticky hit my ass cheek followed by Mauro's groan. I twisted my head around. Mauro's eyes were closed as he pumped his erection slowly, spurting his release all over my ass. My core clenched at the sight.

I'd never thought this would turn me on, but it did.

Mauro opened his eyes and frowned. He reached for his shirt and cleaned himself with it, then my ass. "Are you all right?" His voice was rough with a hint of concern in it.

"Better than all right," I admitted with an embarrassed laugh.

Mauro was bent over me to clean me. He dropped his shirt on the floor. "Is that so?"

I nodded, rolling onto my back so Mauro hovered over me, gloriously naked. "I thought you'd sleep with me when you asked me to get on my knees."

Mauro's eyes darkened. He cupped my cheek. "You know the rules," he said gruffly, then added in an even lower voice. "And when I take your virginity, I won't do it from behind. I want to see your face when I claim you."

When, not if.

Maybe Mauro realized his choice of words too because he frowned.

He stretched out beside me, stroking my hair with an unreadable expression. "How will I stay away from you now that I know how sweet you taste? I want to eat you out again."

"I'm not stopping you," I joked. "There isn't much we can do down here."

Mauro chuckled. His eyes taking in every inch of my face until I had to look away, suddenly shy. It still seemed surreal what we'd just done. With Mauro I'd felt safe, I still did. He kissed me. I tasted myself on his lips. Pressing even closer to his strong body, I knew I wanted to be with him. Not just in this panic room.

I fell asleep in his arms not long after, feeling protected and in love.

"I won't ever let you go."

Seconds before I drifted off, Mauro murmured those words against my skin.

Mauro jerked behind me and practically leaped over my body, grabbing his guns from the floor. It took me a moment to understand why.

The lock of the trapdoor had clicked. With a creak, the thing opened. Mauro grabbed my arm and pushed me behind him, his guns aimed at the ladder.

My heart pounded wildly in my chest.

"Mauro?" a man called.

Mauro relaxed, lowering the gun. "Stella and I are down here."

"Don't shoot. I'm coming down now."

I slumped against his back, finally recognizing the voice of one of Father's men. Realizing I wasn't wearing anything beneath the T-shirt, I quickly slipped into the discarded boxers. Luckily, Mauro had put on his sweatpants before we'd fallen asleep.

"We're safe," I said, relieved.

Mauro turned to me with a small smile. "We are."

This panic room had become our respite from reality, our own pleasurable, safe haven. It had brought us closer, not just physically.

I wanted a future with Mauro, and I would get it.

GIANNA & MATTEO: NOVELLA

CHAPTER ONE

Gianna

"How about we party the night away?" Matteo said as he nuzzled my neck.

I grinned. "I'm in. It's been too long."

"I know," he murmured.

"Sometimes I wish I could just make a girls' night out with Aria and Lily."

"You can."

I snorted. "Yeah with bodyguards watching our every move."

Matteo's dark eyes met mine in the mirror. "I'm trying to give you as much freedom as I can. I'd allow you to go party with your sisters if it wasn't too dangerous. And Luca would never allow it anyway."

"Allow it?" I muttered. "Like I'm a kid or a prisoner."

"You know it's not true," he said. I gave him a look because we knew it was true. Matteo would never let me head out on my own either, and I wasn't entirely sure if it was only because of the Bratva and the MCs breathing down the Famiglia's neck.

"It doesn't matter anyway," I said. "Now that Aria and Lily have kids, they don't want to party anymore anyway."

Matteo grimaced. "I know. Romero and Lily talk about nothing but poo and vomit since Sara was born."

I snorted, shaking my head. "I hope they hold back when we celebrate my birthday this month." It would be a chilled affair in the Hamptons.

"I doubt it," Matteo said. "We'll have a nice barbecue and jump in the pool, and listen to exciting diaper stories."

"I'm so glad we don't have kids."

Matteo kissed my throat, then down to my shoulder. "Hmmm. Then we couldn't have sex in the open bathroom now."

"We're having sex now?" I asked, raising my eyebrows. "I thought we wanted to party the night away."

"Oh, we will," he growled in my ear as his hand snuck into my panties. "But first this."

Two hours later I was dressed in tight black jeans and a sparkling crop top with the words "Sparkly Bitch" across the chest. I put on black boots because no one could really dance with high heels. Checking my eyeliner once more, I walked out of the bedroom and down the staircase into the living area. Luca and Aria had bought a spectacular townhouse with a small yard in the Upper East Side shortly after Amo's birth and had given us their penthouse. Matteo was already waiting, leaning against the kitchen island of our apartment, scrolling through messages on his phone. He was also dressed in all black and the sleeves of his shirt were rolled up, revealing those muscled arms that had held me up less than an hour ago when he'd fucked me against the wall. His dark hair was short but it still took him longer than me to get it in shape with wax.

He looked up and his eyes slowly slid over my body. "Hot as hell," he said with a grin. "Sparkly bitch? I thought you didn't like to be called bitch."

"I don't like to be called bitch by others, especially you when we fight," I said.

Matteo stalked toward me and gripped my hips. "But Gianna, sometimes you are a real b—"

I clamped my hand over his mouth. "Don't you dare say it."

His brown eyes crinkled in amusement. I lowered my hand. "Beast," he finished.

I hit his chest. "And you're a cocky bastard."

He didn't deny it.

"How about we have drinks in the Tipsy Cow first?"

"Deal," I said. "How can I resist a good cocktail?"

Hand in hand, we walked into the elevator and leaned against the mirror as it traveled down. Matteo regarded me. "You get more gorgeous the longer we're together," he said.

"That's because your eyesight gets worse." I was turning thirty-one this month and had found the first gray hair a few weeks ago. I'd plucked it at once but it had given me a small crisis. Matteo, the bastard, still had thick, dark hair, and even if he got gray hair at some point, I just knew it would make him look hot.

Matteo squeezed my hip. "I have perfect sight, trust me. You are sex on legs, Gianna."

I took my burgundy lipstick out and put it to my lips, trying to hide my pleased smile.

Matteo waved at the bartender when we entered the crowded bar. We tried to have a cocktail night once a week and most of the time we came to the Tipsy Cow. Its bare brownstone walls, cowhide booths, and their amazing list of cocktails was right up our alley.

We slipped into our usual spot, sitting beside each other, thigh to thigh, in the booth. Matteo threw an arm around my shoulder and leaned in. "See, the first poor sucker thinks he can eye-fuck you."

I followed his gaze toward a guy sitting in another booth with a woman and still leering at me. I gave him the most disgusted expression I was capable of.

"I love your resting bitch face," Matteo said, then grabbed my face and gave me a deep kiss.

When we pulled apart, the menus rested on our table. I gave Matteo a look, embarrassed that the server had to witness our PDA.

"How about a little adventure?" Matteo asked as he picked up the menu.

I narrowed my eyes. I'd learned to be wary when it came to Matteo's definition of adventure. "That depends."

"We choose each other's cocktails."

"That's tame for you," I said, surprised, but actually liking the idea.

I perused the list of cocktails, trying to decide what I'd order for Matteo. Even though we'd been here countless times, there were many cocktails that Matteo had never tried, mainly the sweet and creamy variety. His usual choice was an old-fashioned. At first, I considered choosing something sickly sweet and girly to tease him but then I decided it would be more fun to try and find a cocktail he never tried because he thought it wasn't what he liked. Smiling, I chose the Chilled Irishman.

Matteo raised his eyebrows but didn't comment. I could tell that he thought I was trying to find the cocktail he liked least.

Eventually he chose a concoction with mint schnapps and white chocolate, definitely not my usual choice.

I settled in his arms as we waited for our order. "Sometimes I'm shocked by how long we've been together."

"Almost thirteen years. A lucky year?" He grinned.

I shook my head. "Did you really believe we'd last this long when we first married?"

Matteo shrugged, looking thoughtful. "To be honest, I rarely thought beyond the next weekend, much less a decade. But I knew I wanted you and that we'd be great together if you'd get over your mobster aversion."

I rolled my eyes. I had never really gotten over my aversion for the business but I'd accepted it as part of my life. The waiter headed toward us with our cocktails. I eyed the green concoction in front of me warily. "You know how much I hate mint and chocolate together, and yet you order this." I motioned at the glass in front of me with sprigs of mint and a mesh of white chocolate as decoration.

"You hated us together at first and now here we are." He took a sip from his drink and nodded appreciatively.

I removed the mesh from my glass and bit a piece off before I put it down on the napkin and took a sip from my drink. My lips pulled into a grimace. "You're lucky we worked out better than this drink."

Matteo squeezed my hip. "I think we're both lucky."

I sipped at his drink and shrugged. "Deal."

"Don't worry, baby."

The hell. His words and the look in his eyes didn't match. We'd been at the dance club for less than an hour and trouble had already found Matteo, or he'd found it…

"Matteo," I said more insistently. He put his palm flat against my bare belly and pushed me a few steps back, behind him.

I looked around. People were starting to build a circle around us in anticipation of an impending fight. They whispered among each other but it was impossible to make out anything over the loud music.

"From what hick town are you?" Matteo asked with that scary smile as he stepped up to his three opponents.

I hooked my fingers in the back of his pants but he ignored me.

The tallest of the three men jerked his chin up in challenge. He looked like a lumberjack with his broad shoulders and full beard. He could probably throw a mean right hook. "What makes you think we're not from here, motherfucker?" He took a step closer to Matteo and so did his two friends, trying to intimidate him.

Matteo's smile widened. "Oh, you definitely aren't from New York."

"Matteo," I hissed. "This isn't your club. There are too many people around. If you get arrested, I'm going to kick your ass."

Tall guy shoved Matteo's chest hard. "Think you are something better?"

Matteo stumbled a step back, right into me, and I let out a startled gasp. Matteo's eyes flashed from me to the guy. Oh no.

"I'm better in every regard that matters," Matteo growled. He smashed his fist into the other guy's face who stumbled back and fell to the ground, clutching his nose, blood sloshing out of it.

And then all hell broke loose. The right guy crashed his beer bottle against the bar, breaking the lower half off, left with a sharp top.

Matteo shoved me back again and reached under his leather jacket, pulling out something and then a silver blade flashed in the flickering overhead lights.

"No!" I screamed over the beat. The crowd jeered, but in the back of the club I could see two tall bouncers pushing their way through the mass of people, and the police probably were on the way as well.

Both guys attacked Matteo. He jammed his elbow into the face of the unarmed one then faced off with the other guy. The guy made a slashing motion with the beer bottle and Matteo sidestepped him, then thrust his elbow down on the crook of the guy's arm. I winced when the arm twisted at an impossible angle. The throbbing beat swallowed the scream of agony.

Matteo shoved the guy to the ground and pressed the knife against his throat, looking scary as hell. "So you think you can touch my wife?"

I rushed toward him and grabbed his shoulder, but he didn't let me pull him away. A bouncer broke through the crowd. "Stop it, you fuckers! The police are here!"

Matteo dropped the knife and I quickly picked it up, closed it and shoved it into my pants. The cold metal rested in my panties.

Matteo stood and raised his arms with a twisted grin.

I was so going to kill him.

Thirty minutes later, Matteo was in an arrest cell and two of the three guys were in the one beside his, the third was in the hospital with his broken arm. I glowered at Matteo but he only grinned.

"What's so funny?" a police officer asked. "You like spending the night in a cell?"

Matteo didn't say anything but his eyes promised nothing good. For a guy who couldn't even see if I wore makeup or not, he had a very good memory when it came to faces, especially of the people who had pissed him off.

I picked up my mobile, seething, and called Luca. This was going to go over well. He'd blame me for Matteo's mishap. After five rings, Luca's gruff voice rang out, sounding as if I'd woken him.

"What did he do?" he asked, already pissed.

"He got himself arrested for beating the shit out of three idiots," I clipped. The one with the swollen nose gave me a nasty look which I returned tenfold until he looked away. *You're playing with a big girl here, idiot.*

"Where?"

"Brooklyn, the police station near Prospect Park."

"I'll be there soon." Of course, Luca knew where that was.

Luca showed up forty minutes later. The moment he stepped in, all eyes turned to him, and how could they not, he was a goddamn giant and that in addition to the murderous look would make most people wet their pants. Behind him, a tall man in a designer suit and with brown, immaculately styled hair stepped in. The Famiglia's new lawyer, a guy from a soldier family who'd used his intelligence to get a degree from Harvard.

The younger police officer asked in a less than friendly tone, "Who are you?"

Luca regarded him like one would a cockroach, then his gaze moved on to me, and didn't improve.

The color drained off the face of the older officer. He obviously recognized the Capo and when his eyes flitted between Matteo and Luca, he got even paler.

The lawyer stepped forward swiftly, his face a mask of cold efficiency. "Francesco Allegri, I represent the Vitiellos' legal interests."

Luca came toward me and together we moved to Matteo's cell. "I'm surprised you didn't pull a knife," Luca said in a deadly murmur.

Matteo grinned. "I can be sensible."

I snorted. "He actually pulled it."

Luca's eyes slanted to me. "Where is it?"

"In my panties," I said.

Luca shook his head, then narrowed his eyes at his brother who watched me with a predatory grin. If he thought I'd let him anywhere near my panties in the near future, he was going to be disillusioned soon.

"One day I won't bail you out," Luca muttered. "I thought marriage would make you reasonable. Of course, I'd hoped you'd marry a reasonable woman."

"Hey," I hissed. "It's not my fault that the assholes over there touched my butt."

As if that explained everything, Luca gave Matteo a nod. Of course, he would understand Matteo's reasoning. Luca would have cut off the guy's hands right on the dance floor if the idiot had touched Aria's butt. Jealous mobsters were the worst.

I didn't say a word to Matteo on our way home. The second we stepped into our apartment, Matteo held out his hand, palm up. "You can give me my knife back."

"I can but I won't," I said angrily, and tried to stalk away, but Matteo gripped my wrist and tugged me back. Then he backed me into the wall, his arms to both sides of my head, and the predator look in his dark eyes went straight into my core. I couldn't believe this was making me wet. Damn it. I didn't want to be turned on by Matteo's brutality, by his dark side, but I was.

"I could just get it," he said in a dangerously sexy drawl.

"I didn't give you permission to reach into my pants."

Matteo leaned down, running his nose over my ear, then growling. "You're my wife, Mrs. Vitiello. That gives me permission to put my hand wherever the fuck I want." He pressed his palm to my naked stomach and my skin broke into goose bumps, my core tightening.

I bit his earlobe. "No, it doesn't."

Matteo drew back. He cupped the back of my head and brushed his lips over mine, then slid his tongue inside, and I almost moaned into his mouth. His hand slid a bit lower so his fingertips slipped inside my pants. He groaned. "Fuck, have you been sewn into these fucking pants?"

I laughed, couldn't help it. Matteo lowered his other hand and popped open the button of my jeans. "Matteo," I warned.

He met my gaze and slowly slid his hand lower. "You have something I want," he said.

Oh fuck. My panties were drenched, the stupid bastard.

His fingertips brushed my pubic bone and then they found his knife, which was pressed up against my folds and embarrassingly slick with my arousal.

Matteo's eyes dilated with desire and he groaned low in his throat. He pressed into me, breath hot on my lips. "Tell me, Gianna, are you turned on by bad boys?"

I glared up at him. "No," I said, which was the truth in general. "But I'll tell you a secret." I made my voice the sexy whisper that always got him. "I'm always wet for a twisted, murderous *gangsta*."

Matteo smiled in a way that tightened my core again. He cupped his knife but instead of pulling it out, he began sliding the smooth metal along my slit, back and forth.

I moaned. Matteo's mouth took mine as he kept rubbing. I rocked against him desperately, seeking friction that the smooth metal hardly provided, and yet the thrill of the forbidden, the wrong of it, drove me higher and higher, and finally I came all over the knife, crying out my release.

Matteo watched me, breathing raggedly. Slowly he pulled his knife out and held it up between us. It was coated with my juices. Matteo pressed the button that made the blade shoot out and even that was slick. Holding my gaze, Matteo ran his tongue along the blade, and I almost came again. I gripped his hand and brought the knife to my own mouth. Matteo angled it so the sharp edge was facing away and then I slowly licked over the smooth metal, tasting myself on the deadly weapon.

"This is so much better than blood," he rasped.

Damn it all, I wanted this man so much. I fell to my knees before him and ripped at his buttons and zipper, then pulled down his boxers until his cock sprang out. Hard and leaking, and fuck, even that piece of Matteo was pretty. Sometimes I really hated him.

I licked over the tip, then took him into my mouth. Matteo moaned and rocked his hips as I sucked him. My eyes kept drifting to the deadly knife clutched in his hand at his side and the sight aroused me in a twisted way.

Matteo jerked back. "Enough."

He pulled me to my feet and pushed me toward the kitchen and bent me over the kitchen island. He tugged my pants down, then pushed two fingers into me. I threw my head back, arching at the delicious sensation.

I huffed in protest when he pulled out.

He clapped my butt hard. I jerked more in surprise than pain. "Next time you give me my knife when I tell you to."

I threw an indignant look over my shoulder. "You—"

My insult died in a cry when Matteo slammed into me. He leaned over me. "I'm going to fuck you now, Mrs. Vitiello."

And good Lord, he did. My hips banged against the marble as he slammed into me over and over again, his balls slapping against my ass. I clutched the edge of the island, needing something to hold on to. Matteo's grip on my hips was bruising. My core clenched, and I screamed out my release, almost passing out from the force of it. Matteo followed shortly after, and then I lay in a boneless heap over the marble counter, breathing harshly. Matteo kissed my cheek.

"I hated seeing that bastard put his hand on your ass," Matteo murmured.

"I know," I said. "I just wish not every other of our dance nights would end with you in trouble."

"I like trouble, which is why I like you."

I rolled my eyes. "Like?"

"Fishing for compliments?"

I jerked my ass back and clenched around his cock. He hissed then chuckled. "All right, babe, I love you."

I sighed, hardly mollified, considering he'd called me by the name I hated the most.

"I'm never going to clean my knife again." He nuzzled my neck.

"Just don't cum in your pants next time you stab someone."

"Hmm. That's going to be hard knowing I'm cutting someone down with your pussy juice on my knife."

I couldn't help but laugh. Maybe I was as twisted as Matteo. We really were a perfect pair.

CHAPTER TWO

Gianna

For a long time, I stared down at the pregnancy test, unable to trust my eyes. We were supposed to leave for the Hamptons in exactly two hours but I wasn't sure I could move. I'd done the test out of paranoia. I was only one day overdue, nothing to get worried about, but I had a stash of tests in the bathroom.

"Gianna?" Matteo called.

I swallowed, my fingers on the test tightening further. "I'm here." I didn't recognize my voice. It was weak and stunned.

I hadn't taken the pill in over a year because it wreaked havoc with my body but I'd used a pessary or condoms. Over the year we'd been too horny for contraception about a handful of times but my OB/GYN had told me that my chances of getting pregnant naturally were minimal. I'd been relieved back then. It had seemed like a sign that my body was as against having kids as my brain.

Minimal chances.

Still the second line on my pregnancy test mocked me with its intensity.

Matteo pushed the door open and found me sitting on the edge of the bathtub.

"Why are you hiding in here?" he asked as he stepped in, then his eyes settled on the test in my hand and he froze.

"Gianna?"

I met his gaze. "I'm pregnant."

Matteo searched my eyes. His expression didn't give anything away as if he was waiting for my reaction. "You're not happy."

"Of course, I'm not," I whispered harshly. "We don't want children." I paused because Matteo actually didn't look unhappy. "Or do you?"

Matteo shrugged. "I always thought we didn't need kids to be happy. But I like being around Luca's kids, so being around my own might be even better."

I scrunched up my face and shook my head. "It won't. With other people's kids you only get to do the fun things, and when it gets tough you can give them back, but this baby, it'll be our responsibility… I never wanted that. I still don't." I cringed at how horrible that made me sound, but it was the truth.

Voicing it aloud, I felt guilty but I needed to say it. Matteo needed to know. He was the one person who would understand. Right?

Matteo came toward me and crouched before me, looking up at me. He took the test and laid it to the ground, then he touched my cheek. "It's still early in the pregnancy," he murmured. I knew what he was saying without saying it. His brown eyes were so full of understanding and love that my heart clenched tightly with gratefulness. In the beginning, I'd thought Matteo didn't deserve me because he was a bad man but now, I often felt like I was the one who didn't deserve him.

I swallowed. "Will you be okay with it?"

Matteo smiled wryly. "Gianna, I'm a killer." Despite his attempt to sound flippant, I caught a hint of strain in his voice.

I tensed. "So you think we're killing the baby?"

He frowned. With a groan he pushed to his feet and pulled me with him, wrapping his arms tightly around me. "That's not what I meant," he said firmly. "What I meant is that I can deal with anything. I'll be at your side no matter what you decide."

"It's not only my decision. This is your child too."

Something flickered in Matteo's eyes. "It is. But it is your body. You'll have to carry a child for nine months, you'll have to go through labor, and you'll be the one the baby will need the most in the beginning, so really it should be your choice."

I was grateful for Matteo's support, but for once I wished he would tell me what to do, would take the decision off my hands, so I wouldn't be burdened with the full weight of my responsibility. "Everyone will hate me if I… if I end this pregnancy. Or hate me more." Because my fan club was fairly small while my haters were in the majority among the Outfit and the Famiglia. I knew it and usually I didn't care. Trying to please everyone was a losing game and I'd never tried but now, now I was terrified of their judgment.

Matteo regarded me closely. "Our family will understand."

"Will they?" I asked. Luca and Aria loved their children. They would never get rid of a baby, nor would Lily and Romero. Our world was a traditional one. Not that there wasn't abortion. If a child was created out of wedlock, abortion was fairly common. But Matteo and I were married, and he still needed an heir in the eyes of his fellow Made Men.

"It's none of their business anyway. We don't have to tell them," he said. "We never cared about other people's opinions. We shouldn't start now. Fuck them all."

I nodded. That was probably for the best. But I knew I'd be devastated if Aria and Lily condemned me for my choice. Other people's judgment I could deal with but my sisters… "I don't want to be a mother."

"Okay," Matteo said quietly. His brown eyes brimmed with understanding but I couldn't help but wonder if he hid part of his feelings from me.

"Are you sure? I don't want you to hate me for it."

"Gianna," Matteo said roughly, cupping my cheeks. "I could never hate you, and this is our choice. I won't blame you."

I took a deep breath. "Will you accompany me to the appointment?"

Matteo kissed me gently. "Of course, Gianna. I'll be there for you."

I closed my eyes and leaned my head against his chest. I waited for relief to set in now that we'd come to a decision but the uncertainty, the fear, the doubts remained. Maybe it would take time to come to terms with everything. "How are we going to celebrate my birthday as if nothing's wrong? How do we hide the truth from everyone?"

"We just forget about it. Try to enjoy a few summer days, all right?"

I nodded, but I wasn't sure if I'd manage to do it.

I kept twisting my wedding ring around my finger, staring out of the windshield as we headed toward the Hamptons. Matteo was oddly quiet and I hadn't said anything either. My thoughts kept whirring, and with every passing moment my worry over being around my sisters and their husbands, and *worse*, their children, rose. I didn't feel like celebrating my birthday. I wanted to hole up in our penthouse and wait for everything to be over—as if that would magically make things easier. My thoughts kept revolving around my decision and the looming appointment.

When we pulled up in the driveway, Luca's and Romero's cars were already parked in front of the beautiful white house.

I reached for the door to get out but Matteo grabbed my hand and kissed it. "Come on, babe. Everything will be all right. Nothing's changed for us."

But it had. I didn't even feel my pregnancy yet but it was a lingering presence in my body. It was there, ever-present.

Together we headed into the mansion. Inside, Amo's and Marcella's voices rang out. When we reached the living room, we were hit with the full force of our family's boisterous presence.

Lily was trying to prevent Sara from getting ice cream everywhere.

Judging from the chocolate covered face of my two-year-old niece and the brown stains on her dress and the floor, she wasn't very successful. It was a good thing that Sara's brown hair was pulled back in a short ponytail so it stayed unaffected by the chocolate mess. The French doors were wide open, letting in the hot August air. Marcella and Amo were already dressed in swimwear, ready to take a dip in either the new pool or the ocean. They too were eating ice cream but at nine and almost six they did it without making a mess.

Luca and Romero stood on the terrace while Aria and Lily kept an eye on the children. Luca noticed us first, followed by Romero. Romero smiled and Luca did something with his mouth that might have counted as a friendly gesture as well.

"Gianna!" Aria exclaimed. She tore herself away from Lily and Sara and rushed over to me, embracing me tightly. "Happy Birthday! I'm so happy that we get to celebrate together!"

"Me too," I said with a forced smile. Aria pulled back, her brows drawing together briefly before Lily took her place.

"Happy Birthday!" She tried to hug me with one arm while holding Sara away from me but the little girl managed to shove her ice cream in my direction and smear some across my cheek.

"Oh no, Sara," Lily crooned, giving me an apologetic smile. "Sorry, Gianna. I should have set her down before hugging you."

My smile became shakier. Even my sister thought I'd have a freak-out because of her kid and wanted to keep it away from me. Nobody would ever consider me motherly or anything close to it. And here I was, pregnant. "Don't worry," I pressed out.

Aria threw me another questioning look.

I was usually better at keeping up appearances but the current situation made my walls crumble.

Matteo took my hand again and squeezed. His eyes sent a clear message *"Do you want to leave?"*

"Hey princess, how is it on the boys' front?" I asked Marcella, giving her a cheeky smile. I wouldn't run off from my family with my tail between my legs.

Marcella rolled her eyes in the direction of Luca who'd entered the living room with Romero at his side. "No boys."

"They are scared of me!" Amo declared. I raised my eyebrows. He was tall for a five-year-old but I had a feeling Luca's towering frame and his psychotic mafia killer reputation had more to do with the boys staying away.

I relaxed. This was familiar.

Romero gave me another warm smile before he joined Lily who'd set down Sara by now. He embraced her and a secretive look passed between them.

"What?" Aria asked at once. She'd noticed it too.

Lily laughed uncertainly, biting her lip, looking at Romero for some kind of sign. He shrugged. They smiled at each other and then Romero put his hand on Lily's flat belly.

I froze.

Aria's eyes grew wide, delight spreading on her beautiful face. "You're pregnant?"

Lily nodded. "But it's only six weeks."

Matteo looked at me and squeezed my hand again but I didn't react. I was in my fifth week if the pregnancy app was correct. My sister and I were both pregnant but our reactions couldn't have been more different. Aria rushed toward Lily and hugged her carefully, then Romero. Luca slanted Matteo and me a suspicious look before he too congratulated them. Matteo tugged at my hand. "Come on, Gianna."

I let him pull me toward my little sister, embraced and congratulated her on autopilot, pretended to be happy. Deep down I was happy for her but having her own joy thrown at me when I felt devastated for the very same reason… I couldn't bear it.

I excused myself to the restrooms and sat down on the closed lid. For a long time, I only stared down at my feet in my favorite sandals, at my toe with the gold and diamond skull ring that Matteo had gifted me this morning, at the small tattoo on the arch of my foot: a Sanskrit symbol meaning *breathe*. I'd gotten the inspiration for it during my yoga teacher training. Breathing came naturally from birth to death, but right now my lungs seemed weighted down by lead.

A soft knock sounded. Too soft to be Matteo.

I steeled myself before I opened the door to Aria's worried face. "Are you okay?"

"I've been feeling off these last few days. Maybe I'm coming down with something," I lied.

"Do you want me to make you tea?"

I shook my head. "I'll drink a few glasses of water to feel hydrated."

The rest of the family had gathered on the terrace, chatting and drinking wine. Matteo's gaze sought me at once, his eyes filled with concern. I gave him a firm smile and joined them outside. Luca held out a glass with white wine to me but I shook my head.

"Headache. I need to drink water first."

Lily pointed at her glass. "Do you want some of my homemade iced tea. With Rooibos, not black tea though."

"Sure," I said and accepted a glass. We clinked glasses and I sipped at my iced tea. Only a few days until the appointment but I couldn't bring myself to drink alcohol, as if it mattered what I did. Matteo snuck his arm around my waist, pulling me against him.

Luca and Aria occasionally threw us curious glances. They knew us too well. I talked to Aria about pretty much everything but this was a topic I couldn't bring up with her, with my sister who loved her children more than life itself, whose motherly nature amazed me every day.

"I love that we're doing this every year," Lily said. We'd celebrated my birthday in the Hamptons every year in the last eight years because it was perfect out here in August.

"Next year, we'll be one more!" Aria said with a huge smile.

One more. She was right. In one year, Lily would carry a newborn in her arms, looking exhausted but deliriously happy. And I? I'd be the same I had been the previous years, the cool aunt.

Even as I wished for that outcome, I knew I'd never be the version of me I'd been before. This pregnancy had already changed me.

CHAPTER THREE

Matteo

I tousled Amo's hair. "Hey!" he shouted indignantly and dashed off. Not quite six and already a huge personality. That boy would be a strong Capo one day.

"He's getting as vain as you are," Luca muttered with a shake of his head.

I sank down on the sofa in the living room. The women and kids were outside at the pool, and Romero had a call with one of his soldiers.

Luca regarded me. "No annoying comeback?"

I propped my arms up on my thighs, fighting the emotion that kept tightening my chest. Ever since Romero and Liliana had announced their pregnancy the noose around my throat had tightened. Their happiness had been like a punch in the gut.

Luca frowned and sat in the armchair across from me. "Matteo, what's wrong?"

"Don't tell Aria," I said.

Luca tensed. I knew he didn't like to keep things from Aria, unless they served her protection. "All right."

I wasn't sure if he meant it, but I found that I didn't care. I couldn't carry this secret anymore. I needed to get it off my chest.

"Gianna is pregnant."

Luca's eyes widened. "I thought you don't want children."

"We don't."

Luca didn't say anything, realization dawning on his face. "Okay," he said simply. "So what's the problem if you both don't want kids?"

His voice was carefully blank, which meant he hid his true feelings on the matter.

"I… fuck."

Luca stood and sat down beside me. "You want the child?"

I closed my eyes. "I don't know. I do not not want it."

"Have you told Gianna?"

"No. I know she doesn't want to be a mother."

Luca remained silent and his expression was tight. I knew he still wasn't Gianna's biggest fan. "It's not just her decision."

"She said the same but it's her body, Luca. She should decide. We men can pretty much keep living our life while the women have to go through pregnancy, labor and later raising the kids. Let's be honest, Aria's doing most of the work."

Luca frowned. "I'm trying to spend as much time with Amo and Marcella as possible."

"Don't get defensive. You're a good father."

"You'd be a good father as well."

I rolled my eyes. "Come on, Luca. It's a miracle that you manage to be a good father after what our father did, but maybe I won't be as lucky."

"You're a good uncle. Amo and Marcella adore you."

"And I adore them. I'd die for them."

Luca squeezed my shoulder. "I know."

I shook my head. "We have the appointment to get rid of the baby next week."

"Maybe Gianna should talk to Aria or Lily. They are mothers, maybe they can help."

"Luca, they are *mothers*. What do you think they will say? Do you really think Aria won't try to talk Gianna into keeping the child? She'll only make Gianna feel bad."

"Of course, Aria won't be in favor of abortion."

I stood. "We are fucking killers, Luca, so don't look so fucking high and mighty. We've killed more men than we can recall."

Luca glared. "We are. But I would never kill my child."

"Fuck you," I growled and turned around.

Before I was out of the front door, Luca caught up with me and gripped my shoulder. "Matteo, I shouldn't have said that. It's your and Gianna's decision, okay? I have absolutely no right to judge you."

"But you do."

Luca sighed. "Having kids changes things. When I imagine that Amo and Marcella wouldn't be here…" He shrugged, but in his eyes, I could see the anguish only the thought caused him.

I nodded because I got it. Or at least I thought I did.

Luca had changed so much since he'd married Aria and again since they had kids, at least part of him had. His murderous, psychotic side was still intact but carefully separated from his life as a husband and father. It was something I admired greatly. My life hadn't changed that much in the last decade, apart from having found happiness with Gianna and being monogamous, I still lived for the thrill but so did she. A child had never been part of the plan.

I wasn't sure if it fit into our life, and even less sure if Gianna and I were capable of being parents, of pushing our own needs back at least for a while.

Maybe we could, and that small flicker of uncertainty was the worst torture when I thought about our appointment next week.

Gianna

I could feel Aria watching me as I prepared tea for myself. "No coffee this morning?" she asked curiously.

"I'm in the mood for tea and I still don't feel all that well." Usually the morning after my birthday began with several espressos to fight the hangover and wake my body after way too few hours of sleep. Yesterday I hadn't drunk any alcohol and I'd been in bed before midnight…

"Usually you're the three espresso kind of girl."

I took a sip from my peppermint tea. I craved coffee. I always drank coffee in the morning. I loved it. My coffee obsession was actually one of the very few things I had in common with Luca. But somehow, I couldn't bring myself to drink anything with caffeine. I knew too much of it wasn't good in a pregnancy. But it wasn't as if it mattered. I didn't even want this pregnancy and soon I'd end it, so I could have had all the caffeine in the world.

Aria still watched me and that's when I realized that she knew the truth. A truth I had barely accepted for myself. I regretted agreeing to come here despite my inner turmoil. Matteo and I should have stayed in our penthouse and gotten deliriously drunk… but even that wasn't really an option anymore.

Sighing, I set the cup down and leaned against the counter. "Luca told you?" It could only be him. Matteo wouldn't have gone directly to my sister. They weren't that close. They were much closer than Luca and I but not spilling your guts about something like this close.

"Matteo talked to him and…"

"And of course, Luca talked to you. Did you tell anyone else? Lily?"

Aria shook her head. "No, of course not." She took a hesitant step toward me. "Gianna." She fell silent. I could tell that she wasn't sure what to say, and I got it. She probably wanted to congratulate me, be happy for me like she had been happy for Lily yesterday, but she couldn't because she knew I wasn't happy.

I looked down at my hands, feeling bad even though Aria wasn't even judging me, at least not openly. But of course, Matteo would have told Luca that we didn't want the pregnancy, and he would have told Aria. I wondered what they'd said behind our backs. Aria and Luca were good parents, *amazing* parents. What did it say about me when a murderous guy like Luca managed to be a good parent, but I didn't even want this pregnancy? I pushed the thought aside.

"Do you want to talk about it?"

I didn't but at the same time I knew it was too much to deal with alone. I gave a sharp nod, hoping I wouldn't come to regret this.

"Let me grab a tea as well and then we can settle on the sofa, all right?" Aria lightly touched my shoulder, waiting for me to say something. I nodded eventually. Grabbing my tea, I went ahead and sank down. Aria soon joined me with her own cup and made herself comfortable next to me. Maybe it was my imagination but it felt as if she was looking at me differently already. As if I wasn't just Gianna anymore, but pregnant Gianna. Aria sipped at her tea. Maybe she hoped I'd bridge the topic but I wasn't even sure where to begin.

"Is there anything you want to talk about? Any questions?"

I set my tea down on the table, biding my time. "It's not that I don't like kids," I said. "I love your kids, you know that? And I love Lily's kid. I just never wanted them myself."

Aria touched my knee. "I know, Gianna. I get it. You don't have to justify yourself, okay?"

"When you and Lily played with dolls and pretended to be their mothers, I never got it. I never wondered how it would be to be a mother. When I saw you with your babies, I never imagined how it would be if I was in your stead. Motherhood just never was the plan. I don't want responsibility for someone else. The mafia takes away so much of our freedom and I worked so hard to carve out small freedoms for myself, but a child would take those away."

"Sometimes things don't work out how we plan them," Aria said.

I gave her a look. "Don't say something like it's fate or maybe this child is something I never knew I needed."

"I wasn't going to. Hear me out," she said quickly. "I won't tell you that you will magically love motherhood once the baby is there, because it isn't like that for everyone. Some women regret becoming mothers. They don't admit it aloud because they fear to be judged. As women, we are supposed to love being mothers without reservation. As mothers, we are supposed to be perfect. The moment we are pregnant, people think our body is their business and the second the baby is there everyone knows how to raise it better than you. Being a mother is hard. I lost count of the times I cried when Amo was a baby and wouldn't stop wailing."

My eyes widened. "You never told me."

"Only Luca knows because he had to talk me off the edge several times," she whispered. "I didn't want to admit that I was overwhelmed. I thought I needed to handle this, after all, Amo wasn't my first child, so why was I suddenly so overwhelmed? But I was, and I was guilty because of it, and worried I was being a bad mother not just for him but also for Marcella because suddenly she had to share my attention..." She sighed. "Without Luca, I wouldn't have gotten through it. Hormones and emotional overload are a dangerous combination. I'm not sure, maybe I was even teetering on the edge of postpartum depression..."

"Should you be telling me this?" I asked confused, but I was incredibly grateful that she did, that she was taking me seriously and not trying to sugarcoat things. "Shouldn't you tell me how wonderful it is to be a mother? That I'll hear angels sing the moment I see my child, that I'll love my shredded vajayjay, my sore nipples, my sleepless nights and all the poop and vomit?"

She let out a small laugh. "I love my children. There are so many wonderful moments I cherish. I love being a mother, and maybe you'll love it too, but maybe you won't. There will be wonderful moments and very hard ones. For me the hard ones are worth it because the wonderful moments outweigh everything else, but I can't tell you if it'll be the same for you. That's for you and Matteo to decide."

I hugged Aria tightly. "Thank you so much, Aria. I don't tell you often enough but I love you."

Aria's arms shook around me and I heard her sniffle and my own eyes watered. "No crying," I said firmly, pulling back.

Aria smiled tearfully. "You should remind yourself."

I frowned. "See, pregnancy hormones are already ruining my life."

She shook her head, then her smile vanished. "When's the appointment?"

I swallowed. "Next week."

"If you want me to come with you, tell me, okay?"

I squeezed her hand. "Thank you, but I think Matteo and I need to handle this as a couple," I whispered. "And Aria, please don't tell Lily. I don't want more people to know about this, and I really don't want to cause her emotional turmoil in her state. I want her to enjoy her pregnancy one-hundred-percent and not feel guilty for sharing her joy."

"I won't. It's your decision if and when you want to share this with her."

CHAPTER FOUR

Gianna

The days seemed to stick together like glue, passing in excruciating slowness. I barely slept at night, my brain working in overdrive. I didn't really feel pregnant and yet I felt different. Something was happening in my body that I had absolutely no control over. Matteo and I didn't talk about the "p" or the "a" word. We tried to pretend everything was business as usual until the day arrived. A day supposed to relieve me of a burden that still felt a burden in itself.

We didn't talk on our way to the clinic. Matteo wasn't the quiet type and I wasn't sure if he was silent for my sake or his. Matteo's hand was firm around mine as we walked into the building and he didn't release me when we settled on the uncomfortable chairs in the sterile waiting area of the clinic. We were alone in the clinic. Luca and Matteo had made sure no other patients would be around when I had my appointment. I knew Luca didn't want word to get out about this. The Famiglia would be in uproar if people found out I'd gotten rid of a baby even though Matteo and I were married. I could guess the kind of speculations that would create. Was she pregnant with another man's child? My reputation was still bad because of my escape all those years ago, and I doubted it would ever improve, but this could ruin me for good. I didn't care. Not about my reputation, that is. I wasn't sure what I felt anymore. The last few days had passed in a blur.

"Mrs. Vitiello, you can come in now," a nurse said. Her voice was polite but her expression held tension and whenever her eyes darted to Matteo, even fear. I didn't even want to know what Luca and Matteo had told the clinic staff to ensure their discretion.

Matteo rose and after a moment of hesitation, I did the same. Matteo's hand around mine was warm and strong, and his face was reassuring. Again I tried to find his true feelings in his eyes but they were guarded in a way I hadn't seen in a long time.

He led me toward the treatment room but I froze in the doorway, my eyes landing on the treatment chair I'd soon find myself in for the examination before the actual abortion. My chest clenched and I could barely breathe. Matteo peered at me, his brows drawing together. "Gianna?"

I swallowed and shook my head slowly. "I can't," I whispered.

The nurse stepped back to give us privacy. Matteo moved very close, shielding me from the room and its occupants, a doctor and another nurse, with his tall frame. "It's okay. Whatever you do, it'll be okay."

I shook my head again. "I don't want to be a mother. I don't want a child."

Matteo frowned. "Okay."

"But I can't do this. I can't get rid of it."

"Okay," Matteo said again but I could tell that he was confused.

"I just can't." I knew I'd feel guilty because it wasn't like money was a problem. We had enough money so a dozen nannies could raise the kid. Matteo's and my life wouldn't even change… but I knew that even that wasn't an option. I was confused and overwhelmed. "I can't," I said again, taking a step back.

Matteo nodded. "All right. I'll settle things with the doctors. Why don't you wait in the car?"

He held out his keys and I took them, then turned and walked out of the clinic. My feet carried me on their own and finally I found myself in the car, on the driver's seat. I felt like everything was shifting, as if the ground was being pulled from under my feet. I needed time to think about this, needed time to come to terms with the raging emotions inside of me. This was it. I'd grow a baby I didn't even want.

I could barely see the street ahead of me through my tear-blurry vision. From the corner of my eye, I saw Matteo's name flashing across my phone screen. I ignored it. I couldn't talk to him right now. I wasn't sure what to say when I barely knew what I felt. Despair and guilt were very high on the list, but so many more emotions battled for attention as well.

I wasn't sure how long I drove around aimlessly until finally my tear-swollen eyes forced me to pull over. I couldn't even remember the last time I'd felt like this, the last time I'd cried this hard.

Eventually, I steered the car back to our apartment building. My legs shook like leaves in the wind as I staggered into our penthouse and sank down on the floor with my back against the wall.

Thirty minutes later, Luca of all people found me ugly crying in the same spot. Of course, he still had the security code.

I'd thought I'd gotten a grip on myself after the car ride but once I found myself back in our home, all walls broke down.

Luca's gray eyes settled on me, his face impassive.

"What? No assholy comment?" I snapped, embarrassed that he saw me like this. Even in front of Aria and Matteo I hardly showed so much emotion.

"Matteo went insane with worry over you," Luca said as he towered over me.

"I sent him a text message." I wasn't sure how coherent it had been but I had definitely showed him I was alive.

"I need time to think, that was supposed to set him at ease?" Luca muttered.

I shrugged and wrapped my arms tighter around my legs. A wave of nausea crept up but I forced it back. I wasn't sure if it was the first signs of pregnancy or my inner turmoil.

Luca released a low breath. "You are not alone. You have Matteo. You have family, Gianna. We have your back."

"I still don't want to raise the kid. I don't want to be a mother… but I just can't get rid of it. What am I supposed to do now?"

"Aria suspected something like that."

Of course, she did. Aria had a sixth sense when it came to me.

"But how can I give birth to a baby and then give it away?"

"You won't give it away—"

I glared up at him but he continued, "Because Aria and I talked about it, and we're going to adopt it."

My eyes grew wide. "You… what?" I tried to understand what he was offering. "But you can't even stand me."

Luca and I got along better than in the past and I was fairly sure he liked me better than most of humankind, but in his case that didn't mean much.

Luca let out a dark laugh. He crouched before me, still a fucking giant. "Aria and I will love that child as if it was our own. We will protect it and make sure it has everything it needs. It doesn't even have to know that we aren't its parents. If you and Matteo want to keep it a secret, the child won't ever have to know it isn't ours. I swear I'll do everything in my power to protect your child, Gianna. I swear it'll be safe and loved." He touched his chest over his tattoo, and for a moment I considered hugging him. Luckily for both of us, he broke the moment and straightened to his full height.

It took a moment before I could speak. "You know, Luca, I like you more than I let on most of the time," I said in a shaky voice.

Luca held out his hand. I took it and he pulled me to my feet. "Same. When you don't say anything annoying I find you more than tolerable," he said dryly.

I choked on a laugh. "Why thank you. How often does that happen?"

He shrugged. "Once or twice per month."

I laughed. Luca's own mouth pulled into a smile but as quickly as it had come it disappeared. "Don't do this again. Don't ever run off like that. It's also Matteo's baby, Gianna, and the asshole loves you with all of his heart. If something happened to you, he'd lose it."

"I know," I whispered. "I was just overwhelmed. I never planned for any of this to happen."

Luca nodded. "It's what it is. You are pregnant and you'll keep the kid, and you and Matteo will give it to Aria and me if you agree on it."

"Does Matteo know what you just told me?"

"No, I haven't talked to him about it yet. First you two will have to settle things between you."

He was right. The elevator began moving and a minute later the doors slid open and Matteo stepped out. His hair was plastered to his head from his helmet and his eyes were wild. Luca stepped back from me and walked away but not before he touched Matteo's shoulder briefly and they exchanged a look. He disappeared inside the elevator and left.

"Fuck, Gianna," Matteo rasped as he stalked toward me and jerked me against him, then kissed me harshly, shoving me into the wall as he gripped my hips in a crushing hold.

He pulled away, breathing harshly. "You promised you'd never fucking run again."

"I didn't run," I protested. "I needed time to myself to think this through. It's a lot to stomach."

"Not just for you," Matteo said quietly.

Guilt filled me. I cupped his face. "I know. I'm sorry. I keep messing up. It's in my nature. That's why I shouldn't become a mother."

He released a breath. "Don't say that. We'll figure this out. Together."

"Together," I agreed. I kissed him again, then pulled back. "Luca offered that he and Aria adopt our baby."

Matteo took a step back, but didn't let go of me. "He did?"

I nodded. "What do you think?"

Matteo frowned. "I don't know. Do you think you can see the child every day and have it call someone else Mom?"

I wasn't sure. "But it's a good option."

"Yeah. The child needs protection, and Luca and Aria are amazing parents."

"They are," I agreed softly and searched Matteo's eyes for a hint to his true feelings. "Will you be okay with it? With Luca acting as the baby's father and not you?"

Matteo glanced to the side, his brows drawing together. "How should I know?"

Yes, how? How should either of us know how we'd deal with this pregnancy and with the aftermath? "We'll figure it out," I murmured.

Matteo kissed me again. "We will."

I linked our fingers. In the last thirteen years we'd gone through so much, nothing as challenging as this would be, but with Matteo at my side, everything would be fine.

Matteo

When I woke the morning after the canceled appointment, I was alone in bed. Immediately my heart rate picked up, worrying that Gianna had gone off on her own again. Yesterday I'd almost gone crazy.

I shoved out of bed and rushed down the staircase to the living area but slowed when I spotted Gianna sitting in a lounge chair on the roof terrace. I headed for the glass door and slid it open. Despite the early morning, the humid heat settled like grease on my skin.

Gianna turned her head, looking my way. She was still without makeup and her eyes were puffy from crying yesterday. "Hey," she murmured.

"Hey." I went over to her and Gianna made room on the chair for me, so I could squeeze in and fold her into my arms. Gianna sank into me at once, which wasn't like her.

"How are you feeling?"

"Good," she said then amended. "Better than yesterday anyway. I thought about Luca's offer all night and about what it would mean for us… and I think it's the best possible solution for everyone."

I stroked her bare arm. "Aria and Luca will take great care of it, and we'll get to watch it grow up."

Gianna's brows furrowed. "Yeah." She searched my eyes.

"If you're absolutely sure, we should tell Aria and Luca so they can prepare for the new situation," I said.

"Are you sure?"

"Like you said it's the best solution for everyone," I said. I wasn't sure how things would change once the baby was there and I had to watch Luca be its dad. I couldn't really imagine myself as a father either, though. I liked the general idea of being a dad. The fun things, but just from watching Luca and Aria I knew there were plenty of hard moments as well.

"Okay, then I'll call Aria."

"I have a meeting with Luca today anyway. I'll have a talk with him then as well."

Gianna stayed in my arms for a few more heartbeats before she pulled away and stood to grab her phone from the kitchen counter. I headed over to the railing and let my gaze wander over New York. We'd said yes to the baby, but at the same time no. I was relieved but at the same time worried.

Luca and I met in his office in the Sphere to discuss a few alarming developments with the Tartarus MC. Since Luca had annihilated their chapter in New Jersey they had laid low for years but now some of the other chapters, especially their mother chapter in Texas, had sent out scouts into the area.

Luca suspected they were rebuilding a New York and New Jersey chapter. Right now they were still a scattered assortment of drunkards and idiots.

I took off my helmet as I strolled through the bar area toward the hidden backrooms. Luca sat behind his desk chair, his open laptop in front of him. He closed it the moment I entered.

"Any new developments?" I asked.

Luca narrowed his eyes. "Business can wait."

I sighed and plopped down in one of the comfortable leather chairs.

"Gianna told Aria this morning that you two decided to give us the baby."

Give them the baby. It sounded like handing over car keys. I nodded. "It's the best possible solution for everyone."

Luca sat back in his chair, watching me with his annoying scrutiny. "All right. You realize that while we take the baby off your hands, Aria and I can't spare you the pregnancy. That's for you and Gianna to handle, and it comes with responsibility."

Was he trying to piss me off on purpose? "We know that, don't worry."

"No alcohol, no sushi, less caffeine…"

"I get it, Luca. And trust me, Gianna gets it too."

Luca shrugged. "You don't want your lives to change but they will, at least in the next eight months. After that, you can have your old life back and Aria and I will take over."

"Can we talk about business now? The more you talk the more I feel like skinning someone, and I have a feeling a few fuckers from Tartarus might just be the balm for my bloodthirst."

Luca sighed but he nodded. "Aria invited Gianna and you over for dinner tonight. Your wife agreed, so be there at six."

I stifled a groan.

When I returned home in the late afternoon, Gianna was already downstairs, perching on a barstool at the kitchen counter. She drank coffee and was reading a yoga magazine. In her tight black jean shorts and black wife beater she looked like the Gianna I knew. Tough and hot as hell. She slanted me a look. Her makeup covered up the last traces of yesterday's tears. My eyes darted down to her flat belly. It seemed unreal that she was really pregnant, that something as monumental as a baby in her belly wasn't yet visible for the eye.

She raised her cup. "Decaf, in case you're wondering."

"Did Luca give you a lecture of all the things you're prohibited from consuming and doing?" I asked wryly as I strolled over to her and kissed her full lips.

She grimaced. "No. But Aria bridged the subject in a subtle but unmistakable way. As if I'd just keep drinking alcohol and espressos. I'll make sure it's safe until it's in their hands." She shook her head.

"Do you want to cancel the dinner with them?"

Gianna considered that. "No, I'm really grateful for what they're doing."

"Me too," I said. "How was yoga today?"

"Great. I could blank out everything for a little while. Luckily I can keep working out during the pregnancy. I just need to tone it down slightly."

I squeezed her hip. "See. This pregnancy will be over before you know it and then we can party the night away again."

"Yeah," Gianna said with a sigh. Her voice mirrored a deep longing I felt as well. Problem was, I wasn't exactly sure what I was longing for.

Liliana and Romero had agreed to watch Marcella and Amo while we had dinner. Luca and Aria obviously didn't want their kids to overhear anything about the new addition to their family, which was probably for the best.

We were halfway through dinner, when Aria spoke up, "Oh, I made an appointment with my OB/GYN next week for a checkup. You'll be in your seventh week then so she should be able to see the heart beating."

Gianna didn't look surprised, so they must have discussed the matter before. I was stunned. "You'll have an ultrasound?"

"I suppose so?" Gianna said, turning to Aria who nodded.

"That's good," I said. "You'll accompany Gianna?"

"Yes," Aria said hesitantly. "If that's okay for you?"

"Of course."

It wasn't that I was keen on going to the appointment but the knowledge that any step of the kid's development wasn't really my business felt strange.

"We need to discuss the matter of hiding the pregnancy," Luca said unceremoniously. "The child doesn't need to grow up surrounded by nasty rumors. We need to make the public believe it's Aria's and mine."

"You are right," Gianna said. "When did you show?"

Aria pursed her lips. "At twenty weeks it was difficult to hide with Amo. But that's because it was my second pregnancy. You'll be pregnant in winter so coats and sweaters can cover up a lot. But your workout clothes won't be able to hide a bump."

Gianna nodded. "That's what I thought."

Aria exchanged a look with Luca. "How about we take it as we go? You keep on giving yoga and Pilates lessons for as long as loose shirts hide the bump, and wear loose clothes as much as possible. I'll start doing the same. I can't really wear a tight dress to our Christmas party when you are in your fifth or sixth month then, and would show."

"I'd have never thought pregnancy means so much logistics," I joked.

"It usually doesn't," Luca muttered.

"Well, Aria has experience hiding a pregnancy so I have faith we can keep it a secret," I said, not able to hold back the jibe.

Luca's eyes flashed, remembering the difficult beginning of Aria's pregnancy with Marcella.

Aria sent Luca a warning look while Gianna did the same with me.

"We'll get through this together as a family," Aria said firmly.

"When should we tell Lily and Romero?" Gianna asked to change the topic. Clever girl.

"That's really up to you. You could wait until you both are past the first twelve weeks…"

"Yeah. I hope she won't be disappointed we didn't confide in her before," Gianna said.

"She'll understand," Aria assured her.

"Will we tell anyone else?"

Luca shook his head. "I don't see why. Every person we involve is a risk."

A risk to the biggest secret of all of our lives.

CHAPTER FIVE

Gianna

THE FIRST ULTRASOUND SHOWED THAT THE BABY'S HEART was beating. It was strange to see the pulsating thing on the screen. I was relieved that there wasn't much more to see yet. There wasn't a baby to speak of yet. I'd worried a little person would stare right back at me. It made things easier. As long as the kid looked like an undistinguishable black-and-white blob in the ultrasound and I didn't feel it, I could pretend I wasn't really pregnant—except for the few amendments to my lifestyle.

In the week following my appointment, Lily surprised me when she showed up in the Famiglia women gym. She hadn't worked out these last four weeks, probably because of the pregnancy. She'd mentioned something about some light bleeding. Like me she wore yoga tights and a loose-fitting yoga tank, not that either of us showed yet. It was actually quite informative to see her since she was a week ahead of me, and always gave me a glimpse of what lay ahead. Her dark blond hair was piled atop her head in a messy bun just like mine.

"Hey stranger," I called across the yoga room as Lily slid her wool socks off and padded toward me barefoot. We hugged before we both sank down on the round yoga pillows. The yoga lesson wasn't about to begin for another fifteen minutes, but I was always early to prepare everything.

"How are you?" I asked.

"Great," Lily said, brushing her palm across her belly. It was something I'd often seen with pregnant women, especially if you asked them about their well-being. As if they always answered for two.

"Are you going to do yoga today?"

She nodded with a smile. "My doc cleared me for exercise. I want to keep doing something for my health."

Lily had been a constant presence in my yoga classes from the very first day. Aria had been in the beginning but she preferred my Pilates classes so she switched to them later. "Perfect," I said with a smile. Lily and I didn't see each other as often as Aria and I did so I'd missed our weekly yoga sessions and chats afterward.

"But I might not be able to do everything. I have to be mindful of what my pregnancy allows. I'll read up on it so I'll know what I can't do."

"Don't worry. I'll give you alternative yoga exercises in case it's necessary or you don't feel comfortable," I said, touching her leg.

Uncertainty crossed Lily's face. "Are you sure you want to do that?"

It sounded like "are you sure you can do it?" to me, but I pushed my annoyance down. "Pregnancy adapted workouts were part of my training. Trust me, I can make sure you and your kid are safe." It wasn't even a lie. Knowing that many mob wives popped out one baby after the other, I'd made sure to be versed in the special needs of pregnant women or women recovering from birth. I didn't mention that I'd read up on the matter again to make sure I kept the secret passenger in my belly safe until its delivery to Aria and Luca. For a moment, I considered telling Lily. But Lily, far more than Aria, had completely lost herself in being a mom. Sometimes it seemed there was hardly any room for anything else anymore. It was something that I'd always considered the most deterrent thing about becoming a mother—losing yourself and everything you used to be, as if by giving birth you lost every right to still have your own needs and interests.

Lily beamed at me. "Thank you!" Then her expression turned sheepish. "I'm sorry if I'm being annoying. I'm just so excited about my pregnancy. I can't wait for Sara to have siblings."

My eyes widened. "Siblings? Are you preggers with more than one?"

"Oh no." Lily giggled, again caressing her flat belly. For some reason the motion made me unreasonably angry, which was completely irrational. "But Romero and I want at least three kids."

I nodded, smiling tightly. I'd never minded Lily's exuberance when it came to being a mom but for some reason, I had trouble being around it now that I was pregnant myself. Yet, I was determined not to vent my irrational feelings on Lily. She had every right to be happy and I wouldn't ruin it.

Matteo and I sat at the bar in our kitchen, drinking coffee and chatting about Matteo's plans to head out with Growl today to seek out a hiding place of the MC giving them trouble.

"Do you really have to join Growl?" I asked.

Matteo's eyebrows rose. I wasn't someone who clucked. I was more like the mother hen who kicked her eggs out of her nest. With Matteo I'd grown used to his thrill-seeking ways. "Are you worried?"

I was, and more than that, I was terrified. Matteo's life was dangerous and while I'd worried in the past as well, I'd usually kept my feelings to myself, knowing that he could handle things.

I glared in response. Matteo grinned and wrapped an arm around my hip, dragging me closer so he could kiss me. "All these hormones are turning you into a softy."

It was the first time we'd mentioned the pregnancy since my doctor's appointment in my seventh week, which was more than four weeks ago. And even on that day our conversation about the pregnancy had only consisted of "Everything okay?" from Matteo and a curt nod from me. We'd kept living our life, minus the club visits and drunk escapades.

"Just be careful," I pressed out. Matteo searched my eyes as he did so often recently, then nodded. "You know me."

"I do, which is why I want you to be careful. Don't leave me alone to deal with this mess."

Matteo smiled, but there was something dark behind it. "Luca and Aria will deal with the mess, babe."

I didn't get the chance to ask what that was supposed to mean because our bell rang. "Aria," I said, because vigilance had taken over Matteo's face. "She made another appointment with her OB/GYN today."

Matteo stood and allowed her to take the elevator up to the penthouse. Aria probably knew the code from Luca but unlike him, she always rang the bell like any decent human being would.

Matteo waited for her with his back to me. Aria smiled hesitantly as she stepped in. "Ready?"

"Sure," I said. I'd tried to avoid another examination for as long as possible, but Aria had insisted it was time for another checkup now that I was twelve weeks along.

I kissed Matteo and he stroked my back in an almost lingering way. Then I pulled back and followed Aria.

At first, I considered not looking at the ultrasound screen but then curiosity got the better of me. The moment my eyes registered the small baby on the screen, I wished I hadn't given in. This wasn't a mere blob anymore. The doc explained what we saw and marked the feet, head, hands… a complete human being in my belly.

I looked away. Aria met my gaze, her eyes alight with joy then slowly she sobered. She reached for my hand and squeezed. I was glad she didn't say anything. I stared at the painting on the wall, some kind of abstract art, because Aria's expression tightened my chest. The doc kept blabbering about how things looked good. I tried to block her out but it was impossible.

I practically leaped off the examination table when she was done and got dressed, desperate to leave as soon as possible. When I left the changing area, the doc held out a string of photos. Ultrasound photos of the baby. I stared at them. Aria gingerly took them from the doc before she touched my arm and led me outside. We didn't talk until we were in the elevator. "Do you want to have them?"

I shook my head. "You and Luca should have them."

Aria slid them into her purse. "Are you still okay with Luca and me adopting the baby?"

"Of course," I said. "That's not it… I just want to pretend nothing changed, that I'm not pregnant, but days like today make that really hard."

Aria gave me an understanding look. "Maybe try to make peace with it. See it as an exercise you need to get through. It won't be long until it'll be even harder to pretend you aren't pregnant."

"My belly's still flat, hallelujah," I muttered, trying to resort to my usual sarcasm that seemed out of reach so often recently.

"It's not just your growing belly," Aria said quietly as we approached the car with our bodyguards. "You'll feel the baby eventually."

I couldn't imagine feeling something inside of me like that. Weren't there women who didn't realize they were pregnant until labor started and a baby plopped out of them? They couldn't have felt the baby inside of them, so maybe I would be lucky too.

Matteo

I wiped blood off my knife while Luca leaned against the wall, watching me.

"While I appreciate your talents with your knife, you realize we'll run out of MC assholes for you to torture to release some tension eventually. Maybe you should ask your wife for some yoga mantras. A few oms might help you relax."

I slanted him a dark look. "Says the man who slaughtered an entire chapter to release tension. And stop reading shit into my actions. I always loved to torture."

Luca's phone rang and considering his softer expression, it could only be Aria. "That's good. When's the next appointment?"

I knew at once that they were talking about Gianna and the baby. Shoving my knife back into the holster at my chest, I approached my brother. He hung up.

"So what did your wife say?"

Luca narrowed his eyes at me. "Everything's fine. The ultrasound showed a healthy baby."

I gave a terse nod. "See, Gianna's taking care of your kid."

Luca didn't say anything for a while. "It's not our kid yet. It can still be yours."

I considered that, becoming a dad, having responsibility for a small human being. Gianna and I loved staying up late and doing whatever we felt like. We loved traveling too—as much as me being a mobster allowed. I loved seeing the joy on Gianna's face whenever she managed to wrangle a bit more freedom out of the mafia life. A kid would take away plenty of her freedom, even more so than mine.

"No, you and Aria should adopt it like we agreed."

When I returned late in the afternoon, Gianna was browsing travel pictures on her laptop. She didn't mention her examination, nor did I. Instead she pointed at a lush green forest and then white beaches and blue water. "Costa Rica."

I kissed her and sank down beside her. "You want to play name a country?"

She rolled her eyes. "I want to flee the cold this winter. Why don't we spend a few weeks in Costa Rica in November? New York is always so depressing in winter."

"Can you fly?"

She frowned. "Of course."

I gestured at her flat belly. "I mean because of the kid."

"I know what you mean, but it's not a problem."

"Then we should fly to Costa Rica for a bit of adventure."

Her entire face transformed. Relief and happiness shone in her eyes. This was the Gianna I wanted to keep seeing, and this Gianna needed her freedom.

Maybe for the first time since we'd agreed to giving Luca and Aria our child, I felt a sense of certainty and acceptance. Some people weren't meant to be parents, and we were among them.

When I told Luca about our travel plans, expecting to be met with resistance, I was surprised when he nodded. "That's actually a good plan. Maybe you'll be more chilled afterward."

I stifled a comment, but his words proved to be correct. Gianna and I really enjoyed the two weeks away from everything. The only thing that occasionally dimmed our joy was when people congratulated Gianna on her pregnancy. In her sixth month, the bump was now visible when Gianna wore only a bikini. Apart from that, this vacation was like all of our vacations before, except we couldn't drink or dive, but Gianna was still fit and eager to do as many activities as possible.

One evening as we watched the sunset in the hammock in front of our beach villa, Gianna leaned her head on my shoulder, whispering, "I wish we could stay in this moment forever. I'm scared of returning to New York."

Gianna admitting to being afraid was a rare event and immediately fired up my protectiveness. I pulled her closer against me. "There's nothing for you to be scared of. You have me."

She looked at me. "I do, don't I?"

I frowned. "Of course."

"Things will get tough. Pretending this pregnancy isn't there is impossible with my belly, and it'll be hard hiding from the public to keep it hidden."

"You'll spend plenty of time in the Hamptons with Aria and Liliana."

Gianna cringed. "I still have to tell Lily. I can't postpone it anymore. It's not fair."

"Then tell her." I paused, knowing Gianna would loathe what I had to say next. "You should stop teaching classes. Hiding your bump in gym clothes is much harder, especially if you do all those yoga poses."

Gianna nodded slowly, surprising me. "I know. It's been hard to avoid ab exercises these last few weeks. Eventually my clients will get suspicious."

Wistfulness swung in her voice. Gianna loved her job. She loved feeling useful. A life as a trophy wife wasn't what she was born to be. She pulled her legs up against her body, her gaze returning to the ocean cloaked in darkness.

When suddenly she jumped, her eyes going wide and darting down to her belly.

"What is it?" I asked, alarmed.

Gianna didn't say anything at first and only stared down her body. Slowly she lowered her legs and met my gaze. "It's nothing. I think my stomach is acting up."

Gianna was lying. "Are you sure you are okay?"

She glanced down at her belly again and nodded slowly. "I'm fine. I'll just do a few detox-days once we're back home, then everything will be okay."

I had a feeling her reaction had little to do with stomach issues and more with the baby.

CHAPTER SIX

Gianna

I'd avoided this conversation with Lily for too long. I wasn't even sure why. Lily wouldn't condemn me any more than Aria had. Maybe she would have a harder time understanding my reasoning, after all she was blissfully happy being a mom. But now in my sixth month I couldn't keep my pregnancy a secret from her any longer. I didn't want to.

As we'd all agreed on, I'd driven out to the Hamptons after we returned from our vacation. The official explanation why I no longer taught Pilates and yoga was that I had broken my wrist during vacation and it needed time to heal. Now I just needed to stay out of the public eye until early April when the kid was due.

I sat wrapped in a cozy blanket on the couch and watched the flames licking at the top of the fireplace. I wasn't really a winter person but roaring fireplaces always gave me a sense of peace.

The sound of a car pulling up caught my attention. Matteo had stayed in New York to take care of business with Luca, but Aria and Lily would join me with their kids today and stay until Christmas so we could all celebrate together. Of course, I wasn't alone in the mansion. Two guards had accompanied me and were manning the security cameras to make sure I was safe.

My belly flipped when Lily entered, followed by her own bodyguard who carried Sara. He sat the kid down who immediately rushed toward me with a grin and climbed on the couch beside me. I smiled at her. She was a much quieter kid than Marcella or Amo. Judging by the line dancer in my belly, it wouldn't be the hesitant type.

Lily joined me, her eyes crinkling with worry. She glanced at my hands, which were unscathed and frowned. She must have heard the broken wrist rumor from one of the women in my yoga course.

"I'm fine," I said immediately. "We needed to figure out a lie for why I'm lying low."

Lily leaned back, waiting, and as usual, her hand pressed to her very prominent belly. Even though she was only a week ahead, her bump was already much bigger. Maybe because it was her second kid or maybe because she wasn't so desperate to hide it from the world. Sara curled up with her head on Lily's lap and my sister immediately began to stroke her hair.

I looked away, losing myself in the flames. "You know I don't want kids."

Lily nodded, but her frown only deepened.

"And I still don't..." I pushed down the blanket, revealing the bump that my sweater and sweatpants couldn't hide anymore.

Lily's eyes shot open, her shock almost comical in its scope. "Wow. I—" She snapped her mouth shut and shook her head.

"Yeah," I whispered.

She licked her lips and touched my shoulder, her gaze full of questions she obviously didn't dare ask.

"At the very beginning of April. You're only one week ahead," I said. I took a deep breath, steeling myself. "Aria and Luca are going to adopt it."

Again surprise then Lily nodded as if it made sense. "So they've known from the start?"

I put my hand over hers. Sara was completely oblivious to our conversation and stared almost hypnotized into the fireplace. "I was worried it would affect your pregnancy. I wanted you to enjoy it without anything disturbing your happiness."

"I'm the youngest sister, but I'm not breakable."

"Don't be mad."

Lily smiled. "I'm not mad, Gianna. This must have been difficult for you. I know kids were never part of your plan."

"Matteo and I weren't careful. It's our fault."

Lily didn't say anything. "And you are sure about Aria and Luca?"

"They are amazing parents. You are, too, of course, but you have a baby on the way yourself…"

"That's not what I meant. Are you sure you want to give it to them?"

"Yes," I said immediately. I'd been tremendously relieved when Matteo and I had finally made the decision. It was the only option.

The weeks until Christmas dragged on infinitely. I seemed to be stuck in a kind of endless loop of boredom, stuck in the Hamptons, without a real purpose. Not to mention that the kid seemed to seriously consider becoming either a kickboxing champion or line dancer. Despite Aria's curiosity I'd asked the doc to keep the gender of the baby a secret.

My boredom was the reason why I almost ran over Matteo in my excitement when he finally joined me in the mansion for a longer period of time to celebrate Christmas. The rest of the family would arrive later the same day.

"Whoa," he grunted as I collided with him. "Someone's excited to see my pretty face." Before I could retort something, he pulled me even closer and kissed me. I deepened the kiss at once. I hadn't seen him in almost two weeks and was desperate for his closeness. I dragged my lips away. I was already wet and aching for him. "Not for that arrogant face, for your skillful tongue and cock."

Matteo's grin got wider. "Your libido's even more potent than usual."

"Shut up, and let's go upstairs."

I grabbed his hand and practically dragged him to our bedroom, ignoring Matteo's soft chuckling. We always had the same room when we stayed in the Hamptons, so it felt like a second home away from home.

He let himself fall on our bed, spreading his arms. "I'm all yours. Use me as you see fit."

I rolled my eyes but knelt on the bed beside him, not wasting any time as I unzipped his pants and tugged at them. Eventually Matteo lifted his ass so I could drag them down. "Won't you help me?"

"You enjoy being independent."

I slapped his hard stomach and finally Matteo got undressed. The sight never ceased to amaze me, but Matteo didn't give me much time to admire him, which was probably for the best. He helped me out of my sweater and my pants before he pushed me down on the bed. Left in my bra and panties, he let his eyes rake over me. For the first time ever, I felt self-conscious. Growing a belly just wasn't something I could really identify with. Luckily, Matteo wasn't one to waste too much time before the fun started. With a devilish grin, he bowed over my breast and snatched a nipple between his lips. He gave a hard tug that had me moaning loudly. He pulled back slightly. "I think my favorite girls have grown."

I rolled my eyes. He was right, of course. They had grown a cup. I grabbed the back of his head and he latched back on to my nipple. I relaxed, my body humming with the first soft pulses of pleasures spreading all the way from my nipple down to my core. Slowly, he worked his way lower, his tongue and mouth worshiping every inch of me. My body practically burst with anticipation when I felt his warm breath ghosting over my pussy.

"I never get enough of the sight," Matteo growled.

"Enjoy the sight before my vagina gets shredded by child birth."

Matteo burst out laughing. "Fuck Gianna, what kind of dirty talk is that?"

I shrugged. "It's the truth."

"I don't want that kind of truth while I'm looking at your beautiful pink pussy," Matteo joked.

"Tough luck. You should take your time worshiping it then."

"Oh I will," he said in a low voice and I shivered. I parted my legs wider and smiled when I felt Matteo's warm breath against my opening before his tongue dove between my folds for one hard lick and I almost came right then. Matteo chuckled. "Very sensitive today, are you? Then I'll have to be extra careful to draw this out."

He was right. I'd become far more sensitive these last couple of months, which led to embarrassingly fast orgasms.

"I have faith in you," I said, then gasped when he suckled one of my lips into his mouth. "God, yes."

Then I didn't say anything anymore because I really didn't need to. Matteo was a fucking master at eating me. He knew every move I liked and he executed them perfectly. I had to sit up farther to watch him, propping up a pillow behind my back, and he smiled against my pussy, then flicked his tongue so I could see it circle my clit. My lips opened with a moan and I parted wider for him. He held my gaze as he flipped his tongue up and down. I loved watching Matteo and he loved watching me. Our eyes locked as he took his time caressing my sensitive folds with his tongue. I raked my fingers through his hair, smiling almost deliriously from the pleasure coursing through me.

He brought his hand down to my pussy and slid the thumb along my slit then he reached up and pushed the finger into my mouth. I suckled on it, tasting myself on Matteo's skin. His appreciative growl almost sent me over the edge.

With that sexy but annoying shark-grin, he took my folds into his mouth and mimicked what I did with his finger. I moaned and his finger slid out of my mouth and lower until he cupped my breast and squeezed. Matteo sucked my folds noisily before he resumed eating me out like his favorite ice cream. I propped another pillow under my head for a better view, past my bulging belly, and our eyes met again. Matteo's brimmed with eagerness, and lust and I knew mine would reflect the same. I was getting closer but I didn't want to come yet. I clenched.

"Not yet," I gasped.

Matteo pulled back slightly and only fucked me with his finger, his shiny lips curled up into a smirk. I relaxed, slowly coming down from almost toppling over the cliff. Matteo added a second finger and I moaned, my eyes fluttering shut as I relished in the skillful way he massaged my inner walls. His tongue brushed across my folds, close to his fingers and far away from my throbbing clit. Matteo drew my pleasure out for a long time until every fiber of my body ached for release. He sensed my need and turned his attention back to my clit, the tip of his tongue massaging it until I arched up with a harsh cry.

"Yes! Fuck, yes!" I cried as my release barreled through my body like an unstoppable force.

Matteo's mouth was practically buried in my pussy as he guided me through my release. Eventually he pushed up on his forearms and I lay like a boneless heap against the pillows, my lower body throbbing gently in the aftermath of an intense orgasm.

"You're so damn good at this," I said with a satisfied smile.

Matteo smiled smugly. "I know." He climbed up and kissed me, allowing me to taste myself on his lips. "But your cock sucking skills are up to par." He slid off the bed and stood in front of it with his cock straining to attention.

I gave him a knowing look. "Thanks for the praise." I stayed on my back.

Matteo raised his eyebrows then curled his hand around his erection and began rubbing himself slowly. A droplet of precum teased me. With a huff, I pushed into a sitting position and perched on the edge of the bed, so Matteo's cock was in front of my face. I shoved his hand away and gripped his length, then ran my tongue over his balls before sucking on them as I began to pump him slowly.

"Fuck," Matteo groaned. "I can't wait to come all over you."

I ran my thumb over his tip, spreading his precum. My own arousal spiked again. Sucking Matteo off was one of my absolute favorites. I ran my tongue from the base to the tip, then circled the velvety head and dipped my tongue in.

"Stop teasing, Gianna. Suck me."

I grinned at his commanding tone. It turned me on like nothing else, even if I'd never admit it aloud. Of course, the arrogant bastard knew only too well.

I slid his erection into my mouth slowly until he was sheathed completely in me. It took a few breaths through my nose to get used to the feel as always. Matteo watched me with pure hunger, groaning low in his throat. His balls vibrated against my chin as he shook with arousal.

It had taken a while before I'd managed to take all of him but I had been determined to master it because he'd once made a comment about deep throating to annoy me.

Matteo tangled his fingers in my hair and when I started to move back slightly, he knew I was ready. Holding me by the hair, he began to thrust into me deep and slow, hitting the back of my throat every time, and every time he did, he moaned low in his throat and his finger flexed in my hair. He held my gaze as he claimed my mouth and I reached for the vibrator on the bedside table, turned it on and touched it to my clit. In the last two weeks of Matteo staying in New York, it had become my best friend, especially during phone sex sessions with him.

Matteo's smile darkened. "Already eager for cock again, my insatiable fury?"

I glared but couldn't say anything because he kept fucking my mouth.

"Having my cock down your throat has so many perks," he teased.

I graced him with my teeth in warning, and he groaned deeply. "God, fuck. Gianna, you are the blow job queen."

I cupped his balls with one hand while my other slid the vibrator in and out of me. I moaned around Matteo's cock and could feel his balls tighten. He slammed into me a few more times before he pulled back.

I grinned wickedly up at him as his body jerked, his eyes darkening with lust and his cum shot out of his cock and all over my throat and chest. My own release crashed down on me and I arched, moaning. Matteo watched me hungrily as I kept pumping the dildo in and out of my pussy.

I let myself fall backward, the dildo still buried inside of me but no longer turned on. Matteo took a few paper towels from the nightstand and held them out to me. I took them. "You always make such a mess," I teased as I rubbed myself clean.

A dangerous smile curled Matteo's lips. "Do I?" He sank down beside me and gripped the base of the dildo and turned it on. I was oversensitive so I twitched.

Reaching for Matteo's hand, I tried to get him to turn off the dildo again. "Matteo," I gasped. "Stop it."

He gripped my wrists and shoved them onto the bed above my head. My struggling was useless, he was too strong so I didn't bother.

Instead I narrowed my eyes at him. "Stop torturing me!" I said, then moaned as he turned the vibrations up another notch. I was on sensory overload but Matteo was relentless.

His expression was hungry and dark as he watched his hand guide the dildo in and out of me. He was a hunter on a trail. "You have the prettiest pussy ever, baby."

I opened my mouth for a snappy comment but he pulled the dildo out of me and held the vibrating tip against my clit.

I gasped, my eyes rolling back. "You're wasting your time, I won't come again."

That was of course the wrong thing to say. Matteo loved a good challenge, which was why we were married at all.

His answering grin was shark-like and a new wave of arousal pooled between my legs. This man was too sexy for words, problem was he was too aware of it.

"Challenge accepted," Matteo growled. "How about three more orgasms?"

I snorted. "Good luck."

He chuckled but then his expression turned intent, predatory. The hunt had begun. Fuck.

Matteo

Gianna's face flashed with desire. She was fucking eager for those orgasms. I released her wrists and she put her hands flat on the bed, surrendering.

I pulled the pink dildo away from her clit and parted her legs farther. That pink pussy was too fucking pretty. I lowered the vibrations to a soft hum and traced the tip of the device slowly over her outer lips. I circled Gianna's pretty folds like that for a few minutes until her breathing was deep and she was glistening with arousal, then I turned the vibrations up and held the tip to her opening.

She moaned. "Oh God, fuck. Matteo."

I smirked, then slowly ran the dildo up along her crease but stopped before it reached her little nub before I returned to her opening. I repeated that over and over again until Gianna was writhing and moaning, begging for release. My own cock was already hard again, watching her take pleasure like that. Slowly I slid half of the dildo into her pussy and Gianna began quivering. She was close.

"Ready for one of three?" I asked.

"Yes," she gasped out.

I crept down her body and bent over her pussy, watching the dildo half buried in her. "Fuck. I think I'm jealous of that pink atrocity."

Gianna huffed but it was breathless and needy.

I turned up the vibrator to full speed and sucked her clit at the same time and Gianna exploded. She cried out, gripped my hair, tugged, bucked her hips.

I pulled the dildo out and dipped my tongue into her. "You're always my taste of the month."

She laughed. "Is that supposed to be a compliment?"

"Fuck, yes," I rasped as I lapped at her, then I pushed up to my arm.

She shook her head. "Sometimes you sound like a madman."

I grinned. "Only sometimes? Then I must be losing my charm."

Gianna rolled her eyes but her smile was warm and my own heart swelled with love for her. "Are you ready for two of three?" I asked.

She sighed, half exhausted, half resigned. "Probably not, but you don't care, right?"

"Right," I said in a low voice as I kissed her. "How about you take my cock up that pretty pussy now?"

"That sounds good," she said in that throaty sex voice that drove me insane. My eyes traced over her protruding belly. We mostly tried to pretend it wasn't there but it was becoming increasingly difficult, especially for Gianna.

"I think missionary is out of the question now," I said with a grin.

"As if that was ever your favorite."

"It's not, and it isn't yours either," I said with a dirty laugh. Gianna loved doing it doggy style or up against the wall or bent over a table. Fuck we had so many favorites, it was hard to choose.

"True."

"Why don't you ride me? I'm feeling like being lazy today."

I stretched out on my back and Gianna positioned herself over me. Her brows drew together as she glanced at her bump.

"My cock's waiting," I teased.

She lowered herself, burying my cock all the way in her. I groaned and so did she, but her movements were out of sync. I could tell that she was getting increasingly frustrated with her body.

"Let me fuck you doggy style. I miss your pretty ass."

She nodded, but the frown remained on her face. Only when she was on all fours in front of me and I started rubbing her slit with my tip did she begin to relax again. I pushed into her, with less force than in the past, not sure if I could hurt the baby. She moaned, and soon everything was forgotten as I fucked her slow but deep, rubbing her clit, and when she came, her clenching inner walls shoved me over the edge as well. I groaned, my thrust becoming uncoordinated.

"Fuck," I growled.

She laughed. "I guess number three is canceled."

I leaned forward and bit her neck lightly. "Give me some time, then I'm up for another round."

She shook her head. "I really don't think I can again, and I mean it. I feel like I'm about to pass out from exhaustion. I just want to sleep."

I kissed her shoulder blade and pulled out of her. "All right. Tomorrow then."

She smiled and stretched out on her side. I lied down beside her, pulling her into my arms, but her bump got in the way. She sighed. "It gets difficult ignoring this."

"Only three more months, then it's over," I assured her.

She frowned. "I know. I hope we can keep it from the public. I don't want people to suspect anything when Aria and Luca pretend it's their baby."

"We're careful," I said. My stomach did that annoying flip when I thought of giving that baby to my brother and Aria, not because they wouldn't take care of it, but because part of me wanted to be the one to do it.

CHAPTER SEVEN

Gianna

"I think I'm going crazy, Peanut," I whispered as I touched the bump. I'd started talking to it in secret a few weeks ago as it had become clear that the baby wouldn't let me ignore it. It was kicking up a storm every time I was trying to sleep or relax. I hadn't told anyone that I could feel its kicks. I wasn't even sure why. Aria had asked me a couple of times about it, but I'd always changed the topic. It felt too… real, feeling this baby move inside of me.

Another kick, and this time even my belly vibrated. It was impossible to miss anymore. On the one hand, I felt relief whenever Peanut showed it was still alive and kicking, but on the other hand its presence overwhelmed me in a way I didn't understand. The worst was all the secrecy, all the hiding in the Hamptons as if I was a prisoner. So far nobody had seen me with a bump and Aria had managed to stay out of the public eyes since Christmas as well. The chances of us pulling off our plan weren't bad.

"You have our temper, Peanut."

Luca wouldn't be happy about that. I smiled but slowly the smile dropped. I pulled my hand away from my belly and got dressed. Aria and Luca wouldn't have trouble handling a wild child. Amo wasn't exactly an easy kid either and they got him under control, mostly. I couldn't help but wonder how they'd raise my Peanut. If it were a girl, which I still didn't know, Luca would probably be a protective berserk as he was with Marcella. If Peanut were a girl, she would never experience freedom, never get to choose her own path, her husband, or even if she wanted to marry at all.

Matteo poked his head in. He'd arrived in the Hamptons this morning and would stay two more nights. "Why are you pulling a face?"

"Do you think Luca will arrange a marriage for the baby?"

Matteo frowned. "I suppose so. It's tradition. So far, he hasn't given any indication that he's going to fight our traditions. The majority of our men are happy with the rules as they are."

"The men, yes."

Matteo came toward me and touched my shoulders, watching me in the mirror. "If Luca and Aria raise the kid, they are the ones who decide how to raise it."

"I know," I muttered. "But it wouldn't hurt if a girl would be allowed a bit of freedom as well."

Matteo wrapped his arms around my ribcage; I didn't like it if he touched my belly. "Luca's controlling and protective with the women in his life. That's who he is. We can't interfere even if we don't like how he handles the kid. We're giving up that right by letting them adopt the baby."

I freed myself from his grip, glaring. "You make it sound as if what we're doing is wrong."

"I didn't say that. How can it be wrong to make sure the kid gets a welcoming, loving home that's ready for it? That's a reasonable decision."

"As if you're ever reasonable," I hissed. I wasn't even sure why I was attacking him, but for some reason I was angry.

Matteo pulled me against him. "Come on, babe, let's watch a movie and relax a bit. Let's not argue over this. We'll cross this bridge when we come to it."

"I hate it when you are the reasonable one. It's unnatural."

He flashed me a grin and like that, I felt better.

Matteo

Gianna's pained gasp made me jerk up. My hand lunged for the knife and I flipped on the lights, fighting the lingering disorientation.

"What's the matter?" I asked, turning to her.

Gianna regarded the blade as she blinked against the brightness. "No need for your knife," she said. Her hand rested against her belly. "The baby is kicking me again."

I froze and slowly put the knife down. "Again?"

She nodded. "It's been doing it for several weeks now. I wasn't sure if I should tell you." She fell silent. I couldn't look away from her hand cradling her belly. She pulled up her chemise and then I saw it, her belly bulging where a small foot must have kicked from the inside.

My throat became dry. So far her pregnancy had been a very abstract concept, one I could ignore most days, but this… I wasn't sure what I felt.

"You can touch it," she said hesitantly.

I pressed my palm to her skin and for a few moments nothing happened but then I felt the kick. I drew back, swallowing. "Fuck."

"Yeah, fuck," she whispered. "It won't let me pretend it's not there. It's kicking and pressing down on my bladder and just being temperamental like its father."

Like its father. I was becoming a father… but Luca would be the kid's father, he'd be the one it would call Dad. "It sounds like it has your temper." My voice sounded strange to my own ears. It wasn't as if I'd ever dreamed about being a father. Most of the tedious tasks linked to the job were rather deterrent.

Gianna lowered her chemise again, regarding me. "Aria and Luca won't know what hit them."

I nodded. "They can handle it."

"I know," she said. "Let's try to get some sleep, okay?"

I kissed her and extinguished the lights but I couldn't fall asleep. I couldn't forget how it had felt to have the baby kick against my hand. Eventually, I gave up and got up, careful not to wake Gianna.

I crept through the dark of the house and went outside onto the terrace where I sat down on a chair. As I stared off into the distance, the horizon slowly turned gray and the sun peeked out. The door slid open and closed behind me. Luca sank down in another chair in only briefs.

"What are you doing out here?"

He, Aria, and the kids had joined us for the weekend, and Lily, Romero, and Sara had arrived this morning as well.

"Enjoying the silence before the storm," I joked, but fuck, it sounded off.

Luca narrowed his eyes. "How's Gianna?"

"The baby's moving a lot so she can't sleep well," I said.

"It's only four weeks now, then you'll have your nights to yourself again."

I glowered at Luca. "I get it. You'll have the sleepless nights then because you have to raise our baby, no need to rub it in."

Luca leaned back in the chair. "I see the pregnancy hormones are rubbing off on you."

I didn't say anything because I was a fucking mess right now and would only talk more bullshit if I opened my mouth.

"Matteo," Luca said slowly. "It's not like you and Gianna have to give the baby to us. If you'd rather keep it, then…"

"Then what? Then you're happy? Is this your way of telling me that you don't want to raise my fucking kid?"

Luca pushed to his feet and gripped me by the shirt, jerking me to my feet. I grabbed his wrist tightly. "Now listen up, you asshole," he growled. "Stop twisting my words in my fucking mouth. I'll raise your kid like my own if that's what you and Gianna want."

"And what does my Capo want?" I provoked him further. I was on a roll.

His hold tightened. "Right now, I want you to pull your head out of your fucking ass and act like a man, not a fucking pussy. If you want to be a father for that kid, then tell Gianna that's what you want and maybe the both of you finally grow up and act like fucking adults and not like horny teenagers."

I jerked out of his hold and swung my fist at him, punching him square in the jaw. Luca stumbled a step back, looking fucking stunned for a second and then he lunged at me. We shoved and hit each other. The chairs tumbled to the ground and something broke.

"What the fuck?" Romero shouted as he stormed out, gun drawn, He tried to get between us but Luca shoved him back, sending him flying into the table. Then Luca was on me again.

Cold water hit us square in the faces. We jerked away from each other but the stream didn't stop. "Fuck!" Luca snarled. I blinked, trying to see through the fog the liquid had cast over my eyes.

The water was turned off and my eyes landed on Aria in a nightgown, looking furious while holding a water hose in our direction. I turned to Luca once more, who was breathing harshly and glaring at me. He seemed as reluctant to stop this fight as I was.

"One move and I'll turn the water on again," Aria warned.

"Holy shit," Amo exclaimed from inside the house as he stumbled toward us in pj's. Marcella stood behind him with wide but curious eyes. Lily gave us a reproachful look before she tugged her little girl away from the scene. Sara was definitely too young for this shitshow.

Romero straightened with a glare, shoving his gun into the pocket of his sweatpants. "What the fuck was that? You woke the kids." With a shake of his head he went inside to help Lily.

Aria put down the hose, then turned to her children. "Go upstairs."

Marcella did without protest but Amo came outside. "Wow, that was cool. I thought you'd pull knives on each other."

"Amo," Aria said firmly. "Upstairs now."

One look at her expression and he turned on his heel, grumbling. She stepped between Luca and me. "What's gotten into you?"

Luca rubbed his chin where a bruise was forming. My cheek was throbbing fiercely where he'd punched me. "Nothing," we said at the same time.

"Nothing?" Aria repeated. "Oh, okay, so you just beat each other for fun?"

"We had a difference of opinion."

Aria shook her head, then her eyes moved back to the living room where Gianna had appeared. She joined us on the terrace, taking in the mess we'd made. We'd broken two flowerpots and thrown over all of the chairs, not to mention that we were dripping wet thanks to Aria.

Gianna's red brows puckered. "What the hell went on here?"

"They had a discussion with their fists," Aria muttered.

"Aren't you too old to brawl like boys?"

"If you ask Luca, I'm like a fucking teenager."

Luca took a step in my direction but Aria stepped in his way and hit his chest in warning. "Stop it, good Lord."

He lowered his gaze to her. "Someone needs to beat the shit out of his head."

"And someone needs to kick the arrogance out of your arrogant Capo ass," I said.

Luca smiled coldly. "At least, I own up to my responsibilities and don't run from them."

"Luca!" Aria shouted.

Gianna's eyes widened, her face flashing with guilt.

Fuck him. I staggered toward him. "Shut the fuck up." I shoved him over Aria's shoulder.

She gave me an indignant look. "Stop it."

I stared into my brother's eyes. "Don't act all high and mighty, Luca. You've had your fair share of fuck-ups. I, at least, never cheated on my wife."

Fury flashed in Luca's eyes. Oh, I had him. He pushed Aria to the side, out of the way, and grabbed me by the throat, but I had expected the move and rammed my elbow into his throat. He coughed but didn't release me. I rammed my elbow upward once more hitting him under the chin and jerked out of his grip, spluttering.

And then we were at each other's throats again. Hands clasped at me, and then a high-pitched cry sounded. Luca and I both froze. Luca jerked back, his eyes scanning the floor, and he fell to his knees beside Aria who sat on her backside, cradling her wrist, grimacing.

"Love, I'm fucking sorry. Are you hurt?"

My own eyes sought Gianna who held her hand protectively over her belly, standing a few steps back. "You almost hit my belly," she said angrily.

"Fuck. I'm sorry," I rasped as I moved toward her and wrapped an arm around her waist. "Are you okay?"

She nodded, and her eyes moved to her sister. Luca was moving Aria's hand up and down gently, looking guilty as hell, and I felt like the biggest asshole in the world for letting it get that far, for *wanting* to let it get that far. I'd wanted to fight someone, had wanted to punch and hurt, and Luca could pack a punch like no one else. Fuck. He only wanted to help me and Gianna.

"I'm fine," Aria said firmly. "It's not broken, just bruised."

Luca kissed her wrist, then her palm before he leaned forward and kissed her lips. Fuck, my brother was one of the craziest, cruelest, most brutal assholes I had the fortune of knowing, and yet he made his marriage work, and was a fucking great father.

And what about me? I couldn't even take care of one kid.

Gianna nudged me lightly. "Hey, what's wrong? Is it because you felt the baby kick?"

"The baby kicked?" Aria asked excitedly from the ground. She let Luca pull her to her feet and came over.

"It is still," Gianna said. "It's going crazy today. You can feel it."

I took a step back as Aria rested her palm against Gianna's belly, then smiled brightly. "My God, it seems to be step dancing in there." She peered over her shoulder at Luca. "You have to feel that."

I took another step back. Luca watched me closely.

"Go ahead, you should really feel it," I said quietly. "I need to cool my fucking cheek. Don't want a bruise to ruin my good looks."

I turned and headed inside but not in the direction of the bathroom, instead I headed for the study where I grabbed a glass of Brandy. I felt like shit and not because of the pain in my face and ribs. I'd had worse injuries. No, my insides were burning up with emotions I didn't understand. I downed my Brandy, hissing as the alcohol burned a trail down my throat, then filled my glass again.

"One for me as well," Luca said as he stepped inside and closed the door. I filled another glass without a word and handed it to him, before downing my second. I hadn't been shitfaced since I'd found out about Gianna's pregnancy, wanting to be ready in case she needed me, but today felt like the perfect day to drink myself into oblivion.

"Did you feel the kid move?" I asked neutrally.

"No," Luca said.

"Why not? You should have. The kid is a wild one. It kicked my palm really strong." I fell silent, remembering this moment, and knowing it was better to forget it quickly.

Luca stepped up to me and downed his own drink. "I'll say this once and it better get through your thick vain skull. You'll be a great father to that kid. You'll love it and protect it, and you'll cherish every fucking second you spend with it."

I glanced up. "I'm not going to be its father."

"Yes, you are," Luca said. "Because I won't be, and Aria won't be its mother. You and Gianna are going to raise this kid, understood?"

I frowned. "Listen, you might be Capo, but that's not something you can demand. We got a deal."

Luca smiled darkly. "You want to raise this kid, and you will, and now you take that pretty face out of my view and talk to your bitchy redhead, and straighten things out while I figure out a way to break the news to Aria, and then I will knock her up so we get our own kid."

I stared at my brother. "You've lost your fucking mind." But his words had lifted the heavy weight that had rested on my shoulders since we'd agreed to have Aria and Luca take the baby. Yet, Gianna didn't want to be a mother, and I wouldn't force her. I wanted Gianna to be happy more than anything else. I wouldn't limit her freedoms even more than they already were, and being a mom would restrain her more than me.

A knock sounded and Gianna poked her head in. "I need to talk to you."

Luca gave me a look before he set the glass down on the desk and moved toward the door. He stopped briefly beside Gianna and muttered something but I didn't catch what it was. He closed the door, leaving us alone. Gianna frowned at the door then slowly turned to me. For a moment we only looked at each other and didn't move. Fuck, how was I supposed to tell her that I wanted this kid, that I wanted to raise it with her at my side?

CHAPTER EIGHT

Gianna

I watched Matteo stalk away.

"Luca?" Aria asked hesitantly. "Don't you want to feel the baby?"

Luca tore his eyes away from the spot where Matteo had been not too long ago and walked up to her, touching her cheek. "Not now, Love. Let me have a word with Matteo to straighten things out."

"No fighting," she warned.

He kissed her mouth and left.

Lily joined us on the terrace, wrapped in a thick bathrobe which couldn't cover up her huge belly anymore. Hers was even bigger than mine and I already felt like a wrecking ball. "What a way to wake up."

"Yeah, it's a miracle that they don't fight more often considering all the alpha male dominance they have going on," I muttered.

Aria laughed but it was strained.

Lily touched my shoulder but I took her hand and rested it against my stomach. She smiled brightly. "Oh! That's wonderful. You're baking a little hothead." She caught herself and glanced between Aria and me.

I gave her a small smile.

"You know that Matteo wants to raise this baby as his own, right?" Aria said suddenly.

Lily gave her a look but I could tell that they had talked about it before. The thought that they had discussed Matteo and me before didn't sit well with me.

I stared down at my belly that I was still cradling. Ignoring a painful truth was something I was surprisingly good at.

"I know," I admitted. "I can see it when he looks at my belly." When he'd felt Peanut kick for the very first time, the wistful look in his eyes had almost killed me.

"Oh," Aria said. She searched my face. "But you never talked about it?"

I shook my head. I'd always considered myself brave but this time I was a despicable coward. Too scared of what Matteo would say.

She frowned. I could see a hint of disapproval on Aria's face but she didn't say anything. Sometimes I wished she'd rage and scream at me. Maybe I needed it.

"Why?" Lily asked gently.

"I don't know…" It wasn't the truth but I was a coward. I was terrified that Matteo's longing would mirror a feeling deep inside of me I didn't want to allow.

"Is it because you don't want the baby?" Lily prodded.

Aria was oddly quiet and she wasn't looking at me. She and Luca had always wanted a third kid and they had stopped trying because they were supposed to adopt my kid. Hell, she'd been happier about my pregnancy than me in these last few months. If I wanted to keep the child now, how would she feel? They'd prepared a nursery for my child. She'd hidden from the public for months to keep up our charade. All for me and Matteo and Peanut. Could I take that from her?

This was a mess, one I wasn't sure I could get out of.

Aria met my gaze. "You want the child as well, Gianna."

I stared at her. "No… I mean… I don't know."

She touched my chest over my heart. "You have four weeks, maybe less, decide if you really still want to be nothing but an aunt for this child. Listen to your heart, Gianna, and then make your decision, be sure of it. Please, if you know deep down that you want this child, then say it before it's born. Don't let me and Luca act like its parents, only to take that from us. Because, of course, we would always give you your baby back but it would rip our hearts out." She stepped back, turned and left.

As I watched her, I started crying. Lily wrapped her arms around me sideways because our bellies didn't allow anything else, kissing my cheek. "You already made up your mind, didn't you?"

I closed my eyes and nodded, my hand touching my belly. "I'm always making such a mess of things. That's the only thing I'm good at."

"Shhh. Aria and Luca will understand. They will be happy for you and Matteo."

"But they want another kid. They stopped trying because of me. And now they don't get my baby. They wasted almost a year because of me."

"They will understand, Gianna. Aria is a mother. She knows what it does to a woman to feel your baby move inside you. This is your baby. It always was." I buried my face in Lily's neck and she stroked my hair. "And Aria will be pregnant in no time, I'm sure. The last two she got pregnant without really trying and when you got pregnant, she'd only stopped taking the pill two months before. Next year she'll have her own baby."

She pulled back with a soft smile. "Now go talk to Matteo."

I nodded. "Thank you, Lily."

My pulse sped up as I walked through the house. It took me a while to find Matteo and only because I heard his voice in passing. I knocked at the office door then stepped in. Luca and Matteo were talking. "I need to talk to you."

Luca set down his glass and moved toward me. I thought he'd leave but he stopped close to me, his eyes hard. "Don't mess this up."

I didn't get a chance for a comeback because he left. I finally faced Matteo and my heart constricted at the look in his eyes. I walked toward him and grabbed his hand, pressing it to my belly. "I want this baby," he said before I could say anything.

I smiled. "I know."

Matteo frowned. "Okay." He hesitated. "I can take most of the responsibility but…"

"Don't be stupid," I muttered. "We will raise this baby together. I want it too…"

Open shock reflected on his face. "You do?"

I pursed my lips. "Am I that much of a heartless bitch that it seems impossible that I would want our baby?"

Matteo smiled teasingly and the knot in my stomach loosened. "I wouldn't put it quite like that."

I punched his abs. He groaned then grinned and moved his palm over my belly. His cheek was starting to swell, making his smile look grotesque. "It's kicking again."

"Peanut."

Matteo's brows snapped together.

"That's what I've been calling it for a few weeks now because I didn't want to think of the baby as "it" anymore."

"Peanut," Matteo said with a small smile. "So we're doing this? Becoming parents?"

I leaned against him, for once not minding that my belly got in the way. "It seems so."

"Good."

"Good," I whispered, then I sighed. "I'm scared."

Matteo cupped my face. "I'm at your side. I'll protect you and the baby."

"I know but what if I'm a horrible mother? I never wanted kids, and at first, I didn't even want this baby. Hell, I still don't want most of the things expected of a mother. I don't want to lose myself completely, or stop caring about how I look. What if I can't be a good mother? What if I don't love it enough? Or what if it knows somehow that I didn't want it at first?"

"We will both love the baby. And we will be good parents. Maybe we won't ever win a parents of the year award but we'll do our best and that's all that matters."

"We cuss too much and we're both too temperamental."

"We are. And the kid will know the best cuss words in kindergarten, so who gives a fuck?"

"The teachers might," I said with a laugh.

"Then they can come to me and talk to me about their concerns," Matteo said with his shark-grin.

"Intimidating teachers… we definitely won't be voted parents of the year."

"I knew being in the mob would be useful one day."

I rolled my eyes. "In addition to the assload of money you make, and the sick thrill you get when people shit their pants because of who you are."

"In addition to that, yes," Matteo said with a wink. "Not to mention all the fun torture I get to take part in."

I sighed deeply. "You are a crazy fucker." I kissed him softly. "But you are my crazy fucker and I love you."

"And I love you, my bitchy redhead."

I narrowed my eyes slightly but then I decided that he had every right to call me bitch. I was a bitch. He was a crazy fucker. So what?

Matteo

A heavy weight had lifted off my chest since we decided to keep the baby. Of course, our last minute change of mind meant a lot of organizing. We hadn't bought anything for the kid yet, and hadn't read up on anything about raising a newborn.

Gianna knew enough about the birth process, due to necessity, but that was it. The only thing I knew was that these little creatures produced more poo, pee, and snot than a body of that size should.

"You can have all of the things we bought. We won't need them anytime soon," Aria said when she led me into the nursery in their mansion in New York. Everything was ready for a child. The walls were decorated with images of giraffes and lions, and a plush lion head carpet spread out under the crib.

Gianna had run off to the bathroom to pee again so it was only me and Aria. Her bladder was pretty much only a funnel. What entered her mouth wanted out not long after.

Aria motioned at the baby crib. "You'll need all these things."

I moved to her side. "Are you sure? You and Luca want a third poo machine."

Aria set the crib mobile, also featuring jungle animals, in motion. "We do, but we can buy new stuff then, or just take whatever you won't need by then." The wistfulness in her voice sent an unpleasant twinge through my chest.

"Aria," I said quietly, causing her to look up at me. "I never said it to you, but I'll forever be grateful for what you and Luca would have done for us, what you *did* for us. We had difficult times but you are the best sister-in-law I can imagine, and the best wife my brother could ever dream of."

Aria touched my forearm with a small smile. "We're family. We'll stick together till the bitter end. Luca and I will always be there for you. If you need help with the little one, you can call us any time."

I nodded, because I had no doubt about it. "Luca's been pissy lately, and I just want to make sure you know Gianna and I are sorry for taking so long to make up our minds."

Aria shook her head. "Don't be. I'm glad you chose to keep your baby. It won't always be easy and there might be moments of regret, but ultimately you'll see it's the right decision."

Gianna chose that moment to waddle into the room. She had only three weeks until her due date and we really needed to hurry up getting stuff done. The last few days we'd spent coming to terms with our decision. "I hope Peanut is as annoyed by our current co-living situation as I am and decides to vacate her room a few days early."

"You still have plenty to buy and get done before you can welcome her into your life. Have you made the apartment child safe?"

Gianna sighed. "No. We haven't even decided which guest room to turn into her nursery."

"The one closer to your bedroom, trust me."

"All right," Gianna said with a shrug, then scanned the furniture. "Are you really sure—"

"Yes, Matteo and I discussed the matter and you'll take everything with you. So maybe you should start organizing transport and helping hands."

"Who knew she could be such a dictator," I said with a grin.

Aria rolled her eyes in a very Gianna-like fashion.

"She's married to your brother and has him wrapped around her finger…"

"True."

Aria shook her head. "Do I need to organize everything?"

"No," I said and picked up my cell phone, calling a few soldiers who were strong enough to help us carry.

Since our decision to keep the baby, Gianna and I hadn't bothered hiding anymore and had walked out in the open in New York. Of course, word about her pregnancy had spread like wildfire and by now every man in the Famiglia knew, their wives and children as well, of course. It was the gossip of the year.

Later that day, every piece of baby furniture had found its way into the guest bedroom on the second floor of our penthouse. The room had been Gianna's workout room but we'd carried all the equipment downstairs into the other guestroom. My soldiers had refrained from asking questions, only congratulated Gianna and me on our first child, as if there were more to come. Everyone had waited with bated breath for us to create offspring. In our circles, a married couple had to have kids as a sort of rite of passage.

"Put the crib there," Gianna instructed. I did as she asked with Romero's help. I'd sent the other men home because it could take hours until Gianna had made up her mind about where to put the furniture.

"Are you sure Liliana can spare you this long?" I asked.

Romero smiled, wiping sweat off his face. "Don't worry. She urged me to help you. She's so excited that she and Gianna will have babies at the same time."

Gianna sent me a panicked look. I knew her worst nightmare was sinking into the mom-life swamp and never getting out.

Eventually, Gianna was happy with the room and Romero left.

Gianna cradled her belly, shaking her head. "I still can't believe we'll really welcome one of these monsters into our home."

"It'll be our monster."

Gianna laughed. "That only means it'll be even more monstrous judging by our character traits."

I wrapped an arm around her. "And you'll have Liliana and Aria for help."

"I'm worried Lily expects me to only do mom stuff. I still want to work out, and I want to teach again eventually. I don't want to be surrounded only by moms who expect me to do only mom things, and worst, talk about poo."

"I trust in your sunny personality to drive most of them away quickly."

Gianna narrowed her eyes at me. "Oh shut up."

"That's what I mean, babe." I rubbed her waist and kissed her neck. "How about a little one-on-one gymnastics?"

Gianna shrugged. "All right, but you'll have to do all the work. I'm feeling like a beached whale today."

I chuckled. "You know just what to say to make me horny."

Gianna grabbed me through my pants and rubbed. My cock reacted as it always did.

She smiled smugly. "Doesn't take much to make you horny."

I lifted her into my arms, causing her to let out a startled shriek. I would never say it aloud but carrying Gianna had become more difficult these last few weeks, but if it meant I'd get to bury myself in her pussy, I'd even take a broken back.

That night, Gianna twisted and turned until I was sure she was troubled by labor pains already. "Gianna, are you okay?"

She sighed. "I can't sleep."

She rolled around to me and I moved closer to her in the dark. "What is it? Do you regret our decision?" It was a thought that troubled me a lot.

"No," she said firmly. "I want to raise Peanut with our values. No offense to your brother but he can be an old-fashioned, protective brute. I want to be the one to determine its future. I want to give it the best life it can have in our world."

"*We* want to give it the best life."

"We, of course," Gianna whispered. "We never discussed what kind of values we'd want to teach a kid because we never planned on becoming parents but soon the life of a little human is in our hands… and I'm just wondering if we're even on the same page."

"And what page is that?" I asked.

Gianna hesitated. I could tell how much this meant to her just by how long it took her to find the right words. "If it's a girl I want her to be free to choose what she wants to do with her life. I want her to go to college, to get a job she loves. I want her to find the love of her life and not be forced into an arranged marriage. I want her to have sex before her wedding night, and the choice not to marry at all…"

I put a finger against her mouth, silencing her. "I get what you mean. And I agree with you, even if I'd prefer if she'd never date any guys at all."

I could practically hear Gianna roll her eyes at me. I kissed her. "I'll do everything in my power to give our child every possible freedom if it's a girl. I swear it. You'll get your wish."

"But?" Gianna asked quietly.

I cupped her neck. "If it's a boy, he needs to follow in my footsteps. He must become a Made Man and part of the Famiglia, not just because our men wouldn't understand it if I spared my own son and not theirs, but also because I want him to be part of the business."

Gianna swallowed. "So a girl gets freedom and a boy will be bound to the Famiglia."

"Yes," I said.

"Okay."

"You sure you won't fight me every step of the way the moment you find out it's a boy?"

Gianna sighed. "I'll hate it, hate it so much, but I'll figure out a way to accept it, as long as you accept it if our girl has a normal teenage life with boys and parties."

"Deal."

I'd never cared much about gender, but right this moment I hoped Peanut was a girl because for me to accept a girl having her freedom would be far easier than Gianna accepting a boy becoming a murderous mobster.

CHAPTER NINE

Gianna

"Still pregnant?" Marcella asked the moment we stepped into their mansion. The little princess in her pretty dress and graceful movements made me want to strangle something.

I glowered at her. "Be careful. Maybe it's contagious," I muttered.

Marcella gave me her "yeah… sure" expression, but she sent Aria a questioning look when she thought I wasn't paying attention. Aria and Luca hadn't had the talk with her yet, even if I thought it was time to do so at almost ten.

"It looks heavy," Amo added, scanning my belly as if it were a fascinating science experiment.

"Have they always been this annoying or is this the newest evolutionary step?" I asked Aria.

"I doubt a combination of you and Matteo will be any less mouthy, so you better prepare yourself," Luca replied instead. He'd been more restrained around me but since my patience was close to zero these last few days, we were still at each other's throats every other day.

Aria made a shush noise and hugged me awkwardly around my belly. "How are you feeling?"

"Fat, immobile, and about to burst."

"It's not long now."

"That's what you said a week before the due date. Now we're two days past the official eviction date and it's still in there."

"The last few days seem to drag on forever, I know," Aria said with a compassionate smile. "And eventually it'll be over. Look at Lily, she's already nine days over."

I grimaced. "I just hope that's not my fate as well. I don't know how she can be so calm about it, especially with the whole home birthing thing. I'd freak-out."

"It helps that it's her second child. She knows what to expect."

"I thought every pregnancy and birth was unique."

Aria laughed. "Well, yeah, but still you feel slightly more prepared going into labor the second time around."

I doubted I'd ever feel prepared for this whole baby producing scenario, and I would definitely never find out if a second pregnancy or birth would be easier, even if Aria insisted that I might change my mind about the whole thing once the baby was there.

"How about we move the party into the dining room so pregnant lady can get something to eat. She almost got me to pull into an Arby's drive-in on the way here because she was about to eat my arm," Matteo said with a grin.

I tried to punch his shoulder but my movements were slow and he was as agile as ever. "You're dead," I mouthed. But he only sent me a kiss.

"I thought fast food is bad for your body?" Marcella asked.

I waddled into the dining room, trying to ignore the sensation of my belly dragging me to the floor. "It is. Matteo is exaggerating. I'd eat him before I'd consume any fast food with doubtful ingredients."

"Considering what Matteo's consumed over the years, I doubt his ingredients are much better," Luca said.

I sank down on the chair that Matteo had pulled out for me then tried to help him as he heaved me closer to the table. Eventually my belly touched the edge. I sighed.

"Marianna has prepared your favorite lamb roast and grilled asparagus and cauliflower mash," Aria said, obviously hoping to lift my mood.

I smiled and sank back against the backrest. "That sounds fabulous."

My belly became hard, pain radiating all the way to my back. I'd been having these Braxton-Hicks-contractions for many weeks now but they'd become more painful and frequent in recent days, giving me false hope that Peanut would actually evict the premises before the due date.

Marianna entered the dining room in that moment, carrying a massive roast lamb leg surrounded by fingerling potatoes and brussels sprouts. Usually the sight had my belly doing excited summersaults but apart from the tension in my lower back and belly, I hardly felt hunger.

Still, I loaded my plate and pushed the occasional morsel of food into my mouth. Aria eyed me from across the table.

"Are you okay?" she asked quietly.

Matteo slanted me a worried look, ceasing his conversation with Luca.

"I'm fine. I just can't eat as fast anymore. The baby is taking up too much room in my belly."

"Tell that to the two veggie-burgers plus sweet potato fries you wolfed down for dinner yesterday," Matteo joked.

I kicked his calf under the table, causing his grin to widen. Unfortunately, the movement hurt me more than him as it sent a twinge through my back.

Marcella tilted her head curiously. "I don't know why you don't want to know if it's a boy or girl. I'd die from curiosity. And you can't even buy anything pink!"

"Not every girl likes pink," I said.

Marcella pursed her lips. "You're the only girl I know that prefers black."

"Your aunt is a special snowflake," Matteo said with a wink.

Marcella laughed.

"I hope it's a boy," Amo said. "Girls are trouble."

"I wish I'd learned that lesson at your age," Matteo sighed.

This time I only sent him a glare instead of a kick.

Of course, it didn't have any effect. Matteo even high-fived Amo across the table much to Aria's disapproval.

I pressed my palm against my belly, wondering when the tension would leave it.

The pressure got even worse before I could decide if I was going into labor, something warm trickled out of me. I froze, clutching the fork in my hand. This definitely wasn't pee. My bladder was empty.

"Why are you making a face like you're pooping, Aunt Gianna?" Amo asked.

I didn't even have it in me to give the little monster hell for calling me "aunt" again.

"Gianna?" Aria said softly.

"Gianna, your expression worries me," Matteo said. He touched my thigh, my wet pants, and slowly pulled his hand back, his eyes widening. "Fuck."

"Matteo said 'fuck' at the table," Amo said, looking at Aria.

"What's wrong with you?" Marcella asked curiously.

Why couldn't they all stop talking?

"I think my water just broke," I got out.

"Ewww," Marcella said, that gorgeous face scrunching up.

Amo put down his fork. "You peed your pants? Can I see?"

I clutched Matteo's hand. I couldn't believe we were going to get one of these small monsters ourselves.

Luca rose, his expression stern. "Marcella, Amo, up to your room."

"But Dad," Marcella whined.

Luca shook his head. "Now."

Finally, the two went upstairs but not without a considerable amount of protesting. For all I cared they could watch. I doubted there was a better way of contraception than having someone watch a kid being squeezed out of a vagina.

My belly cramped and I gasped at the sharp pain that seemed to last forever. I clutched Matteo's hand so tightly, his fingers turned white but he didn't make a sound. Only regarded me with blatant worry.

I was torn between wanting to clutch him and push him away, because somehow this was his fault.

Aria appeared beside me, touching my arm. "Come on. Let's get you into our car." She turned to Luca. "Can you get it?"

Luca nodded and disappeared.

"You have to stand up, Gianna."

I forced myself into an upright position, waiting for the next wave of pain but the contractions still seemed a few minutes apart.

Matteo hovered beside Aria and me.

"You should help her walk." He wrapped an arm around my back and Aria walked on my other side as we made our way toward the front door. The distance seemed so much longer than ever before.

Another wave crashed through me, making me jerk to a stop and clutch my belly. "I changed my mind. This baby can stay inside forever," I grunted.

Aria tugged at my hand. "Come on. Everything will be fine."

Gritting my teeth, I stumbled farther along. I'd read so much about labor these last few weeks but nothing could prepare me for this. I looked up at Matteo in annoyance but that emotion vanished when I saw the helplessness and even fear in his eyes. I forced a smile that probably looked more like a scary grimace. I wasn't the only one who was terrified of what lay ahead.

Matteo

Gianna clung to the doorway. It had taken us more than ten minutes to get there. I didn't know much about labor but I thought Gianna's contractions were coming very frequently.

Her eyes were wide and desperate. "I don't think I'm ready."

Did she think I felt ready? I'd never been so fucking scared in my life. Of a tiny baby, of all things. But fuck, I was. Nothing in my life had prepared me for the task ahead, least of all my own parents. Not that Gianna's parents would have won parents of the year awards.

"I hate to break it to you but your baby is going to come out if you're ready or not," Luca muttered as he strode up the driveway, probably tired of waiting in the car.

Aria sent him a look. "Luca!" Then she turned to Gianna. "It's going to be all right. You're not alone. Luca and I will help you and Matteo. Together, we'll be okay."

I stroked Gianna's back and gently pried her fingers off the doorway before nudging her outside. Soft rain was falling and soaking us all.

I reached for my keys, thinking we'd take two cars as usual, but Luca shook his head. "I think I better drive. You're a madman driver on your best days, and today isn't one of those days."

I nodded only, not even the brain capacity to give a comeback.

Gianna kept clutching Aria's hand and mine in the other.

"Gianna, baby, we don't all fit on the back seat," I said gently. She didn't release either of us. In the end, we awkwardly crammed in the back of Luca's car. Gianna was breathing fast, her brows drawn together.

"Luca, I'm getting your seats dirty," she gasped out when we pulled out of the premises.

"It doesn't matter, Gianna," Luca said calmly. I wished for his calm. Even when Aria had been in labor, he'd been remarkably calm compared to how I felt now. Gianna tensed again, panting.

"Fuck," she whispered, shaking her head. She turned to her sister. "Aria. I—"

She cried out.

Aria's eyes grew wide. "Pull over!"

"What?" Luca said.

"Pull over, the baby's coming," Aria screamed.

Luca jerked the car over but all I could do was stare in horror at Gianna who was gasping and crying.

"Call an ambulance," Aria ordered. Then to me. "Get out of the car. We need room."

Within a couple of minutes, Gianna was stretched out on the back seat and I was kneeling behind her so she rested against my legs, Aria was between Gianna's legs. "Don't push too hard Gianna, or you'll tear," Aria instructed. How could she sound so fucking calm?

Luca stood close behind her, watching our surroundings and trying not to look at Gianna. Cars were driving past us, honking and letting out curses.

Gianna cried out again and her breathing came in short bursts.

"Gianna." A slight edge entered Aria's voice. "Push."

"Why?" I asked immediately.

"The umbilical cord is around the baby's throat," she said. "But it's okay. We'll get it out."

I clutched at Gianna and she clawed at my arms. Fuck, what if I lost her and the baby? Fuck. I began shaking. My vision seemed hazy as if I was caught up in a nightmare. I'd seen so many horrors but nothing compared to this, to the idea of losing everything that mattered.

Gianna tensed as she pushed once more.

"The head's out," Aria said in a strained voice. "I'll try to get its shoulders out."

"Just get it out, Aria. Please, don't let our baby die," Gianna cried.

"I won't," Aria said. And then Gianna jerked and Aria held the baby but it wasn't moving.

"We need to cut the umbilical cord," Luca said firmly, pulling his knife.

Aria tried to push her fingers under the cord, which was wrapped twice around our baby's throat. "The blood in there might be its only source of oxygen," she said, still tugging. "God, why isn't it loosening!"

"Aria, the cord's choking the baby," Luca said, stepping up to her.

Aria looked desperate. "Be careful, please."

Gianna trembled against me. I held her even tighter. Tension exploded through my body when Luca began cutting the cord. Blood spurted out of it and Aria began rubbing the baby's back and trying to clean its nose and mouth. I wasn't sure how long it took but eventually a cry rang out.

Aria met my gaze but it took a moment for her words to penetrate my mind. "Matteo, cut open Gianna's shirt. The baby needs to rest on her skin, it needs the warmth."

My hands shook too fucking much. "I'll cut her."

Luca pulled Aria back and leaned into the car. He carefully sliced open Gianna's shirt. "I never thought you'd see me naked," Gianna muttered tonelessly. She looked pale and weak. I'd sworn to always protect her from harm but in this case, I was completely helpless and I hated it more than anything.

Luca smiled but it was tense. "It's a nightmare come true."

Gianna laughed hoarsely then winced sharply. I kissed her temple and rested my cheek atop her hair.

I gave my brother a grateful look. "Who'd ever thought you'd have to cut something for me one day?"

He smirked. "You're losing your touch."

"Luca, can you get out of the way?" Aria said impatiently and Luca finally stepped back. Aria leaned over and carefully laid a small, blood-smeared baby on Gianna's breasts. "Congrats on your beautiful daughter," Aria said quietly, tears in her eyes.

I stared down at our Peanut. Our daughter. Gianna hesitantly touched her palm to her small back then peered up at me. There was wonder and fear in her eyes, and utter exhaustion reflected on her face. I kissed her forehead. "We can do this," I assured her.

She gave a small nod then let her head fall back against my chest. I put my hand over hers atop our daughter's back.

CHAPTER TEN

Gianna

STARING DOWN AT THIS WRINKLY, SMEARED, BLUISH-RED human being, I couldn't wrap my mind around the fact that this was really my daughter—that I was a mother now. No longer just Gianna, mob wife and yoga instructor. My brain seemed cloaked by thick fog and the pain in my lower body barely registered anymore.

"Babe, how do you feel?" Matteo asked, but even his voice seemed to come from a distance.

I wasn't sure what answer to give him, wasn't sure what exactly I was feeling. "Exhausted," I said.

The baby seemed to push toward my breasts, smacking its lips. The sound of the ambulance briefly registered and the lights flashed in my peripheral vision but I couldn't look away from the baby— my baby. Some people described the moment of seeing their child for the very first time as love at first sight. That's what Aria had called it. I didn't feel anything but a deep sense of responsibility and disbelief. Soon I was hoisted into the ambulance with the baby still on my chest. Matteo joined me, and Luca would follow us in his car. Everything seemed to happen in a blur, so surreal I often wondered if I were still asleep and would wake any moment, and if that was the case, was it a nightmare or dream?

Matteo stayed close to my side and didn't relax until we were finally alone in a hospital room and the doctors had checked on me and the baby, and stitched me back together where I'd torn.

The baby was latched on to my breast but I didn't have much milk yet.

"She looks like you," Matteo said.

I frowned. "Really?" Her hair wasn't as red as mine, it was a strange reddish-brown and her eyes were a kind of blue, but it was still too early to say what she'd end up looking like.

I touched her small back. So breakable and now my responsibility.

"I didn't think I'd ever see you like this," Matteo murmured, his face reflecting the same disbelief I felt, but in his eyes, I didn't find the same panic taking hold of my body.

Matteo took my hand as if he could sense my inner turmoil. "I'm at your side every step of the way. We can do this."

I nodded then winced at the pain in my breast. "A few things I need to do by myself. What if I fail?"

"If you can't breastfeed the baby, she'll get the bottle. She won't remember once she's older, and let's be honest our parents messed up far more, and we still survived."

A small smile tugged at my mouth. "I love you."

Matteo's eyes soften. I didn't say it first very often. I just wasn't a very lovey-dovey kind of person. Matteo leaned forward and kissed my mouth then he glanced down at the squirming baby on my chest. "Do you have a name in mind?"

I shook my head. I'd thought a name would magically manifest itself the moment I saw my child. As if by merely looking at it, I'd peg it a Lorana or Melania or whatever other name the kid would look like. Yet, staring down at my squishy baby now, I drew a blank. I could barely wrap my mind around the fact that I'd squeezed her out of me not too long ago, much less decide on something as important as a name she'd have to carry all her life.

"Do you?" I asked hopefully but a knock sounded before Matteo could reply. Our baby had fallen asleep at my breast. I quickly tugged her away and covered myself before the door opened. Aria poked her head in, her brows puckered in worry. The moment she spotted me, she smiled brightly. "Can we come in?"

"Of course," I said, relieved to have her here. She was a mother. Maybe she'd be able to help me understand this small creature sleeping soundly on my body. She came in, followed by Luca who gave me one of his warmer smiles, a rare sight. He even held flowers in his hand, probably an order from Aria, but I didn't care.

Aria headed over to me. Matteo got up and grinned at Luca who shook his head with an exasperated smile before he came toward me and put the flowers down on the bedside table. "Congrats, Gianna. Your daughter likes a spectacular show, just like her mother."

It wasn't said in a condescending way so I took it as a compliment. "Thanks, Luca."

He nodded and walked toward Matteo who hovered next to the window, watching me and our daughter with that same disbelief he'd displayed when she'd first popped out.

"How do you feel?" Aria whispered.

"I don't know," I admitted.

She nodded. "It'll take time for you to grow together."

"I thought you experienced love at first sight."

She hesitated. "I did, but that doesn't mean we didn't have to find it together. You have to get to know your daughter. That takes time. Don't worry."

"I hope you're right. Have you heard anything from Lily?"

Aria grinned. "In labor. Maybe your kids will share a birthday."

"This is all so surreal. I'm waiting to wake up any moment."

Aria kissed my cheek. "I'm proud of you."

I swallowed, hating how emotional I'd become and yet unable to change it.

Matteo

"Congrats on your daughter," Luca said as he joined me.

I nodded, stunned. "I still can't believe it." I tore my eyes away from our girl whom Gianna cradled in her arm and looked to my brother. "What if Gianna and I are bad parents? You know us, we're bound to mess up."

"Oh yes," Luca said. I gave him a look and he squeezed my shoulder. "Messing up is part of parenthood. You mess up, you try to do better. You fail, you try again. Sometimes your kids hate you, sometimes they love you. If they don't occasionally hate you, you're doing something wrong."

"That sounds doable."

Luca chuckled.

"I'm not sure I like that you've seen my wife's pussy," I said to distract myself from my worry.

Luca's lips curled. "Trust me that sight won't give me any kind of ideas."

I chuckled. Then gestured at his bloody clothes. "I've lost count of the times I've seen you like this."

He glanced down at his ruined shirt. "Usually the prelude is more entertaining."

I nodded. "Yeah, I don't need another birth in my life."

Luca's eyes moved to Aria who had her arms wrapped around Gianna and was assuring her like Luca was assuring me. "You still working on kid number three?"

"Every day," Luca said with a smirk.

"I suppose I can kiss sex goodbye for the next few weeks."

Luca clapped my shoulder with a pitying look. "Make that the next couple of months."

My shock made him laugh. "You're laughing now," I said. "Wait till I become intolerable because my balls are blue."

Luca sighed. "Trust me, you'll be too tired to be intolerable."

"We'll see."

"Don't take it as a challenge."

"I love a good challenge."

Gianna looked up with a hesitant smile and Aria hopped off the bed then walked over to us. "Go to your wife and daughter," she said as she pressed up to Luca who gave her that adoring look few people ever got to witness.

I didn't need to be told twice. I would have stayed glued to Gianna's side if I hadn't gotten the impression that she needed guidance from Aria first. Aria knew how to be a mother after all.

I stepped up to the bed. Gianna nodded toward the free spot beside her and I climbed into bed with her then wrapped an arm around her shoulder. Our daughter was still sleeping on her chest. Maybe sleep deprivation wouldn't be our problem. She looked like an adorable, uncomplicated child. I reached out and gently took her tiny hand. So small, so vulnerable. "So her name?" Gianna asked.

I looked at the soft reddish-brown hair of our girl, at her rosy cheeks, trying to remember the names Gianna and I had discussed. "Isabella."

The moment the name left my lips, I knew it was the right choice.

Gianna considered that, then smiled. "I like that. A lot."

"So Isabella?"

"Isabella," she said, then yawned and winced.

Aria stepped up to the bed. "Why don't you put your daughter—"

"Isabella," Gianna and I said at the same time.

"Isabella," Aria said softly. "Why don't you put Isabella on your chest, Matteo. That'll give Gianna the chance to rest and you can bond with your daughter. Open your shirt."

My fucking fingers still hadn't stopped shaking. Aria pushed my hands away and unbuttoned my shirt for me. "Luca, your wife is undressing me."

Luca gave me a condescending look. He knew Aria was his till the bitter end.

"Oh Matteo, when do you ever shut up?" Gianna groaned, but her eyes were soft when she looked at me. I knew it probably wouldn't last forever but seeing Gianna's softer, more emotional side had felt good, even if I still loved her tough side like crazy.

I flashed her a grin but it fell when Aria reached over me to pick up Isabella and put her down on my chest. I held my breath when I felt the small body against my skin. She was so tiny. I covered her back with my palm and linked my other hand with Gianna's who leaned her head against my shoulder.

Aria gave us another reassuring smile before she and Luca walked out, leaving us alone.

"I'm still scared," Gianna admitted quietly.

"Me too."

"You are?"

"Yeah. It's a new experience."

She huffed, then winced. "We'll get through this, right?"

"Of course. We have each other. And we have our family."

CHAPTER ELEVEN

Gianna

When I'd thought I was scared in the hospital, it was nothing in comparison to the terror I felt when we headed home with Isabella two days after I'd given birth. Matteo drove while I sat with our daughter in the back. She wasn't too fond of the motion and wailed as if someone was poking her with a hot knife. I tried to distract and soothe her but nothing worked and her face was turning increasingly red.

"Do you want me to pull over?" Matteo asked.

"No," I said quickly. "Just get us home as quickly as possible."

I waved a rattle in front of Isa's face but she ignored it, her tiny face scrunched up. My stomach tied itself in knots and when we finally pulled into our underground garage, I was close to a nervous breakdown.

I got out of the car, taking a few deep breaths. Matteo joined me, touching my back with a concerned look.

"I'm fine," I said quickly and walked around the car to get Isa out of her seat.

The moment I held her in my arms, she settled down, and the red color of her cheeks slowly vanished in favor of her usual rosy complexion. Matteo grabbed our bags from the trunk but he kept an eye on us.

We headed for the elevator and when the doors closed, and I stared at our reflections in the wall mirrors, it really sunk in. Matteo and I leaned against the wall as I cradled Isa in my arm. My hair was in a messy bun and I wasn't wearing any makeup. In my yoga pants and sweater, I looked as if I were on my way to the gym but that wasn't going to happen any time soon. Now, Isa would be constantly attached to me, a little shadow I carried more responsibility for than I ever wanted.

Matteo met my gaze in the mirror. "I like seeing you like this."

"A mess?"

"With our daughter."

"We'll see how long that'll last," I muttered, my hormones wreaking havoc inside of me once more.

Matteo wrapped his arm around my shoulders. "I meant it when I said we're in this together. Eventually that has to sink into your stubborn head as well."

I shrugged, but leaned my head against Matteo's shoulder. He had been my rock so far and I had absolutely no reason to complain.

The elevator stopped at our penthouse and we got out. Being back in our home, a place that still looked like it had before I'd given birth felt strange—like a relic from another time. There wasn't any baby stuff anywhere. All of it was hidden in the nursery.

Every step hurt and it would take a while for me to heal. Carrying Isa wasn't helping. Matteo gently pried her off me and held her in his arms. She was starting to wake, probably because she was hungry. I settled on the couch with a soft sigh. The way I felt one might think I'd never worked out in my life. When Isa began to wail, Matteo handed her to me for nursing while he took our bags upstairs.

I stroked Isa's head and back as she drank. I was slowly falling in love with her, but the full-blown love some mothers described still wasn't something I could understand.

Matteo sauntered down the staircase, looking relaxed and at ease, as if this, us being a family of three, was something he'd been born for. I'd probably always been the driving force behind not having kids, but Matteo had always only seen the fun aspects. Still, he seemed to enjoy the hard first days as well.

"How about I cook something for us?"

My eyebrows shot up. Matteo had many talents but cooking wasn't one of them. "How about you order us something delicious?"

He touched his heart as if I'd wounded him deeply. "I'm trying to be a good supportive houseman and you shoot me down like that."

"I'm very hungry and would rather not watch your three failed cooking attempts before you'll order something. Let's just skip ahead." I gave him a tired smile, which probably looked more like a grimace than anything else but I was trying to soften my words.

"All right. What would my lady like to eat?" Matteo asked, grabbing the phone and heading toward me.

"Something with plenty of carbs."

Matteo's eyes crinkled with amusement. "Carbs it is, all right. I'd say we can't go wrong with the classic choice."

I raised my eyebrows. Isa made a gurgling sound.

"Is it bad that I'm a bit jealous of her for having your tits all for herself?"

I cringed but then I shrugged. "To be honest, you've said worse."

Matteo chuckled. "Right. So pizza?"

"Pizza."

Twenty minutes later, Isa was fed, changed twice (her diaper exploded a second after we'd changed her) and slept soundly in her crib, which Matteo had carried downstairs so we'd have her close by. Two pizza cartons sat on the living room table, waiting for us. We settled on the couch and dug in.

"I can't remember the last time we had pizza on the couch. You hated the couch-potato life."

"I did, and still do, but right this moment I'm too tired to consider my life choices."

Matteo grinned and I knew he'd say something stupid. "If I'd known how docile you'd be after giving birth, I'd have knocked you up sooner."

I slapped his shoulder, then settled against him with a piece of pizza. "Shut up. I'll make your life hell soon enough again."

Matteo kissed the side of my head. "I know, babe, I know."

The days and nights that followed our homecoming were filled with vomit, poo, and screaming. Most days I wasn't even sure what time of the day it was. Finding any sort of routine proved difficult. Aria came over almost every day as mental support.

I hadn't left the apartment in a week and barely changed out of my sweats, but on day seven we decided to brave the outside world and pay a visit to Lily and Romero. Like last time, Isa wasn't too fond of the car but she settled down after a while.

Matteo and I drove to Romero's and Lily's house in Greenwich Village, a narrow brownstone building with an even narrower back yard, but the homiest, coziest place I could imagine. While Aria and I kept our places straight and more focused on modern design, Lily had gone all out with decoration, turning every room into a country-style dream. Matteo carried Isabella in her carrier while I followed slowly. I still felt unsteady on my legs, as if I had to find my balance again after my belly had practically disappeared overnight.

Romero opened the door for us with Sara perched on his arm. The little girl beamed all over her face. Her brown hair was styled in side pigtails which gave her an even cuter appearance. I'd never seen a happier, more easygoing child than her. I had a feeling Isabella would be a little piece of work.

He and Lily hadn't visited us in the hospital or in the week since then, which wasn't surprising considering they had their own little newborn to care for.

Romero hugged me carefully. "How are you feeling?"

I kissed Sara's cheek then gave him a wry smile. "As if someone sent my lower parts through a wringer."

He chuckled, his eyes crinkling. Then he bent over Isabella's carrier. She was fast asleep. After her initial crying fit in the car, she'd fallen asleep.

"She's beautiful."

Sara's eyes were wide and curious. "Favio," she said in her cute toddler voice.

Romero laughed. "No, this isn't *Flavio*. He's with your mom. This is Isabella, Gianna's baby."

Gianna's baby, the words still made me pause. Matteo winked at me, probably because I'd made a funny face.

"How did the whole house birthing thing go?" Matteo asked.

"Good," Romero said. "Lily was very happy with it and that's all that matters."

Happy wasn't a word I'd use to describe my birthing story but maybe I was just my usual bitchy self.

"Lily's in the living room."

I walked inside their house and found Lily on the sofa with little Flavio asleep on her. She didn't wear makeup and her hair was pulled up in a messy bun that I was all too familiar with.

"Hey," I said quietly, hoping not to wake Flavio. Isabella luckily didn't mind the occasional background noise but I wasn't sure if that was a baby thing or just an Isabella thing.

Lily gave me a tired smile. I leaned down and hugged her carefully. Flavio was bigger than Isabella and I wondered how Lily could have done the home birth. "You're brave, squeezing him out of you at home."

Lily peered down at him. "It was really peaceful. Maybe because it was my second child. And you did a car seat birth, Gianna. That's brave."

"It wasn't planned."

"Where is she?" Lily asked curiously, peering behind me.

"Oh, Matteo is carrying her because I still have trouble lifting her with the carrier. I'm sure he'll bring her here as soon as he's done chatting with Romero."

Lily gave me a surprised look. "You don't mind her being out of your sight? So shortly after birth, I can hardly stay away to go to the bathroom."

I glanced toward the doorway where the low murmur of male voices could still be heard, wondering if I was being a bad mother because I had no trouble leaving her with Matteo. It wasn't as if I was gone for hours, or even far away.

Lily touched my hand, tugging me down beside her. "I didn't mean to make you feel bad. Mom guilt is the worst feeling in the world. I'm just being very clingy to the point where even Romero is hardly allowed to hold Flavio. My hormones are really bad this time."

"I guess it was love at first sight for you?"

Lily pursed her lips, stroking Flavio's dark hair. "No, it wasn't. Not with Sara and not with Flavio either. It's… I don't know. Responsibility and protectiveness at first but in the days after birth, as we're getting to know each other, it grows quickly to love."

Matteo finally entered the living room with Isabella in her carrier. He set her down on the floor next to me and bent over Flavio. "Looks like Romero."

Lily grinned. "He does."

Sara ran into the room and climbed up beside Lily, leaning her head against her arm to peer at her brother.

"Romero and I want to take a look at his old Chevy," Matteo said as a way of goodbye before he disappeared from view.

"He bought a classic car that he wants to restore," Lily said with a shrug before she turned to Sara who was tugging at her hand. "Can we play?"

Lily bit her lip. "Not now, Sara. Your brother is sleeping. But later Mommy will make some time."

"Okay," Sara said, pouting.

"Why don't you grab a book that I can read to you?" I asked.

Sara's face lit up and she darted away, probably to her room.

"That's my number one mom guilt point right now," Lily admitted. "Sara wants even more attention than before but I don't have as much time."

"I'd have never thought you'd suffer from mom guilt at all. You seem like the perfect mother."

Lily gave me a disbelieving look. "I doubt there's a perfect mother."

Isabella began to squirm and her eyes fluttered open, soon followed by the first mewls and hesitant cries. I picked her up, pressed her against my chest and kissed her temple. She smelled so impossibly good, even though I couldn't even define the scent.

"What's up, Isa? Hungry again?"

She peered up at me. Her eyes were still that strange murky blue and I wondered if they'd darken or turn lighter. I grabbed her small blanket, draped it over me and started nursing her. At night Matteo and I both fed her. Luckily she took both the bottle and my breast, making our life so much easier.

When I looked up, Lily was smiling emotionally, her eyes glistening.

"Don't tell me seeing me as a milk source makes you want to cry?" I asked with a soft laugh.

Lily shrugged. "It does. I never thought you and I would ever sit on a sofa with our babies together."

"Me neither, trust me. This wasn't part of the plan."

"But you're happy?"

I listened to Isa's smacking, trying to determine my feelings. "I'm not unhappy. I love her and would never give her away. She's mine, but it's not my dream life. I miss working out, I miss working, and drinking a glass of wine and dancing and… sex."

Lily laughed. "Sex is the farthest thing on my mind right now."

"Well, it's not like I'm close to being in the mood right now. I'd probably strangle Matteo if he made a move right now, but still."

"Life changes with kids, but you'll discover new things, and raising a baby doesn't mean you won't still have time to do the things you love. It just requires more planning. Give it time."

Give it time was advice Aria had given me repeatedly. Unfortunately, I wasn't the most patient person but since becoming pregnant I'd learned patience.

Lily watched me nurse Isa for a while before saying, "I really love seeing you like this."

I gave Lily a tired smile. "Don't get used to it. After Isa, we'll make sure there won't be another one."

Lily laughed. "I wouldn't mind four or five of these little ones."

My eyes grew wide. "Good luck with that."

Matteo

"So, how do you feel as a first-time dad?" Romero asked me as he led me into the garage.

I let out a low whistle when I spotted his new car, an ancient Chevrolet that would need plenty of attention before it could grace the road with its presence.

"I don't really feel different, just like old Matteo with more responsibility."

Romero chuckled. "Holding your child for the first time and realizing you're responsible for their upbringing makes you grow up in seconds."

"You were always the responsible type. And I don't really feel any more grown-up or sensible than before."

Romero opened the car, showing me the barren inside. No seats or steering wheel.

"I hope you got this as a gift." I'd never been a fan of vintage cars. I loved to have the newest gimmicks.

"This is a rare piece. I would have paid double just to get my hands on it."

"So you think you still have time for such a big project besides work, two kids, and a wife?"

Romero shrugged. "I sleep less and I don't party anymore. The time I wasted on nursing hangovers in the past is now dedicated to other things."

"Could you sound any more straitlaced?"

"After all the shit we see and do in our job, I enjoy the boring, ordinary side of my home life."

I shook my head. "Speak for yourself. I still love the thrill." My phone rang and Luca's name flashed across the screen. I took the call.

"We got our hands on two new recruits from Tartarus. I thought I'd ask if you feel like getting your hands dirty."

My smile widened. "Do you even have to ask?"

"Maybe you're still stuck in the baby bubble. Don't want Gianna to get her panties in a bunch."

"Don't worry. I'll be there in a bit. Where?"

"Warehouse 2."

I hung up.

Romero scanned my face. "That's your torture prelude face."

"Luca got a job for me. You interested in getting your hands on some bikers?"

"I have to pay a visit to one of our bars. And you probably need me to take Gianna home later, right?"

I nodded. "Yeah, probably. I'll see what she says."

I headed back into the house. Lily and Gianna were still on the couch, drinking coffee. Isa slept beside Gianna, her arms stretched out over her head. Gianna looked up, scanning my face with narrowed eyes. "What's up?"

"Luca called and asked if I could help him."

"From the eager look in your eyes, I'm guessing it involves plenty of blood."

"It might." It most definitely would. I hadn't been involved in the business for almost two weeks and felt itchy to return.

Gianna shrugged, touching Isa's chest lightly. "We're good here. I'm sure Romero will give me a lift later. Go have fun."

I leaned down and gave her a lingering kiss. I waved at Liliana, then said a quick goodbye to Romero before I raced off in my car. My pulse began to quicken. For some reason this felt like the beginning, when the prospect of torture and danger still kept my blood pounding for a long time.

When I pulled up in front of our warehouse, I was whistling and eager like a teenage boy before his first fuck.

Luca shook his head when I strode into the warehouse. "You look like you might be peeing yourself from excitement." He clapped my shoulder. "That bad at home? I thought you and Gianna were starting to find a routine with Isabella."

"We are. That's not it. I just missed this… being responsible twenty-four seven is hard. I'm just looking forward to a taste of my old life."

Luca chuckled. "Knock yourself out. These bikers think they are tough." He motioned toward the back of the warehouse and walked ahead. Behind heaps of old tires, two guys, maybe in their early twenties, were bound to chairs. Someone had roughened them up a bit; busted lips, a few scratches here and there, and already forming bruises. Nothing major. Not yet.

I gave them a grin and pulled my knife from its holster.

Growl leaned against the bare stone wall to my left, inked arms crossed and that stoic expression on his face that belied his violent nature. He nodded my way and I returned the gesture but quickly focused my attention back to our two captives.

One look at them told me they weren't the sharpest knives in the cupboard. That wasn't a surprise. The MCs often scraped their recruits from the bottom of society.

I doubted these guys knew anything of worth about the men we really wanted to have intel on: Earl White and his nephew Maddox. But cutting them up and sending them back to the bikers sent them a message even those redneck idiots must understand at some point.

Luca leaned against the wall beside Growl. I wouldn't argue if they wanted me to do all the work. I couldn't wait.

I chose the bulkier, braver looking first. Usually I kept the hard nuts for last, but I was too eager to prolong the fun.

It was early evening when I came back home. I hadn't stayed longer than necessary, not wanting to abandon Gianna. The penthouse was quiet and the lights were out. I set the takeout bags down on the kitchen counter and went in search of my wife and daughter.

Wife and daughter…

Who would have thought I'd ever have a small family?

Following a dim light into the bedroom, I found Gianna. She was curled up on her side on top of the covers in our bed, fast asleep. Isa was stretched out beside her, protected by Gianna's body and a pillow. I walked over to them, and as if she could sense me, Isa opened her eyes and began squirming. Careful to be quiet, I picked her up and cradled her in my arms. I pressed a soft kiss to her forehead.

Dealing with the bikers had been fun, something I couldn't live without, but returning home to Isa and Gianna, it was the peaceful harbor I now craved in a way I'd have never thought possible. I'd always made fun of Luca for his split personality: the loving father and husband, and the batshit crazy, brutal Capo, but I got it now.

Gianna stirred, rolling over onto her back and eyes fluttering open. She was in my sweats and T-shirt, looking completely disheveled. Slowly her gaze focused on me. "What time is it?"

"Almost eight," I said. "I got sushi for us."

She sat up. "You're early. I thought you'd use your chance to have some freedom."

She pushed to her feet with a groan. "Fuck, I feel old."

I grinned. "I'm glad I won't be the only one teaching Isa curse words."

Gianna huffed and leaned against me. I bent down and kissed her but Isa interrupted us with a wail. "I think she's hungry too. I'll nurse her and then we can have sushi."

"Sounds like a plan."

I handed Isa to Gianna before I headed back downstairs and set up the coffee table. Thirty minutes later Gianna came downstairs, dressed in shorts and a tank. Her belly was still slightly curved but she still looked sexy to me.

She sank down on the couch beside me. "You got me Kombucha?"

"Yep, your favorite brand."

Gianna took a sip before she started digging in. After we were done, Gianna settled in my arm on the couch and we watched *Walking Dead*. I still didn't understand why she had no trouble watching it considering her aversion to bloodshed. Judging by the silence of the baby monitor, Isa was soundly asleep.

I stroked Gianna's thigh. We hadn't shared any kind of intimacy in four weeks and I was slowly starting to get horny. Gianna hadn't made a move yet, which was unusual. In the past, she'd been a very active partner, but of course I remembered Luca's words.

She gave me a disbelieving look. "I don't even remember the last time I shaved."

"Don't worry, I'll find what I'm looking for."

She let out an exasperated laugh. "You're impossible."

I shrugged. "I'm horny. You know how much you turn me on."

Gianna searched my face. "I can't believe I still turn you on. I definitely don't feel sexy."

"You're always sexy to me. What about you? Are you in the mood for a little loving?"

Gianna grimaced. "My mind says yes, but every exhausted and healing part of my body says no."

I kissed her temple and leaned back. "Whenever you feel ready, I'm here, waiting for you."

Gianna relaxed back into my arm with a smile. "Sometimes I wish I could tell seventeen-year-old Gianna that you're not as bad as she thinks."

"Not as bad? That's all you'd tell her?"

She nicked the skin at my neck. "Oh no, I'd tell her how amazing in bed you are, with your tongue and your cock and your fingers and every other part of your body as well."

I groaned. "You're torturing me."

"It's something we're both good at."

"You're better at it, babe, much better."

CHAPTER TWELVE

Gianna

MATTEO LET OUT A LOW WHISTLE. "You are sex on legs, aren't you?"

I glanced toward the door, narrowing my eyes. He leaned in the doorway, tight white dress shirt hugging his abs and pecs, dark hair perfectly mussed up, and just overall male perfection.

He was sex on legs, the bastard. I, in comfy sweatpants that didn't squeeze my poor frayed vagina, without makeup, unwashed hair and stains on my shirt where milk had leaked out of my stupid breasts was a full-blown nightmare. Three weeks since I'd given birth and I'd reached a low point. Matteo was back to working every day and I couldn't deny it: I was envious.

Seeing his grin, I considered committing my first murder. I could probably make it look like self-defense. After all, Matteo was a notorious mobster. "Oh shut up, or I'll throw the fucking milk bottle at your head."

Matteo clucked his tongue. "No cussing around our precious offspring, or have you forgotten?"

I raised the milk bottle. I alternated between breastfeeding and milk from the bottle to give my poor nipples time to recuperate. I wasn't sure if Isa was particularly bad at nursing or if my nipples weren't made for mom-life. "Last warning."

Isabella let out a wail and I let my arm sink with a quiet sigh. Matteo came in, kissed my temple and took our girl from me, cradling her in his arm. He took the bottle. "I'm taking over the rest of the night. Grab a couple of hours of sleep."

At first, I'd felt bad because I couldn't only breastfeed our daughter like Lily seemed to be doing with ease but now I was glad that she took the bottle and Matteo or Aria could feed her as well. "Are you sure? You must be tired," I said despite the bone deep exhaustion in my body.

Matteo had been gone all night on some kind of business that he and Luca had to conduct and that usually didn't mean anything good. Most of the time it involved risky attacks on outposts of the motorcycle club they were at war with.

Something dark flashed across Matteo's face. "I'm good. Adrenaline."

"You shouldn't risk your life now that we've got Isabella," I muttered. Recently, the conflicts with the Bratva and the MCs who worked with them had escalated. At least, the Outfit lay low. There was enough money to be made for all crime families so I'd never understood why they insisted on fighting each other, except for pride and testosterone.

"I didn't, Gianna. Luca and I dealt with a few Russians that got caught."

My nose wrinkled because I knew what that meant. Matteo regarded me as he rocked Isabella gently. I gave him a tired smile then kissed him again. I didn't like what he did but I loved him. "Thanks."

Matteo nodded and peered down at Isabella, then gently nudged her lips with the bottle. She latched on to it and began drinking.

Relieved, I moved toward the bed and crept under the covers. Despite the lights, I fell asleep almost instantly.

The weeks dragged on, night and day blurring into each other. I got a better handle on Isa's feeding and sleeping schedule, and even managed to squeeze in a shower almost every day.

I really started feeling more like myself when I was cleared for working out by my doctor six weeks after giving birth. The first time I stepped into my gym, I really felt like past-Gianna, as if there was room for me besides being a mom. Cara waved at me from behind the reception desk. She had taken over a few classes and also the reception duties since she'd been working out in my gym from the very start. She managed to be a mom and to keep doing what she enjoyed. Her two boys spent time with their grandma whenever Cara worked.

I went over to her and hugged her. "How are things going over here?"

"Good," she said with a confident smile. "What about you? How are you doing? I remember the first few weeks of being a first-time mom in a sleep-deprived haze."

"That sums it up. But it's been getting better. Isa only wakes twice per night now. That's a huge improvement."

"Good!"

The bell rang and the wife and daughter of a soldier stepped in. They congratulated me before they headed into the changing rooms. Of course, nobody could enter the building without passing a security check downstairs. Matteo and Luca had insisted on it.

"I'm going to do Pilates by myself for an hour. Just going to get changed."

"Will you return to teaching classes soon?"

"Yes," I said without hesitation. Matteo and I hadn't discussed when I'd start working again. It wasn't as if I was earning any money with it. The gym and classes were complimentary for all the women in our world, but I still felt like I was doing something useful.

Cara nodded. "Your customers will be happy to hear that."

"They enjoyed your aerobic classes as well."

"They do but they definitely miss yoga."

I couldn't deny how good Cara's words made me feel.

After I'd changed into my workout clothes for the first time in almost three months, I headed into the Pilates room. Giving birth to Isa had left its marks. I definitely didn't look as fit anymore and my belly wasn't as flat as it used to be. But worse than the obvious changes were the invisible ones. I felt as if I was doing Pilates for the very first time. My balance was off and my stamina as well. Still I couldn't stop grinning stupidly once I was done with my workout. I felt reborn as the old Gianna.

"I'll be back tomorrow," I told Cara before I left.

I got into my car, a cute Smart, much to Matteo's chagrin, and pulled out of the underground garage. The car with my bodyguards followed close by. It had taken a while for me to win this piece of freedom. I didn't want those baboons in a car with me, much less did I want them to drive me around like chauffeurs. Alone in my car with the music turned up all the way, I felt like a normal woman, not a mob wife.

I pulled up in front of Aria and Luca's mansion, then waited for one of my bodyguards to check the perimeter. Once he gave a nod, I got out of my car and headed toward the massive wooden door with a metal lion claw as a doorknob.

Before I could knock, Aria opened the door with a grin, cradling Isa in her arms. "And?" she asked.

"Everything aches and I'll have sore muscles tomorrow, but I feel better than I have in a long time."

Isa gave me a goofy smile and my heart beat faster. I took her from Aria, gave her chubby baby cheek a fat kiss and pressed her against my chest. Now that she was back in my arms, I realized I'd missed her, but working out had given my mind and body a necessary kickstart. "Thank you for watching her. You seem to have had fun."

Aria could hardly take her eyes off Isa. "Marcella and Amo are already so grown up in comparison. I really miss the baby stage."

I shook my head. "I can't wait for the baby phase to be over so Isa and I can do fun things together. Right now, she can only poo and scream."

Aria laughed. "Do you want to come in for a coffee and some cake?"

"Coffee, yes. Cake, no."

Aria rolled her eyes. "Back to being fit Gianna?"

"You bet. These additional baby pounds won't disappear on their own."

"They did for me."

I gave her a death glare. "Not everyone is graced with your supermodel genes."

"We share the same genes."

I followed her into their ginormous living room with a splendid view into their yard. I still wasn't convinced Luca hadn't helped with the sudden death of the previous owner to get his hands on such a rare property in New York.

A tray with coffee was already set up on the table. I sank down on the beige leather sofa and put Isa down between my leg and the armrest, tickling her belly.

"I fed her about thirty minutes ago but she didn't want to fall asleep."

"She'll do it soon enough," I said. And less than five minutes later, Isa slept fast.

Aria regarded me. "You look happy. I'm glad Pilates is giving you so much joy. Once you start teaching Pilates classes again, I'll be your first customer."

"But you enjoyed the aerobic classes, right?"

Aria laughed. "Yes, I told you before. You really can't give up control. Cara really did a good job, so don't worry."

"The gym feels like my baby too. I worked so hard to convince Matteo to let me do it and then to build it up."

"And you did a great job. The gym is always bursting with customers."

"I really want to get back to teaching Pilates and yoga classes soon," I said hesitantly. In the past, I'd never had trouble saying my opinion straight out, but for some reason, mom guilt managed to wedge itself into my brain.

Aria shrugged. "Why don't you just turn your own workout sessions into classes?"

"I'm not as fit as I used to be and if I work out, I can't give as much attention to my customers. Many of them need guidance to perform the correct moves."

"Then explain that your current classes are less guided. I'm sure many people would still enjoy working out with you. I'm one of them."

I squeezed her thigh. "Thanks."

That evening during dinner I told Matteo about my plan to get back to teaching yoga and Pilates classes.

"Sure, why not? If you feel fit enough, why wouldn't you? It's not like Isa needs you twenty-four seven. She'll survive spending an hour or two with Aria."

I walked over to him and kissed him. Matteo never cared much about what other people thought, that's probably what I loved most about him. He pulled me down on his lap, deepening the kiss at once. His fingers tangled in my hair, and my hands roamed over his muscled chest.

"The doc cleared you for all kinds of physical activities, right?" Matteo murmured against my lips.

I laughed. Matteo pushed his hand between my legs and rubbed me through my pants. Despite the tingling sensation, I also felt a hint of hesitation. I wasn't even sure why. Maybe because my body felt different. My insecurity was probably why Isa's cry blaring through the baby monitor came as a relief.

"She's got the worst timing," Matteo groaned.

I hopped off his lap. Matteo tried to rearrange his bulge in his pants, looking pained. What the hell was wrong with me? Seeing Matteo now, I desired him. I wanted sex.

Shoving those thoughts aside, I headed upstairs to console Isa.

A week later, I had coffee with Aria again after my workout. It was the first time I'd actually taught yoga, even if I'd focused more on myself than in previous classes. Still it had been a big success with the women, especially those who were struggling with their after-baby bodies as well. Eventually I bridged the subject that's been bothering me for a week now.

"Matteo and I haven't slept with each other since Isa's birth."

Aria didn't look surprised. "Why don't you have a date night with Matteo? Luca and I can watch Isabella."

"Are you sure?"

She smiled. "Of course. I know how important it is to make time for each other."

I bit my lip. Then I blurted. "I want to have sex with Matteo but at the same time a part of me doesn't. Does that even make sense?"

Aria nodded. "It takes time to heal, body and mind. It was the same for me. Pregnancy and giving birth are hard work for the body."

"I don't know why you want to do this a third time. It blows my mind really. Maybe you should change your mind."

Aria bit her lip and my eyes widened. "Don't tell me Luca knocked you up already?"

"It's still early, that's why we didn't say anything yet."

I shook my head, then hugged her. "I'm so happy for you." And relieved. I was so damn relieved that Luca and Aria would get a third baby, that they would get the chance to use the nursery they'd prepared for my daughter.

"Go on a date with Matteo tonight," she urged. "Luca and I can take Isa with us to the Hamptons, and you join us there after you've had some time together."

"Okay," I said slowly. "How do I know if my body's healed?"

Aria laughed. "Well, you have to test it out, and see if it works. Some things might still be uncomfortable. It takes time."

"What takes time?" Luca asked as he walked in.

"The healing of a vagina after birth," I said. It was still my favorite pastime to annoy him with my directness.

Luca grimaced. "You and Matteo are the bane of my existence, and I have a feeling your daughter will be just the same."

"Speaking of Isa," Aria said, "I told Gianna we'd watch her tonight so she and Matteo can have their first date after Isa's birth."

Luca looked at me. "Under one condition."

I raised an eyebrow.

"Do me a favor and give Matteo a fucking blow job or fuck him if your vagina allows it. The horny bastard's driving me up the wall and I will put him down like a rabid dog soon."

I snorted. "Anything for you, Luca. Anything."

Aria's shoulders shook as she laughed. I kissed Isa's soft forehead then handed her to Aria who took her with a gentle smile and rose to her feet to walk over to Luca. "Can you believe that we'll have a small human in seven months."

Luca kissed her temple. "Our two small humans are currently tearing my sanity to shreds."

Aria shook her head. "They aren't that bad."

"They are," I said. Amo was seven and a bigmouthed daredevil and Marcella was ten and currently fawning over some boy band and intolerable because of it. She was trying to talk Luca into arranging a meeting with said boy band but he refused. Of course, he did. That girl was so freaking gorgeous, it was a miracle he hadn't locked her up in a tower somewhere to protect her from male attention.

With a wave, I walked away. In the doorway, I risked another glance back. My daughter was still happily sleeping in Aria's hold. Isa loved Aria and my sister took the best care of her, still I felt a tiny twinge thinking about leaving my daughter for several hours. It would be the first time she'd be away from me for more than two hours.

Luca had his arm wrapped around my sister, looking down at her as if she were the center of his world. Those two… their love made absolutely no sense, but it was unbreakable. And tonight, Matteo and I would spend some time together to make sure our love had time to bloom.

I turned and walked out of the house and toward my car. Before I drove off, I sent Matteo a quick text, telling him that we'd go on a date tonight and that he should be home by six.

I felt nervous when I arrived at our penthouse and considered what to wear for our date. I hadn't dressed up in months, and I really wanted Matteo to be blown away. Considering his horniness, naked probably would have worked best.

After trying on half of my wardrobe and discovering that most of my skinny fit jeans and leather pants didn't fit, I had a brief crisis. Luckily, I found an outfit that even though it was on the tight side, looked fabulous.

Matteo took me to our favorite steakhouse. His eyes kept checking me out, sending a pleasant shiver down my back. After I'd taken extra time to look sexy tonight, I was relieved that it seemed to have the desired effect. I felt newly born dressed up in a sexy leather skirt with a daring slit and a silver silk blouse giving a prime view at my still much larger breasts.

"You're killing me with this outfit," he whispered in my ear as the waiter led us to our usual table. "I'll have to wank off at least twice to get you out of my system."

I kissed him, then whispered. "Who says you'll have to wank off?"

Matteo pulled back, eyes darkening with lust. "Are you ready?"

I thought I'd hidden my hesitance well, but Matteo must have picked up on it. He was too perceptive to trick him.

"More than ready." My body better agree with me. I needed Matteo, and I knew he needed me as well.

Matteo squeezed my waist. "Now I won't be able to enjoy my steak. I'll have a fucking boner all through dinner."

"We could have a predinner quickie," I whispered.

In that moment, we arrived at the table but Matteo turned to the waiter. "We'll have to freshen up. Why don't you bring over a bottle of Merlot?"

The waiter nodded then excused himself. Matteo led me away from the table and toward the back of the restaurant and into the men's restroom. He kissed me fiercely, stealing my breath. We stumbled into a stall. Luckily this was the best steakhouse in town and the restrooms were more comfy than usual. It wasn't the first time we did it in a stall so we had plenty of firsthand experience when it came to the quickie-comfort in restrooms. Matteo's kiss became even harder, filled with so much desire my body seemed to vibrate with the sensation. His hand cupped my ass and squeezed hard, making me moan into his mouth. I doubted I could be quiet today. Too much time had passed since we'd last enjoyed each other. Whoever entered the restroom would get a verbal show, but I didn't care.

Matteo's hand slid down my thigh, discovering bare skin through the slit in my skirt. Goose bumps rose all over my body at the skin on skin contact, desperate for more. I pressed against him, clutching his neck, my lips sliding over his. His palm caressed my thigh, slowly finding its way toward my panties, which were already soaked just from our short make-out session.

"That slit has its perks," Matteo rasped as he rubbed my pussy through the drenched fabric. "Turn around and bend forward."

I didn't ask what he had in mind. I needed him so much. Turning my back to him, I braced myself against the wall. Matteo massaged my ass, leaving hot kisses against my neck before he sank down to his knees behind me.

"You'll ruin your pants," I muttered, but really all I could think about was how his mouth would feel on me.

"Fuck my pants, I want to taste your pussy."

He pushed the skirt up until the slit parted over my hip, then he dragged my panties down until they bunched around my ankles. I trembled with need. Matteo pushed my legs a bit farther apart until I was sure my panties would tear and then his hot, wet tongue dipped between my folds. I gasped, shoving my ass backward to feel more of him. Soon I was panting and mewling, completely overwhelmed by Matteo's mouth against my center. Leaning my forehead against the stall, my eyes squeezed shut, I rocked against him, moaning and whimpering. Usually I liked to pretend Matteo had to work hard for my orgasm but not today. I was so eager to come, I was close to losing my mind. I came with a harsh cry, then bit my lip desperately to stifle more sounds. The door opened and steps rang out. I could hardly contain my pants, still completely overwhelmed by Matteo's mouth against my sensitive flesh.

Matteo kept lapping at me and then he pushed a finger into me and my eyes rolled back. Counting the seconds until the guy would finally leave the restroom, I could hardly keep the moans in as Matteo fucked me slowly with his finger, then his tongue returned, replacing the finger and I began shaking again. Finally, the man flushed and left.

I arched back and gasped as my release slammed into me once more. I practically pressed my ass against Matteo's face but he didn't mind. My fingers were stiff from pressing them against the wall and a fine sheen of sweat covered my back. When Matteo straightened, I was still braced against the wall, unable to move. "I think we need to return to our table, it's been a while," I got out.

"I'd rather fuck you now," he rasped, kissing my ear.

"Later," I promised.

It took us another ten minutes to make ourselves presentable. When we arrived at our table, the bottle of wine and the menus were already waiting on us. A few of the other guests gave us curious looks but none of the staff showed any signs that they had noticed something. The Famiglia "protected" the restaurant for a small contribution, how Matteo always put it.

"You look absolutely gorgeous," Matteo said over the main course.

"You don't have to give me compliments. I already promised you sex."

He chuckled. "Fuck, Gianna you have the same dirty mind as me."

I took a sip from the wine and smiled at him over the rim. "Touché."

Despite our desire for each other, we took our time eating dinner. These undisturbed moments as a couple were too precious to waste them with haste. Still I couldn't suppress a naughty smile when Matteo asked for the check. His answering shark-grin only increased my arousal.

Matteo pulled me against his side as he led me outside. I could tell by the tension in his body that he was already eager to continue where we'd left off before dinner. We got into the back seat of his car and kissed, Matteo shoved up my dress and slid his fingers under my panties, finding me ready for him. He unzipped his pants and pushed up my legs, then kissed me again.

"Condom," I pressed out.

I hadn't had my period yet since giving birth but I didn't want to risk anything. Matteo cursed then fumbled in his pants until he pulled out a wrapper. The tear of the material made me shiver, then he was back on top of me again. His tip nudged my opening and I froze up, just like that.

Matteo raised his eyes. "Do you want me to stop?"

"No," I said needily. "I'm ready. I'm just a bit nervous. Ignore it."

Matteo kissed me but this time it was slower, less desperate and hungry, and then he began to slide into me at a torturously slow pace. His eyes held mine and my breathing deepened as I felt him inside of me. It felt perfect. No discomfort, no scary birth memories, nothing.

Matteo groaned when he was sheathed in me. "Fuck. This feels like heaven."

I moaned my agreement.

"Can I move?" he rasped.

"God, yes. Move."

Matteo chuckled and then he slid out of me and thrust back in. With every thrust he hit deeper and harder, and soon the entire car was shaking with our lovemaking and my feet hit the ceiling and the back of my head the door, but I didn't care.

I clawed at Matteo's shoulders, needing him closer and he complied, pressed down on me, sliding even deeper and I exploded around him. Matteo jerked and with a low hiss I felt him release into me.

"Fuck," he muttered.

I giggled. Matteo silenced me with his tongue, a slow and languid kiss as he slowly softened inside me. I loved the feel of it. For some reason the aftermath of sex was when I felt closest to him, I wasn't even sure why.

Afterward, we lay in each other's arms, awkwardly squeezed into the back seat. "I'll make an appointment for the vasectomy," Matteo murmured.

I looked up, surprised. So far he hadn't been too enthused about a vasectomy, or being castrated, how he put it. "Really?"

"Really," he said. "I don't want you to stuff your body with hormones and I hate condoms, so a vasectomy is the easiest and fairest option for both of us. Or do you want the option for kid number two?" His grin told me he knew the answer.

"Hell, no!" I muttered. "I definitely don't want more kids. I love Isa and I'm glad she's part of our life, but if I could live my life again, I'd still decide not to be a mom. It's not my mission in life and it won't ever be."

"Yeah, let's leave the baby producing to our siblings. They seem only too keen to fill the earth with more inhabitants."

I kissed Matteo long and slow. "Thank you. I know most mobsters would lose their shit if their wife suggested something like that. You wanting to do this is the greatest proof of your love I can imagine."

"Do I really still need to prove my love for you?"

"No." I pressed closer to him. "If anyone's got more proving to do then it's me. But I love you so much, it's hard to put into words."

We drove to the Hamptons afterward, even if Aria had given us the option to join them in the morning. I wanted to be under the same roof as Isa in the night. When we arrived at the mansion after midnight, the windows were dark. We headed straight for our bedroom as not to disturb anyone and went for another round of fucking, this time far less gentle, in our bed. Afterward we lay in each other's arms, staring into each other's eyes.

"Maybe we should relieve Aria and Luca," I whispered. It was strange not to have the baby monitor at my side to listen to every sound Isa made.

Matteo chuckled. "Missing our little poo machine?"

I shrugged. "I do. It's the first time we left her with someone else for so many hours."

Matteo stroked my hair. "She's fine. Luca and Aria are taking care of her."

"We're lucky," I said quietly. "Without them, we wouldn't be here today."

"Yeah, they are our better halves," Matteo joked.

"They are." I traced Matteo's tattoo. "Sometimes I worry about Isa."

Matteo's eyes became sharp. "Why? You know I'll protect her."

"I don't mean an outside attack. I worry about her growing up in the Famiglia with all its old-fashioned rules. The outside world changes but our world remains mostly the same. Girls still remain virgins until they marry. Even if we don't teach her those values, she'll be surrounded by them."

Matteo shook his head. "I really don't want to think about our innocent little daughter ever having sex. I can see how crazy Luca gets when anyone comments on Marcella being ten and how it could be time to look for a good match for her."

"As if anyone could ever be good enough for Marci in Luca's eyes. I feel pity for the poor idiot who'll have to marry her."

Matteo grinned like a shark. "Luca and I will have a long conversation with him."

"You two are impossible," I muttered. "But it isn't only that. What about arranged marriages, bloody sheets, cutting the bride out of her dress and all that?"

"How about we try to survive the first ten years before we worry about teenage years, and marriage and bloody sheets?"

I huffed. Matteo pulled me closer and kissed me. "Not all arranged marriages are bad."

"Luca and Aria are the exception."

"I was talking about us," Matteo said.

I opened my eyes in fake shock. He growled and rolled on top of me. "Everyone always said I needed to teach you manners, where did I go wrong?"

He nuzzled my neck in a distracting way.

"Wrong woman," I whispered then sucked in a breath when he licked a particularly sensitive spot at my throat.

"Just the woman I need," he growled, but his wandering hands distracted me from a reply.

We fell asleep in each other's arms but sometime during the night I woke and couldn't fall back asleep. I carefully untangled myself from Matteo and tiptoed out the door and toward the nursery. The mansion was big enough so that every child had their own room and every baby their own nursery.

I hoped Isabella was there and not in Aria's and Luca's bedroom with them. I opened the door and froze at the sight before me. The small night light cast a yellowish glow in the room. Luca was asleep in the armchair and Aria was curled up on top of him. Isabella was fast asleep in her crib but I assumed she had kept them awake most of the night if they'd decided to sleep in the nursery. She'd been a bit fussy these last few days but I'd hoped she'd settle down tonight.

I took a step inside and Luca's eyes shot open, tension radiating through his body, his arm coming protectively around my sleeping sister. Then his eyes settled on me and he relaxed. He yawned and glanced at the clock. It was four a.m.

He rose with Aria in his arms, cradling her to his chest and came slowly toward me.

I mouthed, "Thank you."

Luca nodded. "Will Matteo be more tolerable tomorrow?" he asked in a low voice.

I rolled my eyes at him but couldn't stop a smile from forming.

Luca shook his head and muttered something I didn't catch before he walked off with Aria's sleeping form.

I watched them a moment longer before I moved silently toward the crib. Isabella looked so peaceful and cute, I had to stop myself from picking her up and cuddling her. I didn't want to wake her. I dragged the chair a bit closer and sank down with my chin on the rail so I could watch my baby. I reached out for her and stroked her cheek then her reddish-brown hair. It was a bit lighter than Matteo's but darker than mine. Her eye color was still difficult to determine, a mix of blue and brown, but she had my freckles. They graced her cheeks and nose adorably.

"I knew I'd find you here," Matteo murmured as he came in, his sweatpants hanging low on his hips. Those abs still got me every time. He leaned over me, his chin lightly resting atop my head.

"I still can't believe she's ours. She looks so innocent and peaceful."

"She can scream like a little fury," I said with a small laugh. "She'll drive us crazy soon enough."

"Ohh, I have no doubt about that."

We watched her a little while longer before we returned to our bedroom with the baby monitor and fell asleep almost instantly.

The next morning, Aria and Luca already sat at the breakfast table when we dragged our asses down. We joined them, Isa wedged on my hip. She was clingy this morning, maybe because of our separation last night or maybe because she was caught up in some kind of development phase. I didn't try to let mom guilt overwhelm me. If I wanted to stay sane and protect my marriage, Matteo and I needed the occasional day or evening off.

After some fussing, I finally managed to get Isa to recline into her baby seat and sank down on the chair beside her.

Cradling her still flat pregnant belly, Aria had an expression of utmost baby bliss on her face as she watched my daughter. I stifled a laugh. My sister was the born mother. No wonder she couldn't understand that Matteo and I didn't want more of these little poop machines. She gave me a sheepish smile when she noticed my attention. I winked at her.

"Do you think Lily and Romero will join us tonight? We haven't had dinner together since we both gave birth," I said.

Aria gave a delicate shrug. Matteo of course was less restrained. "Even if they come over, I doubt Liliana can tear herself away from admiring the little poop machine."

"They have two, I doubt Sara is out of diapers yet," Luca commented.

Aria sent both men reprimanding looks. "Lily is a very caring mother."

Matteo's cough sounded remarkably like a cluck.

"What does that make me, a cuckoo?" I joked. Isa laughed as if she could understand what was going on. For a second, I felt horrible because I had almost become the cuckoo to drop her off with Aria. She would have had the perfect life with my sister, but I couldn't imagine giving her away anymore.

Aria looked flustered. "Of course not. I just don't want us to make Lily feel bad for being a bit over caring with Flavio. Every mother handles the newborn phase differently."

"All right, Dalai-L'Aria," Matteo said with a wink.

She pointed her fork at him. "Remember you'll need to be on my good side if you and Gianna want more couple time."

"As if you could ever say no to them, if they ask you for a favor," Luca muttered.

I stifled a laugh at the caught look Aria gave him.

Lily and Romero actually joined us in the Hamptons with their kids that afternoon, and even had an almost adult-only dinner (if you didn't count Marci and Amo) with us. The rest of the kids were already asleep. It almost felt like old times, apart from Marci's pouty-face because Luca had told her to turn her music down in less than favorable words for the band members. He'd compared their songs to castrated cats. Amo of course couldn't shut up about castrated cats since then, making mew sounds all the time to provoke Marci.

Lily was a bit jumpy whenever Flavio made the slightest sound or even when the baby monitor only let out a crackle but apart from that, we had a pleasant dinner. We even chatted about more than diapers and spew incidents. I grinned at Matteo. Old Gianna and new Mom-Gianna could co-exist peacefully.

CHAPTER THIRTEEN

Gianna

We fell into a good routine and eventually I really thought I'd mastered motherhood while also keeping up my classes in the gym. Of course, Aria's warning that especially the first year could be a constant up and down proved right.

At five months, Isa was teething and absolutely intolerable most days. I was torn between worry and pity over her red cheeks. Yet, my worst enemy was exhaustion.

Matteo and I decided to spend a few days in the Hamptons to come down. The ocean air usually calmed Isa but even that was barely working. Aria and Luca had stayed in New York because Aria had a pregnancy checkup and Amo some kind of neck-breaking dirt race. I still wasn't sure how Amo and Luca had convinced Aria to let him choose this insane hobby. Probably Luca's argument that he needed to harden the boy for the mob had worked its magic.

It was late in the evening while Matteo was out to grab us food at our favorite place when Isa had a particularly bad crying episode.

Eventually I began to cry as well, overwhelmed and doubting myself and my decision to become a mother. Aria would have been the better choice.

I was rocking Isa, trying to calm her down when heavy steps rang out. I let out a surprised cry when Luca suddenly appeared in the doorway to the nursery.

I was only in Matteo's shirt and I wasn't even sure if I was wearing underwear.

"Aria decided to spend a few days here," he said carefully.

"What about that race?" I said, trying to pretend I wasn't a crying mess.

"It was in the afternoon. We drove here right after."

"I guess it's Aria's sixth sense," I said with a forced laugh. "She could feel I didn't have my shit together and came to the rescue."

Luca nodded, still watching me. "She's downstairs, trying to settle an argument between Amo and Marcella."

Isa let out a particularly loud wail, her cute face becoming a grimace.

Luca approached me as if I were a spooked horse. "Let me hold her for a bit." In the past, I would have chewed his ear off for the commanding tone but I was glad for his presence. He gently took Isa from me.

"I don't even remember if I put on panties," I said miserably.

Luca regarded me. "Don't worry, I won't lift that shirt to find out. I saw you down there once, that'll last for a lifetime."

I snorted, and a knot loosened hearing his familiar jibe. "Bastard, I was squeezing a baby out of me. I don't always look like that down there."

Luca smirked. "If you say so. Still, no thanks."

I lightly punched the arm that wasn't holding Isabella. "Careful. I'm not too tired to kick balls."

"Good," Luca said, then he rocked Isabella again. When he looked back up his expression was stern. "Go to bed. Get some sleep."

My eyes darted to Isa. "But… I should rock her. I should take care of her. And Matteo will be back with takeout any moment." I wasn't even hungry. I should have been because I hadn't eaten since breakfast but my body only craved sleep.

"And you do care for her. Truth be told, I never expected you to be a good mom but you proved me wrong," Luca said. "But that doesn't mean you can't get help if you need it. Now go to bed before I drag you there. You can eat cold pizza later."

"I really want to hug you right now," I admitted.

"Wait a few seconds, it'll pass," Luca said dryly, but his eyes had softened slightly, which was a rare enough sight that it made me emotional.

Luca narrowed his eyes. "Bed. Now."

I rolled my eyes. "Bastard."

"Bitch."

I gave him a small smile, then turned and walked back to our bedroom. The moment my head hit the pillow, I passed out.

Matteo

Luca's car was parked in front of the mansion when I pulled up. When I checked my phone, I saw his message telling me they'd join us. Grabbing our takeout order had taken longer than anticipated, mainly because I was so sleep deprived that I'd briefly dozed off at the steering wheel and decided to pull over for a minute. That had turned into a power nap of almost forty-five minutes.

Now the car smelled of pizza, which was probably cold by now, and my neck was stiff from the awkward position I'd slept in. I was lucky Tartarus or the Bratva hadn't chosen my moment of weakness for an attack.

I got out of the car, glad for the cooler evening breeze that cleared my head slightly. Grabbing our takeout, I headed into the house. Neither Gianna nor Luca or his family were downstairs. The low murmur of voices came from upstairs. I set the food down on the dining table before I headed upstairs to find Gianna. All doors were closed so

I headed straight for our bedroom. Gianna was curled up on top of the covers in my T-shirt, her perky ass naked and turned my way. Usually the sight would have given me all kinds of naughty ideas, but the last few days of teething and colic had sucked the energy out of me.

Fuck.

Isa wasn't beside Gianna nor in the crib next to our bed. I turned on my heel and stalked toward Luca's and Aria's bedroom, knocking. After a moment, Luca opened the door, already only in boxers. "Is Isa here?"

"Yes," Aria called from the bathroom before she emerged with a squirming Isa in her arms.

"I can take her," I said.

Luca shook his head. "You look like shit. You and especially Gianna need a good night's sleep. With Isa in your room that's not going to happen. She's fussy."

Aria stopped beside Luca. Isa's cheeks were red as she sucked on a teething ring. I ran a hand through my hair. "Who could have guessed that such a small thing could mean so much trouble?" I leaned down and pressed a kiss to Isa's forehead.

"It doesn't get better once they double and triple in size," Luca muttered.

"You're crazy for wanting this again," I said.

Aria smiled. "Go to sleep."

I nodded and dragged my exhausted ass back to our bedroom. For less than a second, I considered lifting Gianna and tugging her in, then I just let myself drop down on the covers beside her and zoned out.

Gianna was snuggled against me, breathing evenly, her red mane all over my face when I woke. I drew back and watched her a moment. She still looked exhausted.

I frowned. How long had I slept? The sun was up and casting its bright light into the room.

I untangled myself and sat up. Where was Isabella? Then I remembered last night. Luca and Aria had taken over. I got out of bed and walked out. When I didn't find anyone on the second floor, I headed downstairs. Aria, Liliana, and Marcella were singing some ridiculous kid song. When I entered the dining room, Aria was holding Isa on her hip and swaying back and forth, while Marcella sat in front of her, making silly gestures with her hands that seemed to match the song. Liliana had Flavio on her lap and was moving his tiny arms in rhythm to the music.

Luca, Amo, and Romero with Sara on his lap, sat at the table, having breakfast, which in Amo's case was the cold pizza I'd forgotten all about, but Luca and Romero were throwing the occasional glance at the girls. I hadn't even heard when Romero and Liliana had arrived. It must have been in the morning. I slanted a look at the clock. It was already eleven a.m.

I headed over to them, shaking my head. "Who would have thought that it ends like this? I remember the days when the three of us were notorious players and party-goers. Now we're only notorious killers."

Amo perked up from his slouch over the pizza carton. "What kind of players?"

"Nothing interesting," Luca said to his son before he smirked at me. "You look like shit. The only women you can have right now are the ten-dollar crack whores in Jersey."

"Luca," Aria whispered, shocked.

Luca slanted a look at Marcella who had stopped singing, and grimaced.

"Never mind," he said.

"I was never a player," Romero muttered.

"I remember you with more than enough women," I said with a grin.

Lily's attention shifted to her husband. "How many?"

Romero gave me a murderous look.

"Why don't we postpone this conversation to tonight?" Aria suggested.

"Romero was fairly tame," Luca tried to save Romero's ass.

"In comparison to you?" Aria asked with raised eyebrows.

Luca sighed. "We men can't win this argument, can we?"

She came over to me and handed Isa to me before she went over to my brother, wrapping her arms around his neck from behind. "No, no you can't."

I kissed Isa's soft forehead, then pressed her up to my bare chest before I sank down. "How was the night?"

"Busy," Aria said.

"She can wake the dead with her screech," Marcella said.

"Maybe she's trying to sound like that boy band you love so much. What's their name again? The Castratos?"

Marcella flushed then glared. "That's not funny."

I sank down beside Amo and grabbed a piece of the cold pizza. "Why's your little poo machine not teething and being intolerable yet?" I asked Liliana.

She pursed her lips. "I think he's just starting to teethe."

Soft steps rang out and Gianna appeared in the room, red mane a complete mess but she'd put on her own pajama bottoms. She scanned our small congregation with a frown. "What's going on here?"

"Family council to vote if we're going to have a second kid or not."

Gianna snorted and dragged herself over to Aria. "Good luck with that. If necessary, I'll glue my vajayjay shut."

"Dad, what's—" Amo began but Luca shook his head. "Later."

Marcella looked mildly disturbed but didn't say anything. Gianna took Isa and cradled her in her arms, kissing her gently. "This girl will remain the only one to ruin my birth channel."

"Ew," Marcella exclaimed.

I winked at Gianna who grinned. She sat down beside me.

"You look better," I murmured.

"I feel better. Sorry about the cold pizza."

"I fell asleep before I could eat a single bite."

Gianna rolled her eyes. "Next thing I know we'll buy a condo in Florida and drive one of those cabs. We're getting old."

"You're growing up," Luca muttered.

Romero stifled a laugh.

"Family… you can't live with them, but you can't live without them either," I muttered.

Gianna tickled Isa's belly, earning a giggle. She exchanged a look with Aria.

No matter how much we all teased each other, we stuck together. I'd never appreciated family more than I did now.

CHAPTER FOURTEEN

Gianna

The day of Matteo's surgery finally arrived. I picked him up afterward. He didn't show any outward sign of being in pain, but Matteo being Matteo that didn't mean anything. I'd tried to read up on vasectomies and, in general, the pain was described as moderate, so for Matteo it could really be nothing.

He settled on the passenger side while I took the wheel, which almost never happened. I wasn't a bad driver but Matteo, like all mob men, preferred to steer.

"Feels as if I got a thumbtack in my balls."

I snorted. "You've had worse."

"True, but those injuries usually didn't have me worried I wouldn't be able to get one up." Matteo touched my thigh. "We should give it a try."

I sent him a disbelieving look. "You just got out of surgery and already want to have sex. You know the doctor said you need to wait a week before we do it."

Matteo's hand moved higher. I swatted him away.

"Come on, babe. One week is a long time, considering I've only been getting regular sex for a few months."

"So sorry, my vajayjay needed time after being shredded giving birth to our daughter," I muttered.

"So that's a definite no to sex?"

"Definite."

"Then lets at least get drunk tonight. Isa is being taken care of. We need to use our evening alone."

We'd had one evening in the Tipsy Cow since Isa's birth, but we hadn't gotten shitfaced, nor had we gone to a club to party afterward, but still it had felt like a major accomplishment.

"You're not supposed to have alcohol either."

"No sex, no alcohol. At least, let's find someone I can cut up."

A laugh slipped out but I combined it with a scowl to show Matteo I thought he was being an idiot.

I patted his leg. "You get my eternal gratefulness for doing this." It wasn't even only meant as a joke. I really loved Matteo even more for taking responsibility.

I'd put Isa down to sleep and headed back to the bedroom but froze in the doorway. Matteo lay spread-eagle, completely naked, on the bed. "Have your way with me. I'm ready."

I cocked one eyebrow. "Seven days. You kept track."

"Come on, babe. Give me a helping hand— or mouth."

Matteo curled his fingers around his cock, which was already hardening.

"Doesn't look like you need help," I said but arousal was already pooling between my legs at the sight of Matteo. His body never left me unaffected. I strolled over to him and tugged my top over my head then shook off my shorts. Naked, I stopped in front of the bed. I felt confident in my body again, which was the best feeling in the world.

Matteo sent me a grin. I climbed on the bed and straddled his head before I shoved his hand away from his cock and sucked the tip into my mouth.

Matteo moaned but fell silent when he buried his face in my pussy. His eagerness showed by the way he shoved his tongue into me. I moaned around his cock. Matteo answered with a groan that vibrated against my clit. Soon we were both panting. I was grinding myself against Matteo's skillful mouth while he thrust upward into my mouth.

When he sucked my clit into his mouth, I exploded. My fingers around his cock tightened and I sucked him even harder until he too exploded in my mouth.

I collapsed on top of him, completely spent. Rolling off his body, I stretched out on the bed, wiping my mouth.

"And, does it taste different?"

I hit his six-pack.

"What? It's a legitimate concern."

"It hasn't improved," I muttered.

Matteo grabbed my feet, which rested on the pillow beside his head and tickled me. I let out a screech and tried to jerk free of his hold but he was too strong.

"You'll wake Isa, babe. Laugh quietly."

I rammed my elbow into his side, causing him to grunt but not to release me. My belly hurt from howling and tears pooled in my eyes. "Stop!" I gritted out. "Fuck me!"

Matteo momentarily stopped the assault. "You know how to distract me." His voice was low and one of his hands traveled up from my ankle to my inner thigh.

"It's not that difficult," I got out and opened my legs.

Matteo pushed two fingers into me and began to fuck me with them, his intense gaze never looking away from my pussy. Soon my muscles began to spasm for another reason. I rotated my hips, driving Matteo's fingers even deeper into me until I came with a hoarse cry.

Not wasting any time, I climbed on top of Matteo who was already hard again. "See, everything's still working."

I reached for a condom and slid it over his cock.

Matteo sighed. "The next few months will be hard."

I lowered myself on him, causing us both to moan. "I hope so."

Matteo chuckled and gripped my hips, but I didn't need encouragement. I loved to ride him, to steer my, and especially his, pleasure with every move of my hips.

When we laid in each other's arms afterward, I asked, "And, do you regret it?"

I could only imagine what kind of comments Matteo had gotten from Luca. Given our traditional culture, a vasectomy was something that might hurt his manliness.

"No. We don't want any more kids and I hate condoms, so it's our best bet to keep Isa an only child."

I smiled. "Growing up with Flavio and Aria's third kid, she'll pretty much have annoying siblings to spend time with."

"No doubt."

I slung my arm around Matteo's chest. Now that Isa was eight months old, things had calmed down. I had returned to giving almost all of my classes and Matteo's and my sex life was almost back to how it used to be. Moments of panic were few and far between but Matteo or my sisters were always there to catch me if they came.

We all alternated watching our kids. That way we all got some much needed couple time, even Lily occasionally let me or Aria watch Flavio and Sara. With Isa under the same roof, sex was limited to our bathroom and bedroom, and we had to be quiet, but on the nights when Isa was with one of her aunts we really went all out.

Right now Aria and Luca still got the short end of the stick because they didn't have a toddler yet, but their third child was due in a couple of months and then things would take a turn.

"You're quiet. What are you thinking?"

"About how far we've all come. When Aria, Lily and I were teens, back in Chicago, and tried to imagine our future, we never imagined it to be like this."

"I thought all girls want true love, a handsome prince and a splendid palace. I think you live every young girl's dream."

I huffed. "You are impossibly vain."

"Why? It's true, isn't it?"

I gritted my teeth but I had to admit he had a point, especially Lily and Aria had often droned about finding true love and a good-looking prince. I'd rarely entertained such fantasies, already too jaded at that young age, and if I'd ever allowed them, I'd kept them to myself. "I was never like that. Disney princes never did it for me."

"That's why you got me."

I pushed up on his chest, narrowing my eyes. "All right, so let's say I really live my teenage self's dream, what about you? Is this your teenage dream come true?"

Matteo grinned in a way that raised my alarm bells. "Every horny teenage boy dreams about a girl that can suck cock like a pro and ride like a cowgirl."

I punched his shoulder as hard as I could.

Matteo chuckled. "Okay, okay. But I never dreamed about having a wife and a kid. I never thought that it was meant to be. Until I met you. I wanted you from the first moment I saw you and only wanted you more with every rude word coming from your mouth. Today, you and Isa are the embodiment of a dream I never dared to dream."

I swallowed, stunned by Matteo's words. "Asshole, why do you have to say something so heartfelt and lovable? Now I feel like the cold-ass bitch in our relationship."

"It's your parade role, babe. Embrace it."

I punched him again but gentler, then I gave him a hard kiss. "You and Isa are something I never thought I needed but all I want now," I mumbled as quickly as I could to get the words out of the way. Then I swung myself on top of Matteo. "Now let's fuck this lovey-doveyness out of my system."

"Your wish is my command."

The screaming and laughter of children filled the back yard of the mansion. We spent a few weeks in the summer together in the Hamptons every year. It was chaotic but also the best time of the year.

"They outnumber us," Matteo muttered as he sank down in the chair beside mine.

I held up a bottle of white wine. Matteo grinned and grabbed a glass from the table. I filled his glass then lifted my own. "To booze, the balm for every parent's frayed nerves."

"Can I have some as well?" Marcella asked as she stepped out onto the terrace in a summer dress that made her look like a runway model.

Marcella had Aria's beauty, only the pale skin against the black hair was even more eye-catching. She was fourteen and men began to notice her. Every time I went shopping with her, I noticed the appreciative looks. Every man who knew of her father kept their eyes to themselves. Anything else would be suicide. I couldn't imagine Luca ever being okay with Marcella dating anyone, much less marrying. The perfect man for her probably didn't exist on this planet.

"Ask again in seven years," Luca muttered from his position at the barbecue.

"Daaaaddd," Marcella moaned with a roll of her eyes and went back inside.

"She's at a difficult age," Aria said.

"When aren't they?" Luca asked.

A high-pitched laugh sounded. Isa was playing hide-and-seek with her cousins Flavio and Valerio. As usual, the boys did what she wanted, she was only four but already very strong-willed. Aria's second son was only nine months younger than Isa, and Flavio one day younger. They were inseparable.

"Dinner's ready!" Aria called as she set a salad down in the center of the massive patio table. Luca carried over a plate with grilled meat.

"Flavio, Valerio, Isa!" I called but they kept chasing each other.

Aria sighed. Matteo waved at Amo. "Come on, Amo, move your butt and help me catch the little monsters."

Amo pushed out of his chair. Only ten and the kid was already taller than Aria. He and Matteo began running after the children who began screeching. Marcella came out on the terrace, Lily's seven-year-old daughter Sara trailing after her like a lost puppy.

Eventually, Matteo headed back to the table with Isa wedged under his left arm. Amo carried his little brother Valerio upside down so the kid's blond hair fell into his face. He reminded me so much of little Fabiano, it sometimes gave me a wistful pang until his gray eyes reminded me that he wasn't my brother. Flavio trotted after them. He was easier to handle than Isa and Valerio but far more trouble than sweet Sara. Lily sometimes said it was a boy thing, but Isa proved that theory wrong.

Matteo set Isa down in the chair beside mine.

I gave her a stern look when she was about to get up again. "Dinnertime."

My tone made it clear that arguments were in vain, so Isa nodded with a small pout. Lily waddled outside, pregnant again, followed by Romero who always kept a close eye on her now that she was about to pop any day now.

Eventually everyone sat at the table, and the food was even still moderately warm.

Soon we all dug in and chatter filled the table. I cut Isa's steak and she eagerly wolfed it down, much to Matteo's delight. The girl loved meat and her dad's motorcycle but she never missed our weekly mother and child yoga either. I brushed a few of her reddish-brown curls away from her forehead and she gave me a grin around her fork, those bold blue eyes getting me every time. So far Isa hadn't encountered any restrictions. She was allowed to brawl with her cousins. The older she got, the more people would speak up to tell her what she could and couldn't do because she was a girl. I'd make sure they all shut up, and if necessary, I'd even let Matteo use his particular scary talents to keep anyone at bay who'd try to make Isa believe her potential had limits only because she didn't have a penis.

Matteo leaned over to me. "You got your fierce mother bear expression. Worrying your pretty head about Isa's future again?"

I gave him an annoyed look but didn't deny it.

"Trust me, babe. I'll make sure our girl has all the freedoms she wants as long as she never brings a date home, unless it's her lesbian lover."

"You are impossible," I muttered, trying to stifle a smile.

"That's why you love me, admit it." Matteo kissed me briefly until Valerio let out an ewww.

"Your mom and dad are being disgusting again," he said with a scrunched-up nose.

"I know," Isa said as if she had to suffer under our PDA all the time.

"You wouldn't be sitting here if your mom and I didn't enjoy being disgusting," Matteo said. I rammed my elbow into his side. Marcella shook her head in disgust and Amo let out a laugh.

"What does that mean?" Sara asked, and the younger kids all looked from Matteo to Romero then Luca.

The latter sent Matteo a death glare. "Ask Matteo."

Matteo leaned back and opened his mouth. He would explain the birds and the bees in every detail if anyone let him so I wasn't sure why Luca provoked him like that.

Aria hit her palm flat on the table. "No disgusting topics at the table. We're having dinner now. Can't we act like a well-behaved normal family for once?"

I shrugged. Luca seemed only amused by her outburst but tried to hide it.

At least the kids all sat up a bit straighter and focused on their food again.

"That's how she got Luca in line," Matteo said.

I snorted. And all hell broke loose at the table again.

I mouthed sorry to Aria, but she shook her head with a badly disguised grin. A normal family we were not, but none of us really cared.

The end

SHORT STORY #2: LILIANA & ROMERO

Romero

It was past eight in the evening when I returned home from a long day doing business. The negotiations with our main distributor of high-quality absinthe and whiskey had taken longer than expected.

Since Luca had made me Captain five years ago, I'd often worked long days. As the son of a mere soldier, not to mention after the war my love for Lily had caused, I had to gain the respect of my men and fellow Captains. I'd come a long way. The men working for me were a loyal lot and they didn't need any more convincing, unlike some of the Captains and Underbosses, but they weren't my main concern. My men appreciated that I didn't mind getting my hands dirty instead of just showing my face at the clubs on the Eastside in my responsibility. Partying wasn't part of my job description after all.

I preferred to deal with the drug and alcohol distributors myself to make sure the prices and quality were right. You needed to know the details in your establishments if you wanted to control them.

Of course, that meant I often returned home later than I wanted. Lily never complained though. As usual a soft glow came from the windows of our home, a cozy brownstone townhouse in a tree-lined street in peaceful Greenwich Village. When our neighbors had found out who was moving in, they'd avoided us like the plague, terrified we might bring war into their midst. That was the farthest thing on Lily's and my mind. We'd moved here to find peace not destroy it. We wanted a normal life despite our background and my job.

Lily had done her best, with tea invitations and homecooked meals for one of the elderly neighbors who'd broken her hip, to improve our standing in the last six months. People still avoided me, which was fine, but I wanted them to like Lily, because it was important for her.

I opened the front door. The scent of a homecooked meal, something meaty from the oven, greeted me when I stepped into the foyer. I hung up my jacket when Lily came into the foyer, her cheeks rosy with excitement. She wore a beautiful long-sleeved blue dress, her dark blond hair framing her gorgeous face.

"You look beautiful," I murmured as I pulled her into my arms, trying to remember if I'd forgotten any kind of special occasion. Usually Lily didn't wear dresses or her hair down for a standard dinner. Something was the matter. It wasn't her birthday, that had been three weeks ago. I'd never forgotten a birthday or anniversary before.

"You sound surprised," she said with a soft laugh, her eyes tender and emotional.

"I'm never surprised by your beauty. I'm just…. Is today a special day?"

She took my hand, biting her lip. Something was definitely the matter. "I'm happy, that's all. Today, Mrs. O'Hara invited me over for coffee."

That our old lady neighbor had finally accepted Lily hardly explained her strange mood. She led me into the kitchen where the scent of roasted meat and tomatoes got even stronger. A casserole with bubbling cheese baked in the oven.

"Your favorite."

"Cannelloni al forno?" I asked.

Lily nodded with a secretive smile. My mother had taught her how to make the dish, which had been part of our family for generations. Candles cast a romantic glow over the table and at my usual place a parcel waited on the table.

Fuck. Had I really forgotten a special date? Something important? But no matter how hard I racked my brain I couldn't come up with anything.

Lily squeezed my hand. "Why don't you open it?"

I sank down on the wooden chair and reached for the red ribbon wrapped around the white parcel. Lifting the cover, I peered in. It took my brain several seconds to process what I was seeing. A long stick stating "pregnant" and a tiny onesie stating "Best Dad in the World".

I looked up, stunned. Lily was crying and nodding.

"You're…?"

"Pregnant!" she exclaimed.

We hadn't been trying for very long. Only once really, even if Lily had stopped taking the pill a few months ago. I shoved to my feet and pulled her against me, kissing her over and over again. "When did you find out?"

"Only today. I couldn't wait to tell you. I have a doctor's appointment in two days, but the three tests I took all showed the same result."

I lifted her off the ground, needing to feel her even closer. Lily and I had often talked about starting a family but becoming Captain and moving into our new home had kept us busy for a while.

"Are you happy?" Lily asked.

"Can't you see?"

She nodded, more tears streaming down her face. I wiped them away and buried my face in her hair. Eventually we pulled apart.

"I need to take the cannelloni out or they'll burn."

I sank back down on my chair, completely stunned as I watched Lily put the casserole on the table. Soon she'd give me a child and we'd become a real family.

Lily caught my gaze and gave me the smile I'd love till the day I died.

She sat down across from me and I put a generous amount of cannelloni on her plate, much more than in the past, before I filled my own plate.

Lily laughed. "I know some people think you have to eat for two when you're pregnant, but that's not true."

"I just want you and the baby to get all you need."

Lily took a bit of the pasta with an amused look. "You realize I'll double in size if I eat like that."

"You'd still be gorgeous with a few pounds more." I shoved a forkful of the cannelloni into my mouth and groaned in delight. "I think you might actually be cooking this better than my mother."

"Don't tell her. She'd be heartbroken you think so."

I chuckled. "My mother loves you. She won't mind." I paused. "When can we tell our families? My mother has been eagerly waiting for grandchildren from me."

"I don't know. It's still early but you know how bad I am at keeping a secret. How about we tell them next time we see them in person. I don't want to share something this important in a message or phone call."

I reached for her hand, stroking her knuckles. "Perfect."

Lily got more beautiful in her pregnancy, even if that should have been impossible. I had to admit I really liked her new curves, especially her fuller hips and bigger butt. As a woman, Lily of course always worried about gaining weight but I did my best to show her how much I desired her pregnant body. The last few summers we'd spent in Italy in a beautiful country house in Sicily and on Luca's yacht but this year Lily didn't want to fly.

Instead we rented a beach cottage in North Carolina in late August for a week. Just the two of us where nobody knew us and we could act like a normal couple. Nobody gave us special treatment or the best table because the mob loomed over us. We were just a normal young couple enjoying their babymoon. I had to admit I enjoyed these days of anonymity. Lily positively loved it.

After dinner at a small rustic fish restaurant with a beautiful view over the ocean, Lily and I returned to our one-bedroom cottage. Lily wore a flowery summer dress that accented her curves and her baby bump. At five months it was unmistakable. Maybe some men were turned off by the sight of their pregnant wife. I definitely wasn't one of them.

The moment the front door closed behind us I cupped Lily's face and kissed her, my tongue slipping in for a taste. The chocolaty note of our dessert lingered on her lips. Lily pressed her palms against my chest and I pulled her even closer, my back against the door as we kissed for a long time without hurry.

Soon my hands couldn't stay still anymore. I stroked Lily's neck, her collarbone before I cupped her breast gently through the fabric of her dress. She moaned softly into my mouth and I couldn't resist sucking her lower lip into my mouth as I kneaded her breast. I was already growing hard, tasting Lily, feeling her.

"I need to make love to you," I rumbled as I pulled away. She nodded with a dazed smile.

I lifted her into my arms and carried her toward the bedroom where I lay her down on the bed. I climbed on top of her, my thighs parting her legs. Careful not to rest my weight on her belly, I kissed her again as my fingers slid down the strap of her dress. She wasn't wearing a bra underneath so her beautiful pink nipple appeared as I tugged down her dress. Not able to resist, I kissed it, feeling it harden against my lips before I drew it into my mouth. Lily moaned, her hips lifting to meet mine. I circled Lily's nipple with my tongue, watching her face. Her eyes were lidded, those pink lips parted. I gently rocked my hips, knowing she wanted to feel me there. But I wasn't in a hurry. I took my time kissing and sucking her nipples until Lily shifted almost helplessly under me.

I let up and pushed into a sitting position then helped Lily get out of her dress. She reclined again and I dropped light kisses all over her belly before I moved lower to the soft triangle of darker hair. When my tongue traced her slit, Lily bucked her hips with a breathless moan. I smiled against her bundle of nerves and gently traced it with just the tip of my tongue. I kept my touch light and slow, teasing Lily until she begged for more, for release.

I swirl my tongue around her clit, then take a long lick along her center. I push a finger inside of her pussy, groaning at the feel of her heat, her arousal. My dick's digging into the mattress and I'm close to losing sight of my main goal: prolonging Lily's pleasure for as long as I can, but my own need burns hotter with every passing second. As I suck her clit, I curl my finger inside of her and Lily snaps. Her cry sent another thrill through me. I pumped my finger harder, faster, wanting my cock to take its place.

I pushed up, unbuttoning my shirt impatiently. Lily quickly sat up to help me until I was finally naked. Bending over her, I slid into her, slower than I would have liked but I couldn't help but be worried I'd hurt the baby after all.

Lily wrapped her arms around my neck, pulling me closer. Her belly bumped against my abs as I lowered myself for a kiss. Every thrust into Lily felt like heaven from the wet heat surrounding my cock to her gasps and moans. Soon our bodies fell into a rhythm. Lily met my thrusts with her hips, driving me deeper. We never stopped kissing even as our breaths came shorter. When Lily dug her nails into my shoulders and pulled away for a moan, I allowed myself to let loose as well. Lily clung to me as my movements became uncoordinated. Eventually, I paused, breathing harshly against Lily's throat. Her lips found mine for another kiss. I rolled off her but pulled her into my arms.

We fell asleep like that not long after. As usual my sleep was peaceful with her at my side. No matter how bad the day, Lily kept the horrors at bay.

Luca, Matteo and I sat in Luca's office, talking business. Even if Luca and I were closer than he was with his other Captains, he expected me to report frequently. He'd put his trust in me by making me Captain despite the many dissenting voices and I wanted to show him that he hadn't made a mistake. That's why I worked hard every day to make sure the clubs and bars under my wing flourished. He wouldn't have a reason to regret his decision.

My phone rang. Usually I would have turned the sound off during a meeting with my Capo but Lily could be giving birth any time now. She was already five days overdue.

Lily's name flashed across the screen.

I jerked to my feet and picked up. "Lily? What's wrong?"

Luca and Matteo both fell silent.

"I'm in labor. I don't think it'll take long."

"Where are you?"

"At home. My doula is here. I'm waiting for you."

"I'll be there soon. Hold on."

Lily laughed. "All right."

I hung up, flustered.

"I assume Liliana is about to have your baby?" Luca asked.

I nodded shakily. "I should—"

"Go ahead. Your wife needs you," Luca said.

"Good luck," Matteo said with a wink.

I turned and rushed to my car. I usually wasn't someone who disregarded traffic regulations as a sport like Matteo, but today I raced through traffic, cutting lines and taking red lights where I could.

When I arrived at home, out of breath and ready to carry Lily to the car or call an ambulance, I was surprised to find her sitting on the sofa, with her doula, the wife of a soldier, behind her, massaging her back. Lily was breathing heavily, her face twisted in pain.

After a moment, her eyes settled on me and she gave a shaky smile. "You are quick."

"I hurried," I said. "Should we head to the hospital now?"

Lily looked at her doula. "We can wait another hour, I think."

I shook my head. I knew Lily trusted the woman but I'd rather have a doctor close by. I walked toward her, causing the doula to stand up and give us some privacy. Sinking down beside Lily, I kissed her hand.

"Let's get you to the hospital. I want you and our daughter to be safe. Next time we can discuss having that homebirth you want."

"Next time," Lily said with a smile.

I helped her to her feet and slowly guided her to the car, glad she'd agreed.

Less than two hours later, Sara was born. She was as beautiful as Lily with big brown eyes and soft light brown hair. Lily nursed her with a tired but loving smile, and I held her in my arms, admiring her strength.

"She's so beautiful," Lily said again.

I nodded, stroking Lily's bare arm. Protecting others had been my job for a long time but now it was suddenly part of my life, because the people who needed my protection were my life.

Liliana

Sara was asleep in her room so Romero and I had some time for us. This happened rarely. Sara kept us busy and so far, I couldn't bring myself to let anyone else watch her overnight or in the evening, even if Aria had offered to babysit several times.

When I walked back into our bedroom, the lights were dimmed and the door to the bathroom was ajar. As I stepped into the doorframe, my heart swelled with love. A dozen candles cast their warm glow on my surroundings and soft jazz music played in the background. Romero waited beside the bathtub, a box with my favorite chocolate truffles in hand and a bottle of non-alcoholic sparkling wine on the edge of the tub. He was only in tight boxers. My eyes took in his muscled chest and strong thighs, feeling a familiar tug between my legs. Since Sara's birth, our love life had taken a hiatus and still hadn't picked up where it had been before my pregnancy.

"This is beautiful," I whispered as I walked toward him and pressed up to his side. Now I wished I'd put on something sexier than a T-shirt and panties.

"Is there a reason?"

There wasn't always. Romero was a romantic at heart and loved to surprise me with candlelight dinners or relaxing evenings in the bathtub. Still I always asked because my brain was frayed since Sara's birth. Neither of us had ever forgotten an important occasion and I didn't want to be the first.

"The anniversary of the night that I made you mine," he murmured before he left a lingering kiss on my lips. I loved remembering our first night together, the moment I'd known my heart irrevocably belonged to Romero.

"That's a good reason to celebrate," I said, smiling up at him.

"Why don't we relax a bit?" His eyes reflected the desire slowly kindling in my belly as well. His hands slid under my T-shirt and helped me pull it over my head before he tossed it away. Despite the warmth in the room, my nipples pimpled. Romero's fingers next hooked in my panties and slid them down slowly. His eyes never left mine, practically devouring me. How could I have worried Romero would care that I wasn't wearing sexy lingerie? I hooked my hands in his boxers and pushed them down. My desire burned even brighter seeing Romero completely naked.

He helped me into the tub and I sank into the hot water with a moan, feeling my tense muscles relax. Romero climbed in behind me and poured us the sparkling wine before handing a glass to me. We clinked glasses, and I settled against his chest and took a sip of my wine. Closing my eyes, I released a soft sigh. "I could fall asleep like that."

Romero's lips traced my throat. "You didn't get much sleep in the last few months. If you want to sleep, I'll hold you."

Despite my body's need for sleep, I also felt another growing yearning, and I knew Romero would feel an even stronger desire. "No," I said softly. "Not tonight." In my words swung my need for more and

Romero picked up on it. As we listened to music, Romero's hands caressed my breasts. The touch was gentle, almost fleeting. His palms and fingertips barely brushed my sensitive nipples but they puckered eagerly. Soon his cock grew hard against my back. He kissed my throat and the tender spot behind my ear as his fingers focused on my nipples, lightly circling them.

Romero's soft teasing was just what I needed to awaken my body. Without meaning to, my legs slid farther apart, pressing firmer against Romero's muscled thighs. One of his hands slid down my belly until his fingertips brushed my pubic bone and brushed over my folds. As with my breasts before, his touch was careful, light. His fingers seemed to discover my folds with gentle strokes, rarely touching my clit, which swelled under the soft ministrations. I turned my head and kissed Romero, tasting him. His index finger rubbed small circles on my clit. Soon I rested bonelessly against him as we kissed and he cherished me. Despite the slow pace my body soon tightened with pleasure. Romero pulled back, our eyes locked, his fingers keeping up their slow caress of my clit and nipple. My lips parted, my lashes fluttered and then my release overwhelmed me. I moaned, my body arching into Romero. He kept up his caress until I sagged against him, spent as if we'd spent hours making love as in the past.

He slid one of his fingers into me, causing me to moan again as he began to fuck me with it slowly. I reached behind myself and stroked his length. Romero's breathing deepened immediately and he added a second finger to my center, making my inner walls clench. My head dropped back against his shoulder as I peered into his eyes.

"Don't stop," I gasped.

"I won't," he promised. I loved the darker, deeper timbre his voice took on when we made love.

I was getting closer and closer, my hips bucking in rhythm with his fingers, and then stars burst in my vision. Romero breathed heavily, his arousal unmistakable at my back.

"Ride me, Lily," Romero murmured.

I turned around and hovered above him, his tip brushing my

throbbing entrance. Our lips met in a gentle kiss as I lowered myself on his cock. When he was sheathed all the way in me, we both paused, our eyes locked.

"This feels so good," I whispered.

"Yeah," Romero breathed. It still amazed me how good Romero could make me feel, how loved and cared for. I hadn't regretted marrying him for a single moment. He was the love of my life and the best father I could imagine.

Romero grabbed my hips, guiding my movements as I rocked up and down. The water sloshed gently around us as our bodies slid against each other. Soon my rocking turned almost desperate as I drove Romero's cock deeper into me. One of his fingers found my bundle of nerves, rubbing it. My hold on Romero got tighter as I got closer. "Tell me when you come," Romero panted.

"Not long."

My movements became jerky, uncoordinated, but Romero's upward thrusts hit just the right angle. "I—" Words died on my tongue as a wave of pleasure radiated through me but Romero knew my body.

He threw his head back and gripped my hips hard as he came with me.

I slumped against his chest, breathing harshly.

A sound came from the baby monitor. Both Romero and I held our breaths, listening but it was silent. I breathed in and giggled.

Romero rubbed my back. "I missed this."

"Me too," I admitted. I hadn't thought about sex as often in the last months but now I realized sex was more than pleasure, it was giving and receiving closeness on another level.

We stayed like that for a while before soft wails rang from the speaker. Sara was waking up. Romero kissed me and helped me get out of the bathtub. I quickly wrapped a towel around myself before I dashed off toward the nursery beside our room. Sara was bellowing by then and didn't quiet until I'd settled on the plush armchair and nursed her. The towel was bunched around my hip and I knew I'd be getting the armchair wet, especially the constant dripping of my hair.

Romero came in, dry and in boxers but he carried a towel. He walked over to me and created a makeshift turban for my hair. "Do you need a blanket?"

"I'm not cold," I said with a smile. "Thank you."

He nodded, then watched me for a little while. "Seeing you like this makes me happy."

He bent down and kissed my forehead, then he walked out. I joined him in bed thirty minutes later. The moment I snuggled up beside him, he put away his phone where he'd undoubtedly been reading work emails. I yawned, exhausted.

Romero wrapped his arms around me.

"I always feel safe in your arms."

He kissed the top of my head. "You are safe. If I could I'd even protect you in your nightmares."

I looked up. "You do. Knowing you're by my side does. I rarely have bad dreams and if I do, they have nothing to do with what happened in the past, only about the crime thrillers I sometimes read. You banished every bad memory."

Romero tightened his hold on me. "I'll make sure there are only good memories in our future."

"And even if something bad happens, I know you're there."

"Every step of the way."

I kissed him, then pressed my ear on his chest, listening to his calm heartbeat as I drifted off to sleep.

SHORT STORY #3: GROWL & CARA

Cara

My stomach was in knots when I knocked at the front door of my former home. I'd moved into Ryan's place only two months ago but his apartment already felt more like a home than this place ever had. Talia opened the door and gave me a smile which soon turned into a frown. "What's wrong? You look tense."

She wasn't the oblivious girl of the past. At only sixteen, too much had happened to her. If Dad were still alive and saw us now, he wouldn't recognize us, not even Mom. But she was a good actress so maybe she'd succeed in making him believe a charade.

"Big news to share," I said.

Talia's eyes widened. "You're going to marry."

I wasn't even wearing my ring yet. It was hidden in my purse for later. Puzzled, I asked, "How do you know?"

"I expected it any day now. You and Growl live together after all. It was only a matter of time."

She was right. Living together in our world before marriage was frowned upon, but my life had gone off the right track a while ago, so I wasn't as obsessed with fitting in anymore. There were more important things, which was why I had wanted to live together with Ryan before marriage. He would have married me months ago, but he'd respected my wish and waited with his official proposal until a week ago. Even though I knew he wanted to marry, his knee-fall and the beautiful ring came as a surprise.

Even if I'd already said yes and would marry him either way, I couldn't deny that it was important for me to get my family's approval, and Talia and Mom were pretty much the only close family I had anymore.

"Does Mom suspect something?"

I entered the apartment. Luca allowed Mom and Talia to live in it for free. It was a nice three-bedroom place in Brooklyn, newly renovated and completely furnished, but less than what we had been used to in Las Vegas. Mom was struggling with this fact. She couldn't accept that the life before Dad's murder was gone. I hoped one day she'd realize that it could have ended so much worse if Luca hadn't taken us in and given us a home in the Famiglia. Even if some people looked down on us for our family history, they mostly kept their opinion to themselves because we were related to the Capo.

"You know how she is," Talia said as she closed the door. "She prefers to ignore unpleasant truths."

She acted and looked so grown up, I had trouble getting used to it.

I followed my sister into the dining room where Mom was setting the table. She looked up, stressed. "Dinner still takes a few minutes. Without staff, things just don't work how I'm used to."

I didn't mention that we were lucky to have a home and Mom didn't really have anything else to do at the moment. Doing housework and cooking should be doable. In the past, invitations to social events and gossip meetings with her so-called-friends had been her main occupation, but in New York most people still avoided us. The only people who invited us were Luca and Aria, and that was mostly Aria's doing. Luca might have taken us in but he didn't care much about us. Not that I blamed him. We didn't know each other. He was a stranger for me as well.

I headed toward her and embraced her briefly. "No rush. We have all evening."

She nodded but I could tell that the words didn't really sink in.

"How can I help you?"

"You're the guest. You shouldn't have to work."

I rolled my eyes. "Mom, I moved out only a few months ago. And we're family. We don't have to stick to social rules when we're alone, don't you think?"

"I still think it was a mistake to move in with him before you're married." Her unsaid "or at all" lingered between us. She didn't like Ryan and she didn't try to pretend otherwise.

"Ryan and I love each other, Mom. You can accept it or not, but it won't change what I'm feeling."

"I didn't say anything," she said, even though she had. "It's your life. You don't want anyone to tell you what to do. I have no choice but to accept it."

"You're right."

Talia gave me an encouraging smile but I didn't feel like telling Mom about my engagement now.

Eventually, we settled at the table and had dinner. Talia had started school again and found a couple of friends. Mom had more trouble, mainly because she wanted to make acquaintances among the higher-ranking mob wives, who still gave her the cold shoulder.

"Why don't you give a few of the soldiers' wives a chance? You'll be lonely if you don't have people to spend time with."

Mom's lips pinched. "We'll see."

That meant she'd keep schmoozing the Captains' wives until the last shreds of her dignity were gone.

"I have something I'd like to tell you." Talia bit her lip, twisting a strand of her brown hair around her finger nervously.

Mom slowly set her fork down.

"Ryan asked me to marry him and I said yes. We want to marry next spring."

Mom blinked then she nodded as if this wasn't news. She didn't look angry, disappointed or happy. "I suspected something like that. It's the logical choice given our current position. We're not accepted by most people in the Famiglia so it's impossible to find a better match for you, especially because you aren't pure anymore. And your Growl is Enforcer under Luca. It could be worse."

She made it sound as if Ryan was some kind of emergency solution, someone I'd chosen because I didn't *have* a choice.

"I didn't say yes because I thought I wouldn't find a better match. I said yes because I love him and know that I can't find a better man for me."

Mom gave me a bitter smile. "I don't blame you, Cara. I understand, believe me, and I accept your decision."

Anger spread in my body, making my blood pound in my temples. "I didn't ask for your approval, but we're a family and I want us to stick together. I want Ryan to be a part of that family, for you to see him for who he really is, for who he has become."

"He was Enforcer and now he's Enforcer again, Cara. He's doing what he does best."

"You loved Dad despite what he did for work," I reminded her because no matter how desperately she tried to pretend Dad had been a good man, that wasn't the truth.

"That's different."

"Is it, really?"

Mom stood with a forced smile. "How about we have dessert now?"

Talia rolled her eyes, but I nodded. "Sure."

Mom turned and hurried into the kitchen.

I sighed. "It's the reaction I expected. I don't know why I hoped for something else."

Talia patted my hand. "She's taking our new situation harder than us."

"But we suffered all the same, yet we're trying to move on."

"She'll learn to live with Growl."

"What about you? You know you don't have to be scared of him. He'd never hurt you. We're his family now."

Talia shrugged. "I don't know him, but I know you and if you trust him then I know I don't have to fear him."

I leaned over and hugged her. "Thank you."

Talia and I were closer now than we'd been before our father was killed. Maybe because I'd stopped being obsessed with pleasing society and my so-called friends, and because she'd become more mature. We'd both changed and now really appreciated each other.

"We could lock them in our bedroom," Ryan said, but in his eyes, I could see his reluctance. I felt the same way. Coco and Bandit were part of our family. Locking them away felt wrong. As if Bandit knew what was going on, he pressed up to my leg. At nine, his black fur was slowly turning gray around his muzzle. He wagged his tail when I patted his back and soon Coco trotted my way, wanting her share of petting as well.

Mother would have to get used to them eventually. "Bandit and Coco will stay."

I wasn't sure who was more nervous about Talia's and Mom's visit, Ryan or I. It was strange seeing my tall, strong, inked-all-over fiancé nervous. It wasn't very obvious, just subtle signs like him checking his watch for the hundredth time or glancing into the oven repeatedly to check on the roast I'd made. He usually didn't have the slightest interest in cooking but today it seemed to calm his nerves.

"We'll have a wonderful Christmas," I assured him as I slid up to him and took his hand, leaning against his strong side.

He nodded, not saying anything. Ryan still wasn't the talkative type, but the days leading up to our first Christmas together definitely reminded me of our early days as captive and captor, when he rarely spoke a word to me, much less opened up about his feelings.

I, too, was nervous. This was the first time Mom and Talia would visit us for dinner—on Christmas Eve no less. Talia had been over to our apartment on occasion when Ryan was home but Mom had only met him a couple of times at social events since she was in New York. She preferred to avoid him.

Ryan and I both kept busy with preparations while the dogs watched us curiously from their baskets. They were still weary of the newest addition to our apartment: a Christmas tree. This was the first time they encountered one, but I'd insisted we have it as part of our Christmas decoration.

The bell rang, making me jump. Coco perked up and Bandit jumped out of his basket with a deep woof before he trotted to the door. Coco followed him half-heartedly.

"You get the door," Ryan said. "Your mother and sister will feel more comfortable if you greet them."

I shook my head and grabbed his hand before I pulled him toward the entrance door. "You and I are together in this."

He squeezed my hand briefly but his face was devoid of emotion. I put on my brightest smile and opened the door. Mother and Talia waited in front of it as if they were about to face their executioner. Luckily, Talia caught herself fast and stepped close to me for a hug.

"Is Mom going to make a mess of tonight?" I whispered.

Talia shrugged. "Probably."

I pulled away and faced my mother. She stood frozen in the hallway, giving me a stiff smile but her eyes kept flitting to Ryan. I didn't get any Christmas mood vibes from her.

"Hello Cara," Mother said almost formally, clutching her purse in front of her belly like a shield.

From the corner of my eye, I saw Talia awkwardly shake Ryan's hand. I couldn't remember if I'd ever seen Ryan shake anyone's hand at all. The sight almost had me bursting out laughing.

I invited Mom in but she was as stiff as a salt pillar, her eyes directed at Coco and Bandit who waited in the hallway behind us. Talia's initial fear during her first visits had been replaced by tentative affection. She even stroked Coco's back who was more approachable than Bandit. His trust issues with humans went deeper.

"It's okay, Mom. They accept visitors as long as we do. They won't do anything."

I had to drag Mom inside and then I led her into the living area with the small dining table. I'd decorated everything in gold and red to give it a cozy feel. Bandit and Coco both headed toward their baskets after a sign from Ryan.

"Good evening," Mom said to him with a stiff smile, holding out her hand.

Ryan took it and shook it very briefly, probably picking up on Mom's obvious discomfort.

"How about we sit down and have dinner?" I said quickly before the tension could rise.

After Talia and Mom had left, Ryan went out to walk the dogs and I cleaned the kitchen. He took longer than usual, a sign that he needed time to think.

When he finally returned and sank down on the sofa, I approached him. His expression was guarded.

"It went okay, don't you think?" I asked softly. It hadn't been the easy-going, warm Christmas dinner other families might have, but events like that had always been a rather formal affair with my family, and that hadn't improved.

Ryan shrugged, stroking Coco's head. "It went better than I thought. Your mother won't ever get over who I was and who I still am."

"You changed. You aren't the person everyone feared in Las Vegas."

"I'm now the person people fear in New York, Cara. I'm still Enforcer. Of course, Luca isn't as depraved as Falcone."

"My mother has no problem with Luca's level of depravity so she can't blame you for what you're doing in his name."

"Fear is immune to reason," he rasped. I stepped between his legs, forcing his eyes to raise to mine.

"My sister and mother will learn to accept you if they love me because I love you. End of story," I said firmly. Ryan grabbed me by the hips, his amber eyes intense. I knew the look and my core answered with a familiar tightening.

"I love you too," he growled.

His big hands slid to the back of my skirt, jerking down the zipper almost brutally. It wouldn't be the first piece of clothing I lost to Ryan's overeager, too strong hands. The moment the zipper was down he started dragging my skirt down my legs impatiently. It dropped to the floor beside my feet. Coco trotted away, knowing what was coming.

Ryan's impatience and lust won out. He grabbed my tights and ripped a hole in them right over my panties before he shoved them roughly aside. He leaned forward and forced his tongue between my pussy lips with a hard lick. I half-gasped, half-moaned, my hands flying up to clutch at Ryan's head. He grasped my leg and propped my foot up on his leg, opening me up for him. The sounds falling from his mouth were almost animalistic as he licked me. I panted, smiling as I watched him. He tugged even harder at my panties so he had better access and could press his mouth against my pussy and suck my lips into his mouth.

"Ryan," I gasped.

"You taste so sweet, Cara. Have from the very first moment I ate you out."

His tongue dove back between my folds for a firm lick before he sucked my clit into his mouth. I cried out from the almost painful sensation and Ryan switched to soft soothing licks that had me relaxing. He cupped my breast, stroking lightly. My body brimmed with a mix of anticipation and anxiety. Then he pinched my nipple hard, causing me to cry out again. The pain battled with the intense pleasure Ryan's tongue created with its gentle circling of my clit.

Ryan enjoyed it if I caused him pain during sex and slowly he taught me to appreciate the play of pain and pleasure as well. This time he didn't release my nipple. He tugged and twisted it but kept up sucking my clit. I scratched over his scalp with my fingernails, causing him to growl, and then stars burst before my eyes as intense pleasure radiated from my core. Ryan pinched my nipple and my orgasm became even more intense. I almost fell backward and would have if Ryan hadn't released my panties and clutched my ass cheek firmly to keep me in place while he shoved his mouth even harder against me, thrusting his tongue up and down.

I barely got the chance to catch my breath before Ryan released me and tore open his zipper, shoving down his boxers and freed his erection.

"Turn around," he rasped.

The moment I had my back turned to him, he pulled me down on his lap, impaling me on his length. I screamed, still oversensitive from my release and almost came again. Gripping Ryan's muscled thighs, I rocked myself back and forth, driving him deeper into me with every move. Ryan gripped my hips, guiding my moves as his hips thrust upward, driving even deeper into me. The sound of our bodies' joining filled the apartment but I didn't care. I'd long gotten over my embarrassment.

Ryan cupped my breasts through my blouse, kneading them. His tattooed thighs flexed under my fingers. So strong. When his strength and harsh exterior had terrified me at the very beginning, it now increased my desire for this man. I leaned forward and dipped down my head, watching Ryan's length slide into me, claiming me.

"Turn around. Let me see your face."

Ryan hoisted me off his lap and I hissed at the loss of him inside of me, but soon knelt over him, our faces close together. I sank back down on his length with a soft moan. This time we moved slower. I leaned forward, capturing his mouth with mine. He tangled his fingers in my hair, tugging slightly until he had me pinned in a way that allowed him to ravish my mouth. His other hand kneaded my ass, guiding my movements. We stayed joined like this for a long time, our bodies barely moving, pleasure only a low burn in our bodies.

The back and forth between the gentle lovemaking and animalistic fucking heightened my senses and lust. Ryan sucked my lower lip into his mouth as his thumb gently traced my clit. We'd stopped moving, but he was buried all the way inside of me, hard as stone, and I knew what would soon happen but never when. Ryan's amber eyes seemed to burn into me as his finger guided me higher. My muscles started clenching around his cock, the first treacherous signs of my approaching release.

His circling became even slower and he released my lip before he kissed me harshly. Grabbing my neck, he tilted my head until he could rasp in my ear, "I'm going to fuck you until you scream."

He hoisted me off his lap. I gasped when his cock slid out of me. Ryan lifted me on the couch, my hands propped up on the armrest. One knee on the sofa behind me, one leg standing, he stood behind me. He grabbed my throat and hip, and thrust into me almost violently. I arched back against him, needing more. Every thrust seemed to reach deeper than before. I clutched the armrest desperately. Ryan leaned closer, his fingers around my throat tightening slightly.

"Fuck, Cara. If you knew what you're doing to me... the power you're holding over me."

I tilted my head and kissed him harshly. Our eyes stayed locked as he slammed into me. His hand slid down from my throat to my breast, kneading it firmly before he pinched my nipple.

I clenched around him and began to tremble.

"Come for me," Ryan rasped. Sweat glistened on his face and inked chest. His fingers tugged even harder at my nipple until I gasped out from the combined sensation of pain and pleasure. Ryan drank in my expression as my orgasm hit me. My lips fell open and my eyes widened as a wave of intense pleasure pulsated through my core and soon my entire body.

Ryan grunted as he kept thrusting into me, forcing my oversensitive body to accept even more pleasure.

His other arm came around me as well, jerking me even closer to his body, and his fingers found my still throbbing clit.

"Too much," I groaned but Ryan bit lightly down on my shoulder. "No."

I squeezed my eyes shut, surrendering to his fingers and cock, and soon pleasure took over again. This time I took Ryan over the edge with me. He growled against my neck, his thrusts becoming less coordinated. My arms gave in until I had to brace myself on my forearms, crying out my release.

Ryan stilled behind me and I panted, my forehead pressed against the backrest, my body pulsating almost painfully. Ryan kissed my shoulder blade as he pulled out of me. He sank down on the couch and pulled me sideways onto his lap. I leaned my head against his chest, trying to catch my breath.

"Have you ever considered kids?" I wasn't sure why the words left my mouth in that moment but it was a topic I'd been wondering about for a while. Ryan and I wanted to spend our life together and for me children were a must.

Ryan stiffened, his fingers on my thigh digging into my skin. "Kids?" he rumbled as if the word didn't even make sense to him.

I pulled away to look at his face. His expression was a mix of confusion and wariness. "I never thought they were an option for me."

"Why not?"

"Because of who I was… who I still am. I never wanted a woman at my side and knocking up random whores and producing bastards was never something I wanted."

"But I am at your side now," I said softly.

He nodded, wonder reflecting in his eyes. "You are."

"And I won't go anywhere."

He stroked my throat with his inked hand. "You will." There was still the hint of doubt in his voice. I cupped his stubbled cheeks.

"I won't go anywhere."

"You want kids?" he asked roughly.

"I do. I always wanted two for as long as I could remember. I still do. I want a happy family."

"A happy family…" He tested the words as if they were entirely foreign to him, something from a language he didn't understand.

"Don't you want that after everything you've gone through?"

"I've destroyed many families in my time as Benedetto's right-hand man. You know that better than anyone."

I swallowed. Ryan hadn't killed my father but he would have and he'd tortured him. He was loyal to Benedetto, a fact that still boggled my mind after what the man had done to him. "That's the past. You can redeem yourself by doing right by our children."

"You really want kids with me? They could be like me…"

"Nothing's wrong with you. You had a horrible childhood, that's why you became Benedetto's enforcer. Our children won't suffer like you did. They'll be raised with love."

"I don't know if I'm capable of doing that."

"You're capable of loving me so why shouldn't you be able to love our children?"

Ryan nodded slowly. "Yeah, maybe."

"Definitely."

"If you want kids, I'll give them to you. I want you happy."

I hugged him. "We still have time. But I want us to be a family."

Ryan hugged me tightly. I breathed in his musky scent, relaxing further.

Our wedding wasn't the splendid feast I'd imagined as a teenage girl, not a way to impress society and friends. It was pure and simple, like Ryan's and my love.

We married on a ship on the Hudson with the Statue of Liberty in the background. Only a few people were present as we were declared husband and wife. Talia and Mom, who'd grown used to Ryan even if he still wasn't the son-in-law Mom wanted, Aria and Luca as well as Gianna and Matteo. While I'd been close to Aria in the beginning, and still was, because she'd helped me and my family so much, I now met

Gianna more often, which had come as a surprise. She'd seemed difficult to get along with during our first few encounters but soon we'd figured out we both enjoyed yoga, Pilates and working out. From that day on, we'd met at least once to work out together and she even asked me to help her with the Famiglia's women's gym she wanted to set up. Naturally, Coco and Bandit were present as well, despite their wariness toward the ship.

It was a hot May day with the sun shining down on us. Ryan was dressed in a white dress shirt with the sleeves rolled up and suit pants but no jacket or tie, and I had chosen a short, sleeveless wedding dress with a high neck. The material of the skirt was smooth like silk but the body had beautiful embroidery. Ryan had asked me to wear a short skirt and no sleeves because he loved the lean muscle I'd worked hard for. Of course, the main reason why was that I could show off my two tattoos that way. They weren't anything like his but Ryan still loved the splashes of color on my skin. Over the last six months I'd gotten two beautiful watercolor tattoos, red poppies across my ankle and lower calf, as well as a hummingbird in flight on my shoulder blade. They were pops of color against my white dress and pale skin. To my surprise, it hadn't caused any kind of stir in the Famiglia. Maybe because Ryan and I were regarded as misfits anyway, or maybe because Gianna had joined me during my first tattoo session to get inked as well. Her much smaller tattoo had been the scandal of the last few months. Even Mom had hardly said anything about my body art, even though I knew she hated seeing me inked.

"You may kiss the bride."

I smiled up at Ryan and he bent down. When our lips met, I knew everything that had led us to this point had been worth it.

Maximus and Primo chased each other through our small yard. At two and four, they were almost unstoppable, which was why Ryan and I would take them to an adventure playground in the afternoon. I did a quick workout on the patio as I watched them to make sure they didn't injure themselves seriously.

Daisy and Buddy, our rescue pit bulls, slept on the lawn, between where the boys played and me, so they could protect us. We'd saved them from a fight-dog breeding factory at only four weeks old three years ago. Coco and Bandit had died only one week apart from each other mere weeks before the raid of the fight ring. Despite our sadness, Ryan and I had seen it as a sign. Not to mention that we didn't want to live without dogs. Taking care of the tiny puppies in the beginning had been a twenty-four-hour job, which wasn't easy considering Max had been a toddler and I had been pregnant with Primo, but Ryan and I had succeeded together and our dogs thanked us with utmost loyalty and love.

"Primo, no!" I called when he hit his brother. Max, of course, hit him back. Ryan was the only one who called our son Maximus. He had chosen both boy names. People had always looked down at him as a child and he wanted to make sure our boys didn't suffer the same fate. For him a proud and strong name was a crucial key. When I'd seen how important the matter was for him, I'd given in under the condition that I'd choose a possible girl name, but I knew deep down that our family was complete with Max and Primo.

"Don't make me come and get you," I warned. They slanted me a look to see if I was serious. I was.

They started chasing each other again, almost stumbling over Buddy's huge white body. Primo climbed on top of him. Buddy barely lifted his head but I had enough. I went over to my boys and they trotted toward me, knowing what was coming.

"The dogs aren't toys. You can pet them and throw their ball, but you don't climb them, don't tug at their tails or ears, and don't tease them. Understood?" My voice was stern.

They nodded. "Okay, Mommy," they said as one, their amber eyes guilty.

I tousled their brown hair and sent them off again. Instead of continuing my workout, I sank down beside Buddy and Daisy. They both immediately put their heads on my crossed legs so I could pat them.

Max and Primo stopped and looked behind me. With huge grins, they dashed toward what they saw.

Growl

I'd spent the day dismembering a Bratva spy, had relished in his screams. Adrenaline still rushed in my ears like static when I got out of my pickup in the driveway of the small house Cara and I had bought shortly before Maximus had been born. I'd never much cared about a place, but this house, our home, held a special place in my heart.

Both our boys had been born here and Coco and Bandit had enjoyed their evening of life on the soft lawn. I had buried them in the soil of their favorite spot with my own hands.

I paused on the porch. I'd never cried over someone's death as an adult, never mourned someone but to this day my chest ached when I remembered the summer my loyal friends died. The memory of that day crashed down on me as it did often on days of inner turmoil.

Bandit and Coco were thirteen years old. When I returned home from work, I found them in the yard in their favorite spot close to a maple tree. Cara grabbed my arm, Maximus asleep in the baby sling against her chest. "I don't think it's going to be long now." Tears brimmed in her eyes.

I followed her gaze toward my furry friends who had both lifted their heads and were wagging their tails. Bandit had been diagnosed with cancer a couple of months ago. We'd done everything we could. Now we made sure he wasn't in pain.

I nodded, swallowing past the lump in my throat. "I'll stay with them. I won't leave their side until—" I couldn't say it. I didn't have to.

I strolled toward them and sank down beside them, patting their old bodies. Bandit met my gaze and deep down I knew Cara was right. It was only a matter of hours, maybe less. Bandit had waited for me to return home. I lay down on the warm lawn, my arm wrapped around Bandit and Coco, who hadn't moved from his side in days.

The sun soon set and the temperature began to cool, but I didn't stir. My own needs seemed irrelevant as I stroked Bandit's side. Cara had only briefly come over to give him a big piece of sausage with pain meds.

Soon I felt Bandit's breathing slow, the fall and rise of his chest under my palm almost unnoticeable now. Coco snuggled even closer to him and then his breathing stopped. I kept stroking his chest, even though it had stilled. Coco let out a low whine. I stroked her ears and neck, trying to comfort her.

Wetness hit my cheek and I looked up, expecting rain until I realized I was crying. Neither Coco nor I moved from Bandit's side until sunrise. Then I began digging a hole and buried my friend. Coco curled up on the grave and I stayed at her side, stroking her soft fur.

I reduced my workload drastically in the following days and Cara stayed with Coco whenever I couldn't, but like Bandit, Coco waited until I was home before she too fell asleep forever in my arms on Bandit's grave. I buried her beside him, so they'd forever be at each other's side.

Taking a deep breath and dragging myself out of the past, I followed the joyful screams of the boys into the yard. The sight before me quieted the violent vibes in my body. Cara sat on the lawn with our dogs, and our boys played with each other.

They looked carefree and happy, something I'd never experienced as a child. Maybe that was why it had taken some convincing on Cara's part before I could see that Maximus and Primo looked like me. They had my eyes and sharp features, but Cara's hair color. My face as a boy had never been filled with so much joy, so recognizing my facial features in them took imagination.

Maximus and Primo spotted me at the same time, and before Cara who was petting Buddy and Daisy.

I opened my arms and squatted. Seconds later both boys flew into my arms, almost causing me to fall back. They were growing so fast. I stood, lifting them up.

Cara glanced over her shoulder and smiled. I walked over to her. Buddy and Daisy wagged their tails excitedly. Cara stood and pressed a kiss to my lips, searching my eyes. The darkness in them wouldn't completely be gone yet. It took a while, especially after particularly brutal days like today. "Why don't you play with the boys for a bit? Then I can finish my workout."

I nodded, grateful that she knew I needed to take my mind off things and didn't want to talk. With another smile, Cara turned and headed back to the patio with the dogs at her heels. She was dressed in only tight workout shorts and a tank, looking ready to be devoured.

"Carousel!" Maximus exclaimed, drawing my attention back to my boys.

I set Primo down despite his protest, grabbed Maximus' hands and started spinning. Afterward, it was Primo's turn. I kept playing carousel until I was dizzy and had to lie down, which the boys used to climb on top of me and try to tackle me.

Cara watched us for a long time until she finally went inside, probably to have a post-workout snack and take a shower.

Primo yawned and Maximus, too, looked tired. "Time for your afternoon nap."

"No!" both cried but I picked them up and carried them inside. Soon they quieted.

Tiredness usually won out after we played together. The boys still shared a room because they slept better with company. Once they were both tucked in, I closed their door and stalked into Cara's and my bedroom. The shower was still running and when I stepped into the bathroom, everything was fogged up. Cara's eyes were closed as she let the water rain down on her. I shrugged out of my clothes and prowled toward her, my cock already hardening. Cara's eyes peeled open a second before my fingers curled around her throat and my lips crashed down on hers for a harsh kiss. I pressed her against the tiles, my tongue thrusting into her surprise widened mouth and my cock digging against her stomach. Her nails trailing over my chest, she sank down. My fingers tangled in her hair and guided her head toward my cock. She took me into her mouth. I braced myself against the tiles, breathing harshly as I watched her work my length.

I pulled her to her feet and lifted her up. She wrapped her legs around my hips immediately. With a hard thrust, I impaled her on my length as I pressed her against the wall.

I lost all sense of time as I slammed into Cara and soon the violence of the day was nothing but a distant echo. When Cara's muscles clenched around me and she came with a cry, I let loose as well. Eventually we both stood under the spray, breathing harshly, wrapped in each other's arms.

"Better?" Cara asked quietly.

"You and the boys are the antidote to my rage. I don't know what I'd do without you."

She took my hand and led me out of the shower. We towel dried quickly before we slipped into our bed. Cara stroked my chest. "You won't ever be without us. You're stuck with me and our boys."

The End

MORE BOOKS BY CORA REILLY

Born in Blood Mafia Chronicles:

Bound by Honor
(Aria & Luca)

Bound by Duty
(Valentina & Dante)

Bound by Hatred
(Gianna & Matteo)

Bound By Temptation
(Liliana & Romero)

Bound By Vengeance
(Growl & Cara)

Bound By Love
(Luca & Aria)

Bound By The Past
(Dante & Valentina)

Luca Vitiello (Luca's POV of Bound by Honor)

The Camorra Chronicles:

Twisted Loyalties (#1)
Fabiano

Twisted Emotions (#2)
Nino

Twisted Pride (#3)
Remo

Twisted Bonds (#4)
Nino

Twisted Hearts (#5)
Savio

Twisted Cravings (#6)
Adamo
Coming 2021

Contemporary Romance:
Only Work, No Play
Not Meant To Be Broken

ABOUT THE AUTHOR

Cora is the *USA Today* bestselling author of the Born in Blood Mafia Series, the Camorra Chronicles and many other books, most of them featuring dangerously sexy bad boys. She likes her men like her martinis—dirty and strong.

Cora lives in Germany with a cute but crazy Bearded Collie, as well as the cute but crazy man at her side. When she doesn't spend her days dreaming up sexy books, she plans her next travel adventure or cooks too spicy dishes from all over the world.

Printed in Great Britain
by Amazon